So Wicked

T0352227

Also by Melissa Marino

So Screwed
So Twisted

So Wicked

A Bad Behavior Novel

MELISSA MARINO

FOREVER
YOURS

New York Boston

Copyright © 2017 by Melissa Marino

Excerpt from *So Twisted* copyright © 2016 by Melissa Marino

Cover design by Elizabeth Turner. Cover copyright © 2017 by Hachette Book Group, Inc.

Forever Yours

Hachette Book Group

1290 Avenue of the Americas, New York, NY 10104

forever-romance.com

twitter.com/foreverromance

First published as an ebook and as a print on demand: May 2017

Forever Yours is an imprint of Grand Central Publishing. The Forever Yours name and logo are trademarks of Hachette Book Group, Inc.

Untitled/Poem excerpted from *The Book of Ryan,* reprinted by permission of R. A. Knipe

The Hachette Speakers Bureau provides a wide range of authors for speaking events. To find out more, go to www.hachettespeakersbureau.com or call (866) 376-6591.

ISBNs: 978-1-4555-6957-1 (ebook); 978-1-4555-6964-9 (trade paperback, print on demand)

To my muffin, my person, Sarah. A piece of my heart, and a piece of yours are all over these pages. #heartcamel

Acknowledgments

This book was a labor of love, and a test of my strength at a level I can't begin to articulate. There were many people who encouraged me, inspired me and carried me through until the end.

I believe there are times in which my agent, **Kimberly Brower**, feels the koala style grip I have imaginarily put around her. It's my attempt to make sure she never leaves me because none of this would ever happen without her.

Megha Parekh, and the entire team of amazing folks at **Forever Romance**, who work endlessly to make every book, including this one, the absolute best it can be.

My dear friend and publicist, **Nina Bocci.** Every single step of my journey, from pre-agent until now, you have helped me in more ways than I could ever repay you for. All the x's and o's.

Ryan A. Knipe graciously allowed me to use his poem that appeared at the beginning of the last chapter. I stumbled upon his beautiful words and moving prose on Instagram while writing this book. The poem used perfectly captured Al and Marshall, and I'm thankful Ryan let me share.

Hawkeye, the fella who sang his way into this book inadvertently, and who aided in helping me find the raw emotions without even knowing it. With all else discarded, I say thank you and I regret nothing.

To my friends at **Addison Starbucks**, who has the most rad employees, that supplied me with endless coffee and treats. They cheered me on almost daily as I wrote SO WICKED and gave me moments of humor to keep going.

My aloof partner in crime, **Court**. You kept me sane and laughing during this process and every day.

Amy Reichert and **Sarah Cannon**, my darlings. You inspire me and lift me. There is no greater gift and I couldn't be more grateful.

To the many San Luis Obispo establishments that were represented: **SLO Donuts**, **Splash Café**, **High Street Deli**, **BlackHorse Espresso & Deli** and especially **SLO Brew**, which was the inspirational backdrop for SO WICKED.

And thanks to a few local Chicago favorites that were represented: **Garrett's Popcorn**, **Vosage Chocolates** and **Koval Whiskey**.

My family, Mom and Dad, brothers and sister-in-law's, and all extended family who not only love me, but walk beside me to remind me of how loved I am.

To L--I couldn't be prouder of the parents we've become, and how we've navigated a difficult path with the empathy and courage that most envy. I'm honored to have been married to you for thirteen years, and know the love we've created around our son will sustain our family always. Thank you for your constant encouragement, and still making me laugh every day.

My sweet, sweet J. You make your mom so very proud. Everything I do, I do for you. Always.

Chapter One

MARSHALL—

In the business world, if you aren't punctual, you can go fuck yourself.

Opening a new bar, in a new-to-me city, was stressful enough, but add in relying on others to show up on time—that made it ten times worse. This chick from the bakery was supposed to be here at ten a.m. Thirty minutes later and still nothing.

"Wells," I shouted to my bar manager.

"Yeah?" he said, rolling his chair, along with his ginger-topped head and beard, out of the office.

It was purely an accident that I hired a ginger-haired bar manager to work at my bar named Ginger. Accidents worked out well sometimes.

"Any calls?" I asked.

"No," he said, reclining his husky body against the back of the chair.

"Shit," I said, pulling the pen from behind my ear and tossing it across the marble bar top. "You better not have set up a meeting for me with someone who is a no-show when I have tons of other shit to do."

A new bar. A new town. An immense amount of pressure.

Not that I wasn't used to pressure. A former career as a day trader, the desire to want to make my parents proud, and a second career as a bar manager were all preparation. Now? With both my parents gone, I was ready to make *myself* proud.

"Just wait until you taste her stuff. Everyone around here knows about Alexis and Tipsy Treats." He took a sip from the straw of his Frappa-whatever-the-fuck he was drinking. "I'm telling you, the whole thing is genius. The different infusion of cocktails that we'll be doing, along with small plates of food and Tipsy Treats? The locals are going to love it."

I was banking on it. This was *my* bar—well, mine along with my best friend Aaron, who was still back in our hometown Chicago. But it was all on me because I was the one here in California. It was my show, and Aaron was allowing me to run with it.

"Look," Wells continued. "It's totally unique to have a bar that only serves small plates, but with a heavy dessert aspect. It's going to work, though." He took another large sip from his drink. "Also, I don't know how it'd be my fault if she's late."

"Because I hired you to make sure you were only hiring the best." I paused, waiting for him to stop slurping up the bottom of his drink. "Plus, you look like a douchebag drinking that thing."

"A tasty beverage from Black Horse doesn't give off douche vibes. There's a reason it's the best coffee spot in San Luis Obispo. You should try one for yourself, and then you can go fuck yourself, boss," he said, rolling back into the office.

A relationship based on mutual shit talk, respect, and trust was the best kind to have. It was why I hired him.

I chuckled, walking to the end of the bar to retrieve the pen I'd thrown. I had a lot of nerve getting drippy when most of what I dished out I deserved in whatever bullshit I got back in return. It went back to having the ideal relationship with your right-hand man. We both could dish out and take.

Ginger was a beauty and I'd fight anyone who thought differently. The expansive two-floor space was in the heart of San Luis Obispo, California. With the walls decorated with paintings from local artists and the oak slate hardwood floors, the vibe was on beat with trendy. I didn't want *just* trendy, though. I wanted comfortable, a place people wanted to stay, drink, and hang out with friends. So I balanced the swanky with relaxed and inviting furniture like leather-bound high-back chairs that were slightly larger than normal barstools and chestnut-colored U-shaped booths that ran the entire perimeter of the bar. Add in small seating with two outdoor patios, one in front for a street view and one in back for a quieter one, and the whole thing was a dream fucking come true.

The pen slid back behind my ear as the front door slammed against the wall behind it, a hip check from the girl coming through it probably marking up my new paint.

"Oops," she said, her red hair matching her embarrassed, flushed cheeks. She looked behind the door to see if there was any damage as she balanced a tower of pink boxes in her arms. "Sorry. I think it's all good."

I sighed, shaking my head, crossing the room to give her a hand. "Let me guess? Alexis?"

"No," she said. "I'm Phoebe. She got held up, so I'm here to drop these off so you can take a look, or rather a taste, first."

I took several boxes, the scent of chocolate and sugar floating from them. "You know, a phone call would've been nice to let me know that."

She followed behind me, mumbling to herself, before saying, "Take it up with her."

"Huh?" I asked.

The vibe I received already, from both the lateness of Alexis and then the attitude of Phoebe, was not getting better. My threshold for bullshit, especially during a stressful time, was close to zero.

We settled the boxes on top of the bar, and she stepped back, placing her hands on her curvy hips. "I said take it up with her," she shouted. "Sorry. Sometimes I don't speak loud enough."

Clearly my "huh" wasn't viewed as rhetorical. It was time to lay down expectations.

"Whatever," I said, rolling my eyes. "I will, but just so you know, I view an owner as only as good as their employee. I'm not sold on either one at the moment. It's not professional to scream at someone."

"Sorry if I hurt your delicate ears," she said with a flippant tone. "But you said 'huh,' and that usually indicates that someone isn't hearing you well."

"Do you interact with all your customers like this?" I asked.

"Dude. Marshall," Wells said, rolling his chair back out. "Loosen up. This is no way to make an impression."

I didn't give a shit. I didn't care who thought I was a dick or not. This was my fucking business, and I expected anyone involved with it to take shit seriously. If that happened, I'd be as cool as a frosted beer mug.

Phoebe retrieved her phone from her back pocket and glanced at it. "Alexis will be here in a minute. She got caught up with another delivery."

"Are these for us?" I asked, poking the top of one of the pink boxes, my finger sliding across the black sticker that had Tipsy Treats printed in white across the top.

"You don't listen very well, do you?" she said, placing her hands on her hips. "I said they were for you to have a taste."

Wells snorted from his seat, and I shot a glare at him. "What the fuck are you laughing at?" I snapped.

"What?" he asked, continuing to chuckle. "Like it's not funny to see someone, let alone a woman, give you all the shit you dish out right back?"

Yeah. Just like I said. Dish out. Take.

"Thank you, Wells," Phoebe said. She smiled and then gave him a wink. "I haven't seen you around in a while."

His face grew serious. "Were you looking?" he asked with his eyebrows raised.

"Maybe," she said, winking again.

"Oh, for Christ's sake," I said, flipping the top of a pastry box open. "Will you two stop? I'm not hosting *Love Connection*."

"What's that?" Wells asked.

"You know, *Love Connection*. The dating show that used to be on," I said. "Remember 'two and two'?"

Both Phoebe and Marshall looked at me blankly. They didn't know. "Fucking children," I said under my breath about the two twentysomethings.

I focused my attention on the baked goods in the first box

I opened instead of the pathetic attempt at flirting that Wells was throwing at Phoebe. On initial look, they were impressive. A large cake-like brownie with shiny frosting on top, a few small, but not too small cupcakes with swirly tops and decorations, and some cookie bar things. It all looked amazing. I was deciding between the brownie or chocolate chip bar when the front door flung open, slamming into the wall behind it.

"What the fu—" I shouted, but stopped when I saw who made the noise.

What the fuck?

What the actual fuck?

The woman, glancing behind the door looking for damage, resembled someone I knew from many years ago. Her blond hair hung longer than I remembered, and without her facing me, I couldn't discern the rest of her features. I moved closer, and as her body shifted away from the door, I saw everything I needed to see.

"Holy shit," I whispered in shock. "Lexie Matthews."

Her head whipped around, and her hand went to her chest.

I couldn't believe it was her.

She had almost been erased from my memory. She had to be because the anger I had toward her for leaving Aaron and their daughter was enough for me to go homicidal.

And now she was standing right the fuck in front of me.

And all that anger was rising.

Rapidly.

She knew it, too, because her own shock had her frozen until she finally spoke.

"No one has called me that in over six years," she said.

Chapter Two

ALEXIS—

There are moments in life in which your breath is literally taken away. It isn't clichéd or a timely saying. No. The air rushing from your body with a force so powerful, your vision goes dark and your legs can barely hold you up.

He was completely covered in tattoos. His arms, reaching beneath his short-sleeved shirt. His chest from what I could see from the V-neck. His legs from his cargo shorts. He looked so different, but there was no doubt it was him.

Nausea came over my body, and my senses were in overdrive. It was a true blast from my past, and I didn't know how to wrap my brain around it. We were so far from Chicago. I'd made sure of that when I left there, to be as far away as possible so no one could find me.

When I could finally focus on his expression, I saw he was no doubt experiencing what I was: shock and confusion. The life I'd left so many years ago never crossed my path ever. Our eyes shifted across each other, narrowing and widening as it all sunk in.

Hell. Marshall Jones. I tried to forget them all, every single one I'd left behind, and I succeeded most of the time. I never, ever completely forgot anyone. You can run from your past, but you can't hide.

My past was staring me right in the face, and it was mad. Crazy mad.

"What the hell are you doing here?" he shouted. "*How* are you *here*? Right now?"

Wells stepped out of the office and approached us. "You two know each other?" he asked, waving a finger between us.

"We used to," both Marshall and I said in unison while still staring at each other.

"Why did he call you that?" Phoebe asked.

Marshall smacked Wells's shoulder. "Don't even fucking tell me this is the baker. How did this happen?"

"Ow," he said, rubbing the area where he was hit. "How did what happen? Why are you mad at me?"

Phoebe stepped up next to Wells. "Yeah? Why are you mad at him? In fact, why are you mad at all?"

Marshall ignored Wells's and Phoebe's questions and returned his annoyance back toward me. "Jesus Christ. Never in a million years did I expect this. What the fuck?"

"You're really kind of an asshole," Phoebe said, her porcelain skin turning red. "Why would you want to work with this guy, Wells?"

They all stopped their questions, and their heads turned to me for the answers.

And I didn't have any, so I went with the first thing that popped into my head.

"Phoebe? Did you bring the new cherry moonshine turnovers? I wanted him to—"

"Lexie," Marshall shouted. "What the hell?"

My head snapped back to look at him, furious at hearing that name again. "Marshall. I go by Alexis now."

His lip curled up in confusion. "You changed your fucking name?"

"First of all, you don't have to look at me like that. Second, what did you think Lexie was short for? I go by Alexis now, not Lexie."

Wells nudged Phoebe and gestured with his thumb toward the office. It was just as well since the awkwardness in running into my ex-husband's best friend was enough for anyone watching it to want to hide. Marshall and I followed with our eyes as Wells and Phoebe entered the office, shutting the door halfway behind them.

"There's a little something happening between those two," I said, trying to lighten the mood. "They're always bantering and making eyes at each other. Guess they knew better than to close the door completely, huh?"

Marshall saw no humor, nothing to smile about what I'd said. He was still breathing fire with straight malice shooting from his eyes. I'd never known him to be violent toward women, an asshole, yes, but never violent.

I knew if a moment ever came when someone from that time in my life was in front of me, I'd have to face all that I left behind. I'd have to stand tall and take whatever anger and hate came at me.

And it would all be completely justified.

I sighed and ran my hands across my vintage pale pink shirt, my fingers brushing over something sticky I must've spilled in the kitchen earlier. It wasn't an everyday item I wore; it was mostly for when I was going to meet new customers.

"So?" Marshall said, folding his arms across his chest. "You're Tipsy Treats?"

I nodded. "I am. And you are what? The manager of Ginger?"

"Owner," he snapped. "Co-owner actually. You want to take a fucking wild stab in the dark who my partner is?"

Marshall always drove me crazy with his filthy mouth and overzealous womanizing, but despite all that, I'd always liked him. He was one of the few people that would cross my mind from time to time.

However, my anxiety kicked in with the mention of a co-partner. No doubt it was Aaron, my ex-husband. His restaurant and bar businesses were flourishing when I left Chicago, and I had no doubt his success would expand further someday. I just didn't think it would be right in my line of vision, halfway across the country from his home base in Chicago.

"What are you doing here? I mean, how did this happen *here*?" I asked.

"Aaron's girlfriend is from the central coast. After they came for a visit, he put his feelers out, and you know how good he is. He knew this was the right place."

Aaron's girlfriend.

Of course he has one. I was glad. No, I was more than glad because I never wanted anything but good things for him.

"This is obviously not going to work," Marshall barked. "I don't care how fucking good your shit is."

"It isn't shit, and I don't think you should be so hasty."

His eyebrows lifted. "Hasty? It's not hasty to not want to have anything to do with you."

I winced at his words, the razor-sharp intent hitting me in the heart. I paused, waiting for the burn to subside before moving forward and in a different direction.

"Okay, this is a shock for both of us," I said, leaning against the doorframe.

"Ah. Yeah."

"How are you?" I asked.

A dirty look passed over his face. "What the fuck do you care?"

I shrugged. "I was trying to be polite."

"You weren't so polite when you ditched your kid and husband," he said in a low, menacing voice. "By the way, they're fine."

I inhaled deeply, letting his words, his anger settle into my bones. I'd wished I'd had time to prepare for this, and in some ways, I guess, I had years to. But I just never thought I'd ever have to deal with him or anyone from Chicago. If I'd known, in any capacity, I would be running into him, I could have processed how I would deal with it.

Or maybe not. I don't think anything could've prepared me.

"I'm glad they're well," I whispered.

"*Well?*" he spat, his voice raising as he dragged out the word. "You're glad they're well? What the fuck kind of thing is that to say? You aren't talking about the weather or how your lunch was. And please excuse the spite in my delivery, but there's no way I can be anything else. Not after what you did."

I twirled the bottom strands of my hair around my hand, a nervous habit I couldn't break. "I wasn't…prepared…and—"

"Oh, please," he said, rolling his eyes.

And this was when I snapped. The part that held everything I'd endured was safely tucked away for no one to see, but seeing him again made it break right open.

"Enough!" I screamed. "I'm no happier to see you than you are me. I didn't think I'd have to see you or be reminded of…everything…ever again. So, I get that you're angry at me, but this is *my* territory. I built a life, a business—and a damn good one—here long before you, or more than likely Aaron, wisely chose the Happiest City in America to open a bar."

I paused, my chest expanding and contracting from the force of my words. You'd think he would've been shaken by my outburst, or at the very least, startled. He was neither.

"Are you done?" he asked calmly. "I'm not going to wait for you to respond to that. You are. I don't give a fuck how long you've been here and what kind of life you have in this happy place. I'm here now and I don't want to see your face around my bar."

I heard a gasp and turned to see Wells and Phoebe poking their heads out of the office door. Phoebe whispered something in his ear as he nodded in agreement.

"And what are you two gossiping about?" Marshall snapped. "If you have something to say, then—"

"Fine," Phoebe said, stepping out of the office with Wells following. "I was trying to be discreet, but since you called me out, I'll be honest. I was telling Wells it was obvious by the way you two are bickering at each other that you must have boned years ago. This is obviously some past-due lovers' quarrel."

"No way!" I said as Marshall shouted, "Fuck no!"

They both recoiled, something between shock and disgust written all over their faces. I sighed deeply again, trying to clear my head and regulate all my emotions. This was a disaster. As the silence between us all began to grow, it seemed like the walls were closing in around us.

"Well, I really don't think there's anything left to say," Marshall said. "I'd say it was nice to see you, Lexie, but—"

I stomped my foot. "Alexis! Geez!"

"Alexis," he shouted back. "I don't want to see you in my bar again."

Phoebe gasped again as Wells whispered under his breath, "Damn."

It was all deserved. I didn't have to like it, and Phoebe and Wells didn't have to understand it, but it was all warranted. Even though I told myself all this, it didn't soften the blow enough. My instinct was to give it right back to him and not be talked to that way.

My instincts, in all areas except for business, were much different than they were years ago. I was no longer that woman who would level anyone, even a man, with a ferocious retort. I gave all that up when I gave up Lexie Matthews.

I stared him straight in the eye, allowing him to see I got it, but I could still stand tall. "The best to you, Marshall. I'm sure our paths will cross at some point. Small town and all."

I turned my back to him and headed to the door, calling to Phoebe over my shoulder. "See you back at the house," I said.

I pushed my way out the door, but it didn't shut before I

heard Marshall shout, "Holy fucking shit, Lexie Matthews."

I stopped in my tracks. "Alexis," I whispered.

* * *

The early afternoon sun was pleasantly warm as I made the drive home through the winding roads between San Luis Obispo and Arroyo Grande, where I lived. Five years living here, and while there were times when I missed such a drastic change of seasons, like in Chicago, I never missed it enough to give up this place. There was a comfort in knowing that while it always varied slightly, there was no need to plan for weather. The mid-seventies temperature, the sunny sky, and beautiful landscape added a peacefulness to the surroundings in a way I'd never known.

As I pulled myself off the twisted road and onto the gravel path to my home, I finally was able to breathe. As clichéd as it seemed, my home was my sanctuary. The converted barn house on five acres was surrounded by farms, ranches, and rolling hills. Far enough away from the downtown craziness of San Luis Obispo, but close enough to be able to make daily trips for deliveries. I came to a stop in front of the U-shaped driveway that was centered in front of a massive wraparound porch.

It was much too big of a house for me the architect had said.

I told him I knew what I wanted and I *wanted* the house.

It was too much house for one person, but when I laid eyes on it, I knew it was mine. Living a life alone didn't deter me from purchasing, renovating, and running a business out of it.

As I walked through the screened front door, I was reminded of why I did it all. Original oak beams preserved the authentic nature of the barnlike qualities while I added modest touches of modern. Warm, neutral colors throughout the living room, along with an oversized couch situated near the brick fireplace, was one of my favorite places in my home. I continued my path, meandering my way through the house across French limestone flooring that guided me to hardwood floors in my kitchen and work area.

I entered my spacious commercial kitchen, which was nothing short of picture-perfect, one fit for *Architectural Digest*. An enormous walk-in pantry and stacked rack-style bakery ovens were the focal points, while the deep, side-by-side basin sinks were flanked by oak cabinets and beams.

The scents of the cooling Fireball whiskey apple puffs and bananas Foster pastry cups I'd made earlier hung in the air. After stopping in front of them to give them a glance, I plopped myself on one of the island stools. My hands settled on the cool soapstone top, my fingers tracing the engrained patterns, and my mind rewound eight years as I allowed myself to think about the past.

"Only Chicagoans would flood the beach on one of the hottest days of the year," Sydney says, rolling onto her back, her body stretching across her beach towel.

"I don't mind it," I say, looking up to the sun and basking in the heat. "It will be twenty below before we know it."

She sits up slightly and moves her sunglasses down to the bridge of her nose. "Check that out," she says. "Yum."

I glance over to where she is pointing at the volleyball game happening. A two-on-two match between what appeared to be a set of college-aged kids and a midtwenties duo. Shirtless, board shorts, and sweaty, they all were eye candy.

"The youngsters are too young," Sydney says, pushing her sunglasses back in place. "However, that other pair. I wish I didn't need my shades so I can start making eyes."

Both tall, the dark-haired one is slightly taller, with an insane body and smile to match. The dirty blond is equally hot, but there is something about him that I'm drawn to more. I take him in, but before I could indulge further, Sydney taps my arm—

"Dibs on the blond," Sydney says, making my choice easier.

My eyes drift back over to them, the sun beating down on their tan, toned bodies, their muscles tightening with every bump, set, and spike. The blond sees us ogling and gives us a quick wave before nudging the one I've come to know as mine.

The whole scenario brings to mind a certain movie sequence, and before I even tell Sydney, she beats me to it.

"We never get to see so much hotness, aka Top Gun, action in real life," she says.

"I was about to say the same thing."

"Well," she says, perching from her beach towel. "Dark hair and light hair. Maverick and Iceman."

I shrug. "I don't know. I always thought Iceman was hotter. I think I'll call the dark-haired one that."

"You can't just switch the names like that!"

"Why not? I can do whatever I want."

We sit quiet as we watch the rest of the game unfold. The college boys are good. They're really good, but Team Top Gun is better. When they spike the game point, Sydney and I cheer, letting them know we'd been paying attention. After they celebrate, Iceman starts to jog over, and I know I have to play a bit of hard to get.

"Hi there," he says when he approaches me. He smiles, and now that it's directed toward me, I know that smile probably gets this guy anything he wants.

I look at him, up and down. "Hi."

He stretches his arms above his head, further accentuating his tight abs. "Hot enough for you?"

I shrug. "I can take hotter."

"Can you?" he asks before sitting down next to me.

He is confident and sexy. Two very attractive qualities. He is also sporting an enormous ego I am going to need to put in check so I can get him right where I want.

I laugh. "Don't waste your time, lover boy. Those lines and the pretty boy face don't do shit for me."

He smiles again, unfazed. "If my face or lines don't do it for you, what would?"

He won't back down, and I know this is as level a playing field as we are going to get. Either he'll be a happily-ever-after guy or the biggest regret of my life. My gut tells me so. It's too tempting of a scenario to shy away from.

I shield my eyes from the sun to look at him better. "Offer to buy me a drink. That's a good start."

He nods. "That I can do. The vodka lemonades at Castaways might put me in an even better position."

I stand and brush off some sand that has stuck to me. I take my time, twisting just so, so he can get a better glimpse of me standing. After bending down to pick up my shorts, I glance at him as I pull them on.

"Come on, Iceman. I'm thirsty."

We start walking toward Castaways, the North Avenue Beach bar, as we steal glances, checking each other out.

"Why Iceman?" he asks as we near the bar. "No Maverick?"

I pause and turn to look at him. "Iceman was way hotter."

The slamming of the screen door brought me out of my reminiscing. Phoebe was standing with her hands on her hips, shaking her head. The curvy girl, with the fiery red hair and personality to match, was going to want answers. Not only was she my friend and employee, she was someone who was never a bystander. It was what I liked best about her. It was what drew me to her in the beginning. When the business began to get busier, I knew I needed the added help. She is a hell of baker, and we work side by side with ease. Her becoming my friend, too? It was an added bonus.

"What the hell happened back there?" she asked.

Chapter Three

MARSHALL—

I couldn't shake everything I was feeling after seeing her. It was so fucked up. Out of all people, out of all places, Lexie—or Alexis I guess she was called now—was the one to show up. I hadn't seen her since before she left Aaron and their daughter Delilah so many years ago. And she didn't just leave, she *abandoned* them. She gave up all rights and custody of Delilah and was never seen again. I was hoping I'd never see her again after witnessing what her selfish, fucked-up act did to my best friend.

Fuck. Aaron was going to lose his shit when I told him. In a way, I couldn't wait.

She looked almost the same—tall, pretty, and long, wavy blond hair. There was one thing that was different, and it was the one thing I was having the hardest time shaking: She had the saddest eyes I'd ever seen. It was almost haunting. There was so much hidden behind those eyes, and I knew a lot of it. The "Ice Queen," the name we all jokingly called her, always had a hard exterior that no one, not even Aaron, could crack through completely. There was never a lot of emotion out of her ever, but now? There was definite sadness.

Abandoning your husband and baby was one way for someone to be sad, and it showed.

Good. She deserves it.

I had to sit back and watch my best friend get his life destroyed. I had to see Delilah, the daughter she gave up and never saw again, begin to grow up without a mother. Yeah. Things were better now with Callie, Aaron's girlfriend, in the picture, but how could Lexie ever justify that? She couldn't. No fucking way. I'd done a lot of questionable shit in my life, but taking off like she did and just leaving a note was something you didn't do.

I glanced at one of the boxes she left. TIPSY TREATS was written in fancy, blue lettering across the pink pastry box. I flipped the top open, and fuck if the pastries inside didn't smell as good as they looked. I was stubborn enough to want to refuse to eat any of it because she made them.

But I wasn't stupid.

So, I picked up the goddamn brownie with the shiny frosting and took a bite.

"Christ," I mumbled.

I was so fucking pissed with how good it was. In fact, it wasn't just good. It was the best brownie I'd ever had. I glanced at the bottom of the wrapper where it read "Stout Brownie" and realized that was what made it so unique. It had this deep chocolate flavor with a, like it said, background of stout. And while I knew I'd never had anything quite like it, there was something familiar about it. Maybe it was the beer flavor. Whatever it was, it was fucking delicious.

"Damn it," I said, before setting it down and deciding on what to try next.

Well. Good for her. She made good shit. At least she could do something right.

I selected a small doughnut, yellow with a white glaze, next. "Margarita Doughnut." Again, after tasting, I was blown away. A sweet yellow cake with a tequila chaser. I wanted to throw it on the floor and step on it because it was so amazing and so perfect for this bar. Too bad the woman who made them made me angrier than when people put the toilet paper roll on wrong.

Always over. Never under.

"Whatever," I said, slamming the box cover down while finishing the rest of the doughnut.

"What did that box ever do to you," Wells said, walking through the front door.

"Where the hell have you been?" I snapped.

He stopped midstep. "I was walking Phoebe to her car."

"That was like forty-five minutes ago."

"It was a long walk," he said with a dumbass smile.

He stood there, grinning like a jackass eating cactus. I shook my head because I didn't even have the energy to give him shit after the whole Lexie…*Alexis*…debacle.

He came up next to me. "Oh! The cherry moonshine turnover," he said, yanking it from the box.

He was about to bite into it when I slapped his hand. "Put that down!"

With his mouth hanging open and the turnover inches from lips, he asked "Why?"

I jerked it away from him and tossed it back in the box. "We are not eating any of these."

"You did."

"How do you know?"

"Because the brownie is the best, and it was gone. Plus, you have chocolate on your face."

"Fuck," I said, wiping at my mouth. "In any case, I don't want to see anything from that woman, including herself, in my bar again. Got it?"

"What is the deal with you and her?"

I folded my arms in front of my chest. "She's Aaron's ex-wife."

Wells's face went to shock, and for added drama, he gripped his chest. "Are you kidding me?"

"No. So, there's no way she'd work out here."

His eyes shifted around like he was contemplating something before he shrugged his shoulders. "I dunno."

"You don't know what?" I snapped again. "There's no fucking way."

"I mean, was it terrible? Is there a reason we still can't do business?"

"Yes, it was and that *is the* reason."

"Too bad," he said. "She's the sweet queen of San Luis Obispo. Everyone I told about her being a possible addition was stoked and thought our infusion drinks plus her liquor treats were an awesome match."

"Well, it's not. No way would—"

"Business is business, boss," he said, interrupting me. "I'm not in any way trying to tell you how to run your bar, but you should consider it if it is best for the business."

Before I could stop him, he snatched the turnover from the box and bolted toward the office.

I was so irritated by everything. For starters, the fact that Wells was right and I fucking knew it. She would be good for business, but there was no way I could see her all the time without having to be on some sort of blood pressure medication/ vodka IV combination to keep my shit together. Not only did she fuck over my best friend, but also she left everything behind in Chicago. Her job, her friends, me included, and her life meant so little to her that taking off without so much as a good-bye hurt us all.

I could never, ever forget that. I didn't know if there was even room to possibly understand. The thought of her being around me daily was too much for me to consider, even from my own personal standpoint. We were such close friends, the three of us, and watching the destruction she left behind was one of the most fucked-up things I've ever had to witness. I couldn't be reminded of that every day.

And even if I did, I couldn't do that to Aaron. He was like a brother to me.

Unless.

I was adamant about running this place with Aaron as the silent partner. It was my chance to prove myself, to not only him, but also to my own self. I had been working with Aaron for years, and Ginger was originally going to be his joint venture with his brother, Abel. When Abel needed out of the partnership, Aaron came to me, and I bought out Abel's share with the money I'd been squirreling away for years. Some from work, but most of it was my inheritance from my parents since I was their only child.

While major decisions were a thing we discussed together, the everyday goings-on was all on me. While the bar wasn't open yet, I had done a decent job so far, and I didn't want that to change. However, Aaron was the pro. He had successfully opened, funded, or oversaw several of the most elite bars in Chicago, along with a few high-end boutique hotels.

The most recent "business" development was going to warrant an immediate fucking phone call to him.

I retrieved my phone from my back pocket and pressed my finger to his name in my contacts.

"Hey," he said, answering. "How's the Chicago-turned-California boy?"

I snorted. "I'll never be California. There's too much Chicago blood running through me. How's things there?"

"Good. Hot as hell, but that's August in Chicago for you."

"And the girls?"

I could practically hear the grin before he even answered.

"Perfect," he said. "Well, Delilah asked me yesterday when I was going to have to start using a walker since I'm getting so old."

"Wow. Seven years old and already getting her uncle Marshall's sass. I love that little girl," I said.

"Having you and Abel as prominent male figures in her life doesn't exactly sit well with me. I'm glad I'm as straightlaced as I am to give her some balance," he said with a laugh.

I, of course, understood his concern. His younger brother Abel walked the line of dumbass enough to warrant his supervision around children. However, since landing the sweetheart of Chicago, Evelyn, he had chilled out a bunch and, dare I say, matured. Now me? There was almost room for me to be offended with Aaron for lumping me into the same category as Abel's idiot ways, but with my crass mouth and "gives no fucks" attitude, I could see his point.

"And Callie?" I asked.

"Great. School's out for summer so she's resting up her overworked teacher brain. Things are really good here," he said.

That guy had been through the fucking wringer with Lexie. While things with Callie hadn't always been smooth sailing, it was nice to hear.

"So?" he asked. "What do you have for me?"

I took in a deep breath. "Dude. You are not going to fucking believe who came in—"

"What, Delilah?" Aaron shouted. "Sorry, man. Hold on a second."

I paused, preparing to tell him about Lexie as he dealt with Delilah.

"What is it?" Aaron asked.

"Where's Mom?" Delilah's small voice said. "I need to ask her something."

"Your mom isn't here right now," Aaron replied.

Their voices muffled during the rest of their exchange, but it gave me enough time to digest what I'd just heard.

Mom.

Your mom.

I'd heard Delilah call Callie "mom" before, but something struck me this time around. And it all had to do with Lexie, Delilah's biological mom. Anger flooded through me recalling the months and years that followed after Lexie was gone. There were no words for the pain and confusion that encircled Aaron, while doing his damnedest to be the best father he could. And he was. He was the most amazing fucking father I'd ever known aside from my own.

The years rolled on, and Aaron created a life for just him and his daughter, but you could sense his loneliness. It wasn't until he hired Callie to be the nanny and sparks flew that everything changed.

He found his soul mate. He found fucking *peace*. And he found what I thought he was missing the most—a mother for his daughter.

That wasn't Lexie. It never was.

And who the fuck was I to invite all that hurt and pain back into his life by telling him our paths had crossed? He'd been through enough anguish. He didn't deserve any more, not when he had Callie and his daughter had her mom.

"Sorry," Aaron said, returning to me. "Always girl drama. There is so much estrogen in this house, I'm actually considering getting a male dog to help balance things out. What were you saying?"

My eyes scanned around the bar, taking it all in. "Man, we've done well here."

"We haven't done anything yet but decorate, Marshall," Aaron said. "Cosmetic shit and a catchy hook will only get you so far."

"I know that, but…" I trailed off as I picked my next words. "I can just feel it. We have something that's solid."

Aaron let out a small sigh. "This is your first baby. For all intents and purpose, it's completely yours. You've put it all together yourself. I'm just the silent partner. However, I've done this enough times to know there is only one thing for certain."

"And what's that?"

"In the bar business, nothing is certain."

"Well, that's both logical and a major buzzkill. What happened to plain old optimism?"

"Of course be optimistic, but you also have to do a lot of other things. You need be smart and savvy. You need to work relentlessly and leave no room for error. Most importantly, in my opinion? Surrounding yourself with the best staff, and I do mean best. You will see potential in some, but there will be others that hit you hard with an impression. Those are the ones you want to hold on tight to."

I let his words sink in, but he said one final thing before I had the chance to respond.

"I'm trusting you Marshall to do what is best, not for yourself, but for Ginger," he said. "I gotta run, but let me know if you need any more help."

His words stung my heart, but mostly at my ego. Aaron and I had been friends long enough, and been through enough shit together, for me to get he wasn't trying to be condescending when he mentioned needing more help. It was only my interpretation. However, his words echoed through my brain.

"I'm trusting you, Marshall."

"If you need any more HELP."

I wasn't going to let Ginger or Aaron, who was trusting me so completely, down.

I wasn't going to let *myself* down.

I wasn't going to fail.

This was my time to do something I was proud of, to have a passion for my work. A white-collar job years ago left me unfulfilled and bored as hell. It was too uptight and suffocating. So I left it and took a job as a bartender, working for Aaron. Bartender then turned to manager to now owner. I'd worked toward something of substance for so many years, had been waiting for my time, but I didn't even know it was opening my own bar until the opportunity was presented to me. Now that I knew my purpose, I was going wrestle it into a success. I wouldn't stop at anything less.

I knew what I had to do.

"Wells," I shouted. "Call Lexie—shit, Alexis—and tell her to get back here."

I probably should've gone to her, but this is where everything was happening. If she was going to see what I was doing, she needed to be part of the whole damn thing.

"All right!" he called back.

"Fuck," I mumbled. "Wells?" I called to him again.

I sighed and slammed my fist against the marble surface of the bar. "Say fucking please to her."

* * *

I was staring at the blank screen of my iPad, pretending to be doing something important while I waited for her to come back. Wells said she was pleasant enough and that she said she'd be on her way soon.

That was a fucking hour ago.

This was going to be temporary thing. I was going to let her do her dessert thing with us until the opening, and when everything was up and running, she was out. This was strictly a business move and nothing else.

And at this rate, if I was going to have to keep waiting for her, I was—

"Marshall," she said in an annoyed toned as she walked in the front door. "Ready to play nice?"

"Are you always so fucking late?"

"Late for what? Coming back here after you all but kicked me out and then summoned me back?"

"Whatever," I said with a roll of my eyes. "Can we just do this?"

"Answer my question first," she said, tapping her foot. "Play nice?"

"Work. I'll work nice with you, okay?"

"So you've decided we can work together?" she asked.

"I haven't decided shit yet. I haven't seen if we can even be in the same room together, but I need to do what's best for my business. I can only assume the same goes for you."

Her chest lifted against her folded arms as she inhaled deeply. As she blew her breath out, she grasped at the end of her hair, twirling it around her finger. "Fine."

I walked around to the back of the bar, picking up a highball glass. "Drink?" I asked.

She gave me a dirty look as she approached. "It's what? Not even one o'clock in the afternoon?"

"So the hell what? Never had a liquid lunch?"

"No. I have a job," she said, sliding onto one of the barstools. "I've always had a job."

"Whatever," I said. "It was a fucking gesture. I had some of your shit to eat. I was extending the same to you in drink form."

"Well, perhaps I should. Wells has certainly put your cocktail making at a level of something special."

"Do you want one or not?"

"Sure."

"Shit," I huffed.

"Did you always swear this much? It's not very becoming for a business owner."

The sides of her light-pink-glossed lips turned up as she tried to hide a laugh. She was pressing my buttons, pushing to see how far she could until I snapped. My grip on the glass tightened with annoyance, and I knew it would break in my hand if I didn't chill out.

"My…language," I said, setting the glass down gently, "is a little more colorful these days than when I was a trader."

"Not the only thing that's colorful. That's some serious ink, Marshall," she said, motioning her hand across my body.

"Yeah. Didn't you throw a tantrum when Aaron got one?"

She winced at the mention of his name, and while there was satisfaction in seeing her in pain, I wasn't enough of a dick to fully enjoy it. If there was any lesson learned, it was that I could push her buttons, too. Also, Aaron's name was off the table. It was better off that way. Considering I was lying to my best friend until the business was thriving and he could see how it all worked out, I'd rather his name stay out of any conversation.

"We had some ice earlier, but Wells had to bring that in for training of the new employees. The machine isn't up and running yet so, it's not a completely functional bar at the moment," I said, changing the subject. I glanced at the fruit and garnish tray to see what we had available. I knew I had some extra fruit and shit from the training for the cocktail infusions.

"That's fine," she said.

"Whiskey? Vodka? I don't remember—"

"Gin."

As soon as she said it, I did, in fact, remember. I remember thinking all those years ago how odd it was for a woman to drink gin straight up. No tonic. Just ice and a few limes. All the girls I knew would sip their beers to try and keep up with the boys or would get foo-foo fruity drinks while pounding shots.

I mentally went through the gin drinks we'd be offering, and after a glance to see what fruit was left over, I knew what I'd make her. I grabbed a cucumber and a couple limes, setting them down on a clean cutting board reserved for making garnishes and add-ins.

"I know you're not usually a tonic person, but this drink is with club soda, cucumber, and lime. It will be right up your alley," I said.

She narrowed her eyes at me. "How did you know about the tonic?"

"I remembered when you said gin," I said, shrugging. I grabbed a small knife from under the bar and started cutting several thin slices of cucumber. "Plus, we used to hang out a lot and drinking was involved often."

She didn't answer me, but rather sat quiet, watching me make her cocktail. I dropped the cucumber and lime rinds that I cut into strips into the bottom of the glass. As I began to muddle them together, my eyes glanced in her direction. Her gaze had moved from my hands to the mirrored shelves lining the wall behind me. Turning my head to see what she was staring at, I could tell that aside from the neatly arranged bottles of booze reflecting off the back, there wasn't anything but her own reflection to look at.

I added some sugar to the glass, along with some lime juice, the only sounds surrounding us were the muddler hitting the glass and Wells's barbaric chuckle from the office. Another covert peek at her and I saw that the gawking she was doing at her own reflection hadn't changed.

What the fuck is she staring at? Yeah, Lexie. You're still hot.

A chill ran across me as I added gin to the glass, when the impact of my thoughts hit me square in the chest. It almost knocked me off balance, the almost vulgar path my brain took me to—*You're still hot.*

Well. Of course she was. She always was. You'd have to be blind not to notice, and people always did—men and women couldn't help but look at her. Deep down I knew that thought that passed across my mind was just that: a thought. It didn't mean a damn thing aside from it being a simple observation.

Besides, I never looked at her like *that* once Aaron staked his claim. She was always Aaron's girl, and even if she was the one that caught my eye first, it worked out the way it was supposed to.

But now? She wasn't Aaron's girl. She was the girl that broke my best friend's heart and left her daughter. At the moment, there was nothing attractive about that.

"What are you daydreaming about?" Lexie asked, breaking me from my thoughts.

"What were you?" I snapped back. "You've been staring at yourself in the mirror for God knows how long."

My attention turned back to her drink. After I added some club soda, I dipped a straw into the cocktail. Squeezing the top of the straw, I then lifted it to my mouth to taste it. Perfect. I tossed my straw in the garbage, plunged a new one into the drink, and slid it across the bar to her.

She narrowed her eyes down at it and then up to me. "Are you allowed to do that?"

"Do what?"

"Taste it first?"

I tossed the muddler and knife into the sink. "Ah. Yeah."

"Isn't that like double-dipping?"

"I gave you a new straw," I said, raising my voice. "And I, or we, don't do it all the time. We're trying out a lot of different things here and what's important for quality control."

She shrugged her shoulders, lifting the glass to her mouth. "Whatever you say, Marshall."

"Jesus," I mumbled.

She wasn't going to rest until she drove me to the point of insanity. Was I going to be able to handle this?

Chill the fuck out, Marshall. Just stand your ground and let her know she's not getting under your skin.

I busied myself cleaning up, avoiding her reaction as she tasted my drink. I knew she'd come at me with some smart-ass remark about it or complain about this or that, so I was biding my time until she did.

At one point she set the glass down, without saying a word, and turned her head around to avoid again looking anywhere but at me.

It was the last straw.

"Well, just sit there and continue daydreaming," I said, tossing the rag I was wiping the bar down with across its length. "No 'thank you'? No 'it's okay'? And why the hell were you gawking in the mirror while I was making that drink, anyway?"

Her indignant eyes opened wide, showing no mercy toward mine. "Thank you," she said sharply. "It's okay. And I wasn't gawking, I was thinking."

"About what?" I snapped.

She twirled the straw around her drink before lifting it out of the glass and tossing it on the bar. Droplets of gin and lime juice sprinkled across the surface that I had just fucking cleaned, that she watched me clean, right in front of her.

She took another sip. "Not that it's any of your business, but—"

"You know what? If you're going—"

"Marshall. Shut up and don't interrupt me," she cut in. "Man. Throw a few tattoos on a boy and all sense of being the gentleman I remember goes out the window."

"Or maybe fucking over my best friend makes me a little cranky."

Another sip.

Another deep breath.

"I was going to say, I was thinking of the perfect pairing for this drink," she said. "*That* is what I was pondering."

Oh.

"Sorry," I mumbled.

"A mini mojito cheesecake," she said.

"Huh?"

"To pair with it. This tastes like a mojito, but without the rum."

"And mint."

"Whatever," she said. "Maybe I should clarify. It has a…vibe…like a mojito. In any case, the citrus with the lime would match the lime in the cheesecake. Plus, the sweetness and rum would complement the cucumber and gin nicely."

I nodded my head, reluctantly impressed with her thought process. It was the first hint of hope I'd had since the moment she walked through the door. Maybe we could make this work if we both just kept our fucking mouths shut and kept it to business.

"I dig it," I muttered.

I extended my arm and grabbed the rag I had thrown. I thought I heard her mumble a "thanks" back, but I wasn't sure.

And I wasn't going to fucking ask her.

"I'm going to need a menu of all the drinks," she said. "I can give my input on what would pair well or if you wanted to do sampler plates."

I dragged my hands through my hair, swallowing her assumptions and carefully choosing my words. "And you think this can work? You and me working together?"

She smiled, a genuine grin, and I was transported back so many years ago. While she always had a rough edge, a no-bullshit attitude, when she smiled, the world saw it. Again, it was another first of the day. Perhaps two more. She smiled for one, and two, I saw the old Lexie.

"I tried your drink," she said. "Did you try my stuff?"

"Why do you think I asked you back?"

"Answer my question."

"Yes, I did."

"And?"

"Like I said, I asked you back, didn't I?"

"I guess that's the best I'll get out of you, but I have one more question. What are you going to tell Aaron?"

There was no hesitation behind her question, and because of it, it was shocking. I'd assumed she wouldn't care what he thought or what my role would be in mediating the situation. It also meant I was going to have to stomach the fact I wasn't being entirely truthful with Aaron, not that I needed to explain a goddamn thing to her. It was more for my own peace of mind. Ginger was the first thing I ever felt so passionately about, and I wanted it to be the best. If it was as big of a success as I hoped for, then Aaron would never need to know about her. His life was complete now. For the first time in fucking years. I wasn't going to mess that up, no matter if it was for business or personal reasons.

"For now? Nothing."

She bit the bottom of her lip, not in a sexy way, but to stifle a laugh. She shook her head and tried to gain her composure. "Sorry. I'm not laughing. It's just ironic."

"How so?"

"You're the one lying to Aaron now."

"I'm not lying. I'm just not telling him. He has the life he wants now, the life he's fucking sacrificed everything for. I'm not going to drudge up everything from the past, everything to do with *you*, and get him all riled up back in Chicago. I'm the one handling shit here."

"One might say not telling is still lying."

"And I say you're wrong."

"That's your business," she said, sliding out of her seat.

She stood up, brushing her hands down her uniform whatever. The pink dress thing looked like she stepped right out of a retro diner. It was cute or catchy, I guess. This was a girl who I never saw in anything that didn't have a designer label or a suit jacket. Her high-powered career in her previous life was a complete one-eighty from what she was doing now. It made me wonder what else was different.

"So," I said, leaning against the bar. "What's up with Sydney?"

She shrugged. "How would I know?"

"You were like best friends."

She stepped in, picking up her drink and taking a long swig. "We drifted apart," she said, after she swallowed.

"Did you drift apart from everyone in your life?"

"I don't see how that is any of your business. Plus, if you're so interested in what she's doing, why don't you ask her. You were the one dating her."

"That was fucking years ago and I never dated her."

She laughed loudly, bending at her waist with how funny this was to her. "That's right," she said through struggled breath and giggles. "You screwed around with her and then on her."

She had so much fucking nerve.

Maintain, Marshall. She's trying to get a rise. Don't let her. I don't care if she tells me I'm as useless as a knitted condom.

"We weren't exclusive, Lexie," I said.

She sighed. "Please stop calling me that. And did Sydney know that? That you were sticking it in every—"

And that was where I snapped. It hit me right in a sensitive spot, the spot where I knew all the pain she caused Aaron and Delilah and couldn't believe her fucking indignation.

"I'm going to move right the fuck past this entire conversation," I said, moving down the length of the bar to get away from her. "I was only trying to make conversation, keep shit as civil as possible."

"Me, too. I can maintain professionalism, so maybe you shouldn't bring up stuff from years ago," she said.

Anger exploded inside of me, and if it wasn't for my office view in front of me, leading me away from her, I would've lost my shit. Steps away from the office door and she came at me with one last round.

"Marshall? Sorry," she said in a tone only above a whisper.

The hell she was.

I spun around. "You know what? I won't bring up shit from the past. That's fine with me as long as you aren't a bitch if I ask a simple question like how a friend is or how you're enjoying the weather."

Her shoulders slouched, her eyes to the floor. "The weather is always perfect here. Even when it rains, it's perfect."

"I have a hard time believing that, but whatever you say."

"What's not to believe?"

"Anything you fucking say, Lexie."

Her head popped up. "Anything but that name. Please," she said.

She drew in a deep breath, closing her eyes as she exhaled with a slow, controlled measure. When her eyes flickered back open, the sadness I saw earlier had returned. It occurred to me it wouldn't take much to break her. There was a vulnerability I'd never known or seen from her before, and because of that, I was confused. There were parts of her, the hard exterior and ice-cold interior I once knew, that were still firmly intact. But this other side? It made her familiar features distort in such a way that the past Lexie and present Alexis were both right there, but hidden at the same time.

"So," she said, breaking through my thoughts. "About the mini mojito cheesecakes."

Chapter Four

It was always quiet. It wasn't only because I lived alone in seclusion. It was because it was how this town was. Arroyo Grande was twenty minutes from downtown San Luis Obispo. It was far enough away from the college kids at Cal Poly and the hustle and bustle of the town, but still close enough for my daily deliveries.

The quiet was what I wanted all along and I found it.

There was no time it was quieter than just before the sun began to rise, an explosion of fiery oranges and buttery yellows lifting from the darkness into the periwinkle sky. It wasn't beautiful. It was breathtaking. I never knew a sunrise could look like that until I moved here. There simply wasn't time, or even the desire, to stop to glance at one.

But now?

It was my morning ritual. My prayer. Mediation. Whatever it was called, it was for me.

The heat and steam from my morning coffee warmed my

hands that wrapped around the mug. Still in my pajamas, I lazily swung on my porch swing, a blanket, a white chenille with little rainbows all over it, thrown over my legs to keep out the morning chill. At a little after six o'clock in the morning, my workday would begin soon once the sun was in full bloom.

I picked up my phone to scroll through my schedule for the day, even though I had looked at it right before bed. All those years in finance as an investment banker, when working eighty hours a week was the norm, primed me for early mornings and late nights. The difference? I traded in my conservative dress and pantsuits for jeans, T-shirts, and my baby-pink vintage waitress/bakery girl button-down dress.

I traded in more than my attire. So much more.

My morning was fairly normal. Phoebe would be here in about an hour and we'd start baking. My orders weren't vast like a regular bakery, but rather made-to-order for the local farmers markets, small restaurants, bookstores, and other specialty retailers. Ginger was my first venture into the bar business and it was going to be a large undertaking. Instead of small deliveries on various days of the week, Ginger was going to require daily drop-offs. It wasn't a venture I was going into lightly.

Especially now.

Damn. I didn't want to work with Marshall. Granted it had been many years, but his personality had taken a nosedive. Looking further down my schedule, I knew I wasn't going to forget what I had to do: Ginger. Before I left there two days ago, I told him I'd be by today to drop off additional samples for his employee training class that night.

I was just going to have to get used to it, both being there and seeing him. My only hope was he'd start to lighten up to make this venture everything I knew it could be prior to knowing him and Aaron were owners.

Aaron.

Delilah.

What if they came here?

No. I couldn't think about that. Not only would Marshall warn me, but he obviously wasn't going to risk his friendship with Aaron over this. It was why it was so odd that he was lying to Aaron about it at all. If there was one thing I knew about Aaron, it was that he had no tolerance for, *hated*, being lied to. He would've never forgiven me for hiding what I did from him, so I decided to run away first. It was what I did, except with him, I ran from my daughter, too.

My thoughts had lasted through to my favorite part of the sunrise, the sun, blinding, brave, and ready to burn up a new day. I pulled the blanket from my lap and wrapped it around me as I headed into the house to refill my coffee. The day was starting.

* * *

"And I don't care what that dicknose says to you, don't let him take your power," Phoebe said as we headed toward the entrance of Ginger. The gravel parking lot was unsteady as we navigated with boxes of pastries and treats.

"Okay," I said.

"I'm serious, Alexis. If he sees you get all riled up with his macho, ego-ridden shit talk, you stand back and smile. He'll hate that."

"Okay," I said. "I get it."

Phoebe didn't know the whole story, though. In fact, she knew *none* of the story. She was part of my life here in California, and I never shared with her about my old life in Chicago.

Phoebe never knew me in my days as an investment banker. In a field where men outranked women by 80 percent, I learned, and learned quickly, to not only stand my ground, but also dominate it. That never left me. In fact, the cold-as-ice exterior was part of me for all of my adult life, and when it came to career choice, I had no fears. However, it was never my passion. So, I took my no-fear attitude and started Tipsy.

We approached the door, and Phoebe pushed it open with what appeared to be a very tame hip bump, but the door overreacted, crashing into the wall behind it. We stepped inside and were immediately assaulted by Marshall's shouting.

"What the hell?" he screamed from somewhere he couldn't be seen. "How hard is it to open a fucking door?"

"It was an accident!" Phoebe said.

Marshall emerged from the office, shaking his head. His messy, dirty-blond hair shook around his face, and his blue eyes glared at us. Even though I'd seen him, he was still *so* different. The Marshall I remembered was this clean-cut, smiley smooth talker. He could charm the pants off anyone or anything. Women, men, customers, and even dogs were putty in his charismatic hands. Outside of WET, Aaron's bar that Marshall managed, he was always dressed in top men's fashion. Now? Jeans and a fitted, plain black T-shirt, every inch of his skin on display covered in tattoos, only reminded me a fraction of the guy I once knew. There was such a mystery surrounding him now, and while I had no right to ask, I wondered.

"Accident my ass," he mumbled, heading over to us. He grabbed a few boxes from me, without even a hello, and turned to walk away.

Or maybe I didn't wonder that much.

"Well, it was," Phoebe said. "You need to put some door stoppers on that or something."

Marshall placed the boxes on top of the bar with a little more aggression than I was comfortable with, considering the delicate nature of what was inside.

Phoebe and I placed the remaining treats next to the others, and I began to open the tops of the boxes. "Phoebe? Can you run out to the truck and grab the serving trays and displays?"

"And watch the door on the way back in," Marshall huffed.

The thing I loved most about Phoebe was she didn't take shit. If I was comfortable with holding my ground against men, she was a rabid animal unleashed if she thought a man was talking down to her. No doubt he got a taste during their first meeting, but now he was in trouble.

She stomped over to him, tossing her wild red hair behind her. As she stepped up to him, he probably could've missed all five foot one inch of her if he hadn't been looking.

"Listen, Asshole Casserole," she hollered, her head lifted as far as she could to try and stare him down. "I don't know what your deal is, but you're going to shove that self-righteous, spunk bubble of an attitude up your ass, leave it there, and act a little more goddamn pleasant, okay?"

"Phoebe!" I said.

His jaw dropped open in shock, but he shook it off. "Spunk bubble, huh? Good one," he said, cracking a hint of a smile.

Phoebe stepped backed, rounding her shoulders in pride. "Thank you. Now if you excuse me, I'm going to go get the stuff to set up the display."

"You know," Marshall called to her. "All I meant was, if you could be a little gentler with your hip check into the door, I would—"

Phoebe spun around, her face turning the color of her hair. "Are you calling me fat now?" she screamed. "Because you may think of that as an insult, but it's not. I'm proud of who I am and—"

"Phoebe," I said. "That's enough."

"No!" Marshall shouted, interrupting her right back. "I didn't call you anything."

And of course, at that moment, Wells rushed in from the back, anger seething from every orifice. "You called her fat?" he exclaimed. "You can be a dick sometimes, boss, but that's a whole other level lower than you."

"I did not call her fat!" Marshall said.

"You implied it," Phoebe said. "What with my overly ample hips checking into your precious door."

"You said that?" Wells screeched. "Dude."

"I did not!" Marshall said. "Lex— Alexis, I mean. Tell him. Tell her!"

Once again, all eyes were on me. The scenario seemed funny enough, but this was business, a business I was trying to run with Marshall.

I turned to Phoebe. "Chill out, he didn't call you fat. He didn't say ample. You made your point. Please go get the display things."

Her face softened, and I saw her anger begin to lift away. A working relationship with Marshall would prove to be volatile, both of them with their strong personalities, but they were going to have to deal with it. I was going to have to deal with it between them, while trying to manage however things were going to evolve between Marshall and myself.

I turned to Wells. "He didn't call her fat. They were riling each other up, and they both need to stop. You also need to mind your own business. If you're into Phoebe, just ask her out and get over all the cat and mouse."

I turned to Marshall. "Phoebe was right. Shove the attitude where the sun doesn't shine, once and for all, or I'm calling it done. This is unhealthy for all of us, and it's not worth it. I get it, okay? You hate me. You hate what I did to Aaron. I can't change it. Neither can you."

"Who's Aaron?" Phoebe asked.

"You don't know?" Wells exclaimed. "He's the other owner here *and* Alexis's ex-husband *and* Marshall's best friend."

Phoebe began giggling. "Alexis doesn't have an ex-husband, and I find it hard to believe Marshall has any friends."

I winced at Phoebe's words. They stung and right in a place I wasn't prepared for. My heart.

He did have friends. He always had a lot of friends. *I* was his friend for many years.

Marshall raked his hands through his hair, shaking his head. "All right," he said. "Enough of all of this. Family meeting."

"Family?" I asked.

"Yes," he said. "We all work together. We may argue and bitch at each other, but in the end, I view it as a family."

"Could've fooled me," Phoebe said under her breath.

"Hey?" Marshall asked in my direction. He crossed the space between us, coming up next to me. He leaned in to whisper in my ear, the closest he had gotten to me since we found each other again. "I want them and *only* them to know about Aaron. For now. Cool?"

My heart began racing. I knew we couldn't keep it a secret from everyone, but I had for so long. My head tilted back to look at Marshall, to inspect his eyes for sincerity. His eyebrow raised because he knew that was what I was doing.

No relationship was sound unless you could trust, business or otherwise. I had to try with him.

Unfortunately, I hadn't tried hard enough with Phoebe. She didn't know the truth, not about Aaron, Delilah, or anything else. A logical, albeit deceptive, train of thought had kept me from divulging my past to her. In the back of my mind, the place so far away it was rarely visited, I knew there might be a time I'd need to explain to her because she was the only friend I had.

"What do you think?" Marshall asked.

Phoebe's demeanor shifted once again. Her worried expression shifted between Marshall and me, as she rung her hands together in front of her. "Please tell me what is going on?" she asked in a small voice.

I sighed because I didn't want to do this, especially not right now, but I had to.

I whispered back into Marshall's ear, "Nothing about Delilah yet, okay?"

He nodded and stepped back from me. "You want to take this?"

No, but I wasn't going to leave it up to him.

"Phoebe," I said, walking toward her. "I was married. Marshall is his best friend. We both had no idea each other was going to be involved. I'm sorry I never told you, but it was a long time ago, and things did not end…well. In fact, they ended pretty ugly. You can probably understand now why Marshall was so angry when he saw me."

"Huh?" she asked, shaking her head in disbelief. "You were married? You told me you weren't or had never been."

"I know, and I feel bad about that. It is a part of my life I want to forget."

Her eyes shifted to Marshall. "So that's why you don't like us?"

He shrugged. "I don't dislike you, Phoebe. Just your hip checks to my door. And Alexis and I agreed we'd see how we can work together. The vibe between the two businesses is too good to not see what happens. And because of that, we want to keep it between the four of us. Deal?"

I didn't see the reactions of Wells and Phoebe because my ears were only focused on one thing.

Alexis.

It was the first time he called me my name without me telling him to or him correcting himself. It showed a level of respect, a small, tiny extension of the olive branch.

And it was completely in my hands as all their eyes were on me once again.

"Phoebe? The displays?" I asked her.

She nodded before carefully opening the door and slipping out of it. Wells let out a deep sigh before retreating toward the office.

And then it was just us.

Him.

Me.

The energy had changed once the truth was released. Maybe it was because I admitted it, and that the air breathing it in was freed of lies. My stomach turned, a nausea rising from my gut and radiating everywhere. It was a reminder from a time when it was common, but now it was no longer familiar. It was all the things I held on to and only kept to myself. I swallowed it down like I always had. The nausea would pass. It always did until it came back again.

I shook my head, freeing it of all that happened. "Anyway, I think you'll be happy about the cheesecakes. Plus, I adjusted a few other things. Like the mint julep cupcakes? I think with your watermelon mint sangria—"

"Can I ask you a question?" he said, interrupting me.

"Yeah."

"How did this," he said, waving his finger toward the Tipsy Treat boxes, "happen?"

Confused, I asked, "How did what happen?"

"How the hell did you go from an investment banker to a…baker?" He spit out the last word like it was dirty.

This did not sit well with me.

"Oh? So, because an investment banker is considered a high-ranking job, more important because it deals with money, I should be ashamed I'm a baker now? Let me tell you something, Marshall. I built this business by myself, *all* on my own. I didn't have a best friend or anyone helping me. I would never and didn't ever think less of you because you were a bartender, and furthermore—"

His laughter cut me off, a full-on encapsulating crack-up. "Do you ever shut up?" he asked. "It's times like this I see the old Lexie."

And I saw the old Marshall. It was the grinning, pleasant Marshall.

I wondered where the old one went to that I only caught glimpses of. Maybe the same place I went? Years spent apart left a lot of room for change. I knew I wasn't the same person I was the last time he saw me. I couldn't expect him to be either.

"All I was trying to ask, before you bit my head off, is what made you make the change? You have to admit the jump from a finance career to culinary is a little unusual."

"It was, but you know what? When you trade a life of work for a love, a passion, for the work you do, it all makes perfect sense."

He was no longer laughing, but was calm as his body leaned back against the bar, his arms resting on the top of it. "Okay," he said, seemingly still confused. "That part makes sense, but how did you get there?"

How did I get there? No one had ever asked me that before. How could they when they didn't even know? I didn't know quite how to answer him without bringing up so much from the past—me leaving, not a word since, moving to Boston and then to California.

"I didn't know baking was a passion," Marshall said.

"How did you not know?" I asked.

"Huh?"

Maybe it wasn't obvious. In retrospect, I guess a lot wasn't then, or even now.

I searched my brain for an example until it came to me, and I had no choice but to smile as I recounted it to him.

"Do you remember WET's one-year anniversary party?" I asked, referring to Aaron's speakeasy bar in Chicago that Marshall had managed.

"Ahh," he said, his eyes looking up as he tried to recall. "Vaguely?"

"Okay. Aaron had the Blackhawk players in, and Oprah stopped by?"

"Was that the year Aaron brought sixteen-year-old Abel to help with shit in the back, and Abel drank whatever was left in the glasses?"

I laughed. "Yes. He got so wasted, and man, Aaron was so pissed."

He joined me in chuckles. "Oh yeah, he did! Aaron had to leave to drive him home. Abel puked in his car and all over himself. Leslie and Daniel read them both the riot act."

Leslie and Daniel Matthews, Aaron and Abel's parents, were never pleased with Abel's shenanigans.

"Abel," I said, recalling my ex-brother-in-law. "How is he?"

He shook his head, smile still in place from his laughter. "That fucking guy. He's awesome. He's a teacher, if you can believe that."

"No way!"

"Right?" he exclaimed. "But he's a damn good one, too. It took him a while to get all his shit together, and let's face it, Abel will always be Abel. A sweet kid with just a side of dumbass."

I nodded. "That's Abel."

"You'd be proud of him, too," he said, his tone and expression softening. "He's become a man. He's got a sweetheart of a girlfriend, and she's the best thing that ever happened to him."

"I'm glad," I said. "Really, because he was still a teenager when I left."

"Hence why you remember him wasted and barfing in Aaron's car."

"Didn't Aaron try and make you clean up his car?" I asked. "I seem to recall a little best friends' quarrel between you two that night as well."

"He sure as hell did. I told him to go find someone else to do his dirty work."

"So, you do remember that night, then? Do you recall the dessert bar? It went with the whole 1920s theme, to go along with the whole Prohibition vibe?"

"Yeah?"

"I made that."

"You made the decorations?"

"No. I made all the sweets."

Once again I could see the wheels turning in his brain. That sweet table was the talk of the party. I had convinced Aaron to let me do it when he was looking for suggestions for a place to hire for the party. For a week before, I worked my regular fourteen-hour-plus day and stayed up through most of the night, prepping for the party. I ran on pure adrenaline and it was the most amazing feeling.

"Holy shit!" Marshall said, slapping his hand on a pile of twisted napkins on top of the bar. "The brownies!"

"My brownies? What about them?"

"The stout brownies!"

"What. About. Them," I repeated slowly.

"When I tried them the other day, they seemed familiar to me, but I knew I'd never had anything like it. But—"

"You did," I said, smiling.

"But it wasn't that night!"

"I know. I remember. In fact, the first time I ever made them was for you."

Marshall had knee surgery, and while in recovery at home, Aaron would bring him food and things. One day, I had an idea based off a recipe I saw for a pumpkin ale brownie to try it with a stout. Both Aaron and I thought they were good, so I packed up some to send over to Marshall. It was all I heard about for weeks after from him.

"Damn," he said, shaking his head in disbelief. "I can't believe that shit."

And I almost didn't notice, with his beard covering his cheeks, but he was indeed blushing.

"There was some good times, Marshall," I said softly. "With all of us."

His eyes held to mine, and it was almost uncomfortable until it wasn't. The shock of seeing him, someone from my past, had worn off, and if this conversation had taught me anything, it was that there were many good times. It wasn't all bad.

He ran his fingers through his hair. "You still have a thing for rainbows?" he asked.

And he did remember things.

I'd had a love of rainbows ever since...

"I do," I said. "Always."

Phoebe opened the door slowly, careful not to bang the wall, and I turned to watch her slide through a crack of an opening while carrying the first box for our display setup. I went to go help her, but Marshall stopped me.

"Alexis?"

"Yeah," I said, calling over my shoulder.

"We did," he said with a shrug before looking down at his shoes. "Have some good times."

* * *

After I left Ginger, I told Phoebe I would head back to the house and that if she wanted a break, she could join me there in a few hours. She never asked for much in terms of time off or anything, so I tried to be appreciative. I also had some ulterior motives. I needed some time to myself after the exchange Marshall and I had.

I couldn't put my finger on it, and I couldn't shake it. He was familiar to me in so many ways, but he was someone I didn't know at all in more ways. I didn't know if that was why I was sensing such a draw to him, a pull, or if it was simply the proverbial blast from the past that had roused buried emotions.

He knew me then.

He was there for all of it.

He was there for the after.

I knew before the plus sign even popped up. The vomiting in the morning, sore breasts, and exhaustion weren't subtle red flags. They were full-blown sirens, blasting their enormous volume into my crumbling soul.

I knew it.

Pregnant.

It wasn't supposed to happen.

Ever.

Not with Aaron. Not with anyone.

I couldn't be a mom. I shouldn't have been.

But with all the precautions taken, the universe still had to get a good laugh in. Hadn't I suffered enough for so long?

There was such clarity as I recalled the day I knew for sure, which began with me hiding in the bathroom to confirm my fears.

I remember taking the pregnancy test and shoving it back in the box before tossing them both in the drugstore plastic bag I brought it home in. I glanced into the mirror above the sink. My red-rimmed eyes were going to be a giveaway. I knew Aaron would know. I wasn't ready for Aaron to know.

I wasn't ready to know.

Allergies. That was what I had decided my excuse would be.

There were little details I always recalled, too. Like how I ran my nude-colored manicured fingertips under my eye to wipe away the mascara that smeared from running and noticing that my polish was chipped.

The plastic bag went in my Louis Vuitton purse, alongside my BlackBerry, as I considered my next move.

I never needed help, advice, or whatnot.

I still didn't, but I needed *someone*.

But it was Leslie, Aaron's mom, who was the person I needed to talk to. Leslie was the only person I could talk to.

And then when Aaron walked through the door, his T-shirt damp, and sweat beaded across his forehead. I put my game face on and went on with what I had planned.

It worked except for my brain screaming: *Tell him, Lexie. Tell him now.*

Later.

Later was going to be better.

It was later. It was almost a month later and only after Leslie helped me to find my courage.

His reaction made me even more confused. Disbelief, shock, and finally complete elation.

I know I shouldn't have married him.

I didn't think I could—even up until the moment I said, "I do," I didn't think I could.

But I did.

My belly grew. My denial and dread at becoming a mother grew as well.

Her nursery was ready, but I was not. Every time I walked past the room, the walls painted blue, the color of a perfect sky, with white, puffy clouds and a rainbow extending across them, I felt…nothing.

Of course, there were rainbows.

I wasn't a religious person at all, but I'd catch myself through the day, at random moments, whispering, "God help me," to myself.

Or maybe it was to the universe because I knew I couldn't do it. I *shouldn't* do it.

And when my water broke on May 11, two weeks before my due date, there was no denying it any longer.

Hours and hours of labor with blinding pain and fear so deep my only focus was that—the agony and the terror.

And they laid her on my chest, and a part of my heart, a place I didn't know existed, cracked wide open and was flooded with the most euphoric emotion I'd ever known. It was indescribable. All I knew was…

Love.

I loved her.

Delilah Leslie.

She was named after the song "Hey There Delilah" that played in the bar the first time Aaron kissed me.

Leslie after Aaron's mother. She was so thrilled, tears in her eyes the first time she held her.

It was like I bundled up all the emotions I had, all I was hiding, and shoved it in a box. I carried it with me for so long already, and while heavy, I knew it was what I had to do. There were so many times I thought I could open the box, all I was hiding, to Aaron, but I knew it would be too late.

I knew he wouldn't understand.

How could he after I'd hid something so ugly, so unforgivable, from him during our entire relationship?

The expression on his face when he looked at Delilah, the pure joy he had when her tiny hand held on to one of his fingers, was the most beautiful thing I'd ever seen. Aaron was made to be a dad.

I was made to give him to her.

That was my purpose. My heart told me so. I just didn't know how to make sense out of it, to know that I was never going to be the wife, specifically the mother, everyone thought I could be.

I was damaged.

When I was seventeen, I'd been reckless, and lives had been ruined. A domino effect all because of me. I couldn't, I wouldn't, do that to Aaron and Delilah.

Despite all my precautions, I was never supposed to be a mom.

Her smile. Her cry.

It made me want to be her mother, but I knew I'd ruin her because I wasn't good enough for her.

Depression, or a word deeper for the kind of despair I had, began to swallow me. I knew I needed to get away. I knew I couldn't live a life like this.

It wasn't postpartum depression.

No. No, it wasn't.

What it was, was something I had long before Delilah. It was something I kept hidden, even from Aaron, a secret so horrible I made myself believe it was a nightmare.

It wasn't, though. It was real, and it had happened. It was the reason I couldn't, I *shouldn't*, be a mom.

But you can't, you *don't* leave your baby, your child.

Only mothers could relate to this. That child that you grew in your body and birthed left something behind. It was something only a mother and child shared. A piece of myself, my heart, went with her when she left my body, and a piece of hers stayed with me. We would always be connected.

I didn't know if the parts that connected us were enough to stay, knowing I'd eventually break her heart someday, just like I did to my parents.

I was drowning.

Aaron's eyes, his continued sadness, was only amplified by my inability to function anywhere but at work or when I was baking. So that was all I did. It was all I could do.

Just when my head was about to go under for good, when the current was going to keep me from breathing, someone reached out to me and made it okay.

She told me it was okay to let go.

So I did.

"Alexis?" Phoebe asked, entering the kitchen, breaking me out of my thoughts.

"Huh?"

"What are you thinking?"

I looked to my hands, my fingers. "I was just thinking…how it's been such a long time since I had a manicure."

Her head tilted to the side in confusion.

I'd thrown so much at her today, and it made the guilt I'd reawakened with my recollections that much worse. As I stared at her, it occurred to me for the first time ever that she was the closest thing I had to family. I had disappointed all other family, both blood and otherwise, I'd ever had and left.

She was my only friend and I'd lied to her.

"I want to tell you everything," I said to her.

Almost everything.

Chapter Five

Anyone who said opening a new bar or any new business was exciting never fucking did it. Sure, it was the culmination of so much work, seeing the vision you had come to fruition. There was a lot of energy associated with that. I guess some could call it exciting, but not me.

It was stressful as fuck.

Hiring, training, scheduling, payroll, deliveries, and another million other little things had to come together at once. At once was happening tonight—our grand opening.

Wells was my eyes and ears and everything else in between when I couldn't do it. My temper was short, while my energy level was off the charts. I put everything I could into my new employees, who were saved from my short-temperedness, creating a baseline of respect between me, them, and one another. It was as I said to Alexis—we were going to be a family. It was the way Aaron taught me to run WET. Ginger was going in the same way.

I rolled over in my bed, exhausted, but letting the early morning sun rouse me. I needed a few minutes of quiet, a few moments of no one calling me with questions or without my mind running in a million different directions.

I was a dude. There was one surefire way to relax and to replace whatever was going on in my mind.

My hand ran down the front of my boxers, palming my morning wood, as my eyes drifted closed to visions of my fantasy girl moving above me. Her long blond hair cascading across her pale skin, the edges brushing against the top of her breasts.

I yanked the sides of my boxers down, kicking them off the rest of the way. My hand wrapped around my cock as I began pumping to the rhythm of how she was pushing herself into me. Harder and harder we both went, and when I was about…

Ring. Ring. Ring.

Ignore it. Ignore it. Ignore it.

It could be about work. The opening today.

What if…

Shut the hell up, Marshall. Get back to dream girl.

I tried to continue the fornication fantasy, but…

"Motherfucker!"

I yanked my phone from the bedside table, ready to rip whoever was calling a new one. It was Aaron. He maybe was my partner and best friend, but he wasn't immune to my wrath.

"Can you wait until a decent hour to call?" I snapped. "Two hours behind, Aaron."

"I know you're not a morning person, but it's a little after seven there, and you have a bar opening today. There wasn't a damn way you were still sleeping."

Asshole.

"Fine. I wasn't sleeping, but I was trying to give myself a few minutes of chill before everything today," I said.

He laughed, this mixture of condescending and truthful humor kind of chuckle he was famous for. It irritated the hell out of me.

"What the fuck is so funny?" I asked.

"You're so transparent, Marshall. I obviously interrupted something this morning."

"Ahh, I…no, well…wait."

"Oh, relax. It's not the first time I've called you and you've had company. Frankly, I don't know why you answer at all if she's still there. It's really rude, Marshall."

"For fuck's sake, Aaron. There's no one here. Just whatever. Why are you calling?"

"Because we have a bar opening today."

Thanks for the reminder, asshole.

"Yes, we do," I said as whatever was left of my hard-on deflated. "And it's going to be fucking flawless."

"Well," he said. "Nothing is ever flawless, especially an opening. I'm bummed I can't be there, and you know I was planning on it, but I just couldn't step away from Chicago with the new restaurant I got here opening next week. However, I'm excited for you."

"You mean us. You're excited for us."

"Of course, but…" He trailed off before continuing a moment later. "This is all you, Marshall."

"Yes, physically. But this wouldn't have happened without you."

"At this very time? Maybe not. But this is all you. Everything that Ginger is and will be is a result of your hard work and inspiration. I'm proud of you."

While I understood his sentiment, I knew if he found out about the Lexie-Alexis situation, he'd flip his shit. In a way, I knew she was right. I was lying to him, my best friend, and that had never happened before. In fact, I didn't take to lying to anyone. There wasn't a point. They almost always found out, and if they didn't, then it was me who had to carry around the guilt, just like I was doing right now.

It made me more nauseous than drinking orange juice after brushing my teeth…with a hangover.

But I needed to remember why I was doing it.

I was doing it to save him from revisiting all the shit he had worked so hard to get over.

"It's normal to be nervous, you know," Aaron said. "Any new endeavor I enter into I get anxious."

"I'm not…anxious."

"Whatever you say, buddy," he said with his signature chuckle. "Hey. Delilah's here and wants to say hi."

I listened as Aaron called for Delilah, her whisper of an adorable voice becoming louder the closer she got to the phone. "Is it Uncle Marshall?" I heard her ask Aaron.

"Hi!" she said when she reached the phone. "Have you seen the dolphins yet?"

"Hey there, Nutter Butter. No, not yet. I've been super busy and haven't had much time to go to the beach. What's happening with you?"

"I have some big news," she said.

"You do? Well, I'm always up for big news, but tell me this first. Is it really big news? Or just kinda big news?"

"No. It's really big news, Uncle Marshall. It's like bigger than when the Cubs won the World Series, even though that wasn't exactly news since everyone was watching it happen. Is it only news if only some people know? Because I think what I need to tell you only some people know, but I don't want to call it news if it isn't. What's that called, then?"

I laughed because oh, could this little girl make me laugh every single time we spoke. "I'm not sure. I think we can still call it news."

"Are you paying attention, Uncle Marshall?" she shouted. "I need to know if it is news or not. I don't want to call it something it's not. Geez. It's like when Mom makes me a peanut butter and honey sandwich, but I asked for jelly. It's the same but different."

I'd heard her call Callie "Mom" for a while, but there was something different about it now. For everything that mattered, Callie *was* her mom, the only mother she'd ever known. Now, after seeing and being around Lexie, her *birth* mother, so many damn emotions came at me at once.

"You are totally not listening to me," she said, breaking me from my thoughts. "Are you watching television instead? If you are, Dad says that's rude to do."

This girl. She was already such a spitfire that when I imagined what she'd be like when she was older, all I could do was smile. She had two uncles, Abel and I, one by blood, one by choice, and there was no way in hell that between us and her dad any dude would think about fucking with her. But it was conversations like this that reminded me she was going to hold her own just fine. She wasn't going to need any man to kick ass. She was going to do it all on her own.

"So tell me the big news, Nutter Butter," I said.

"I figured out this morning that muffins and cupcakes are the same thing. They are both just cake. Both of them. But people call muffins 'muffins' because it's an excuse to eat cake for breakfast."

It was such an obvious and oddly profound statement for a seven-year-old that there was no bullshit when I responded to her.

"You know what?" I asked.

"Huh?"

"That is totally news to me."

"Right?" she exclaimed. "I mean, frosting on a cupcake is what makes cake dessert, I guess, but a muffin is only a cupcake without frosting. I can't believe I didn't know this until today!"

"Which do you like better? Muffins or cupcakes? They're both cake, I know, but if you had to choose which one?" I asked.

"Duh, Uncle Marshall. The frosting is what makes them better. Cupcakes obviously! Plus, Mom is teaching me how to make different kinds. She says I'm really good at it. I think I want to be a baker when I grow up."

Her last sentence, coming from her tiny voice, hit me in the heart with the force of a semitruck carrying a trailer full of iron. It momentarily took my breath away that she was talking about baking, that it was what she wanted to do when she was older, just like her mom.

Not her mom Callie.

The mom she didn't even know existed.

"Dad says I have to go," she said. "Can you send pictures to me when you see the dolphins?"

"Of course. Love you, Nutter Butter."

"Love you, Uncle Marshall," she said.

A momentary handoff of the phone happened before Aaron returned.

"All right. Talk to you tomorrow to see how it all went, but I already know you're going to kill it tonight. Wish I could be there to see it," he said.

If he was only going to be there to see it.

To see *her*.

My mind circled with all that was on the line, all that I could lose.

I didn't remember saying good-bye to Aaron. He was gone by the time my mind returned to the present, my hand still holding the phone to my ear.

* * *

The warm August wind blew our hair around, or what was left of my hair after I decided to cut it all off earlier that afternoon, as I gave my staff a pep talk on the outside patio of Ginger. They were ready for the opening in that first-day-of-school kind of way. There was no way of knowing how they'd do until they were thrown into it. However, looking at their eager early twentysomething faces, I had faith.

"Thanks for all the ironed black button-downs and straight

ties. You're all looking very sharp. Please keep it that way," I said. "I think—"

I paused because I couldn't believe I was going to have to go there again with these guys.

Two of my kids (yes, I had come to refer to them as my kids because they were and because like I'd told Alexis, this was a family—I was the Papa Bear) started making eyes at each other. It was more than lovey-dovey shit or less. Whatever. It was straight-up eye fucking.

"And to wrap up," I said, staring at the couple with my own serious, *don't*-fuck-me eyes. "Don't make me go over the whole business about fraternization between you guys. What I don't know, fine, won't hurt me. If I hear about it or, God help me, I see it, I won't be happy.

"You're all ready," I said. "And I have your back no matter what, okay? No one expects perfection tonight, but I know you're all going to give it all you have."

Wells came up behind me and whispered in my ear. "Line is down the block. There's media here, too."

"Showtime, kids," I said.

They scattered like I'd called them for recess, and seeing their excitement only fueled my own.

I worked it as hard as I could, schmoozing with important people, smiling for cameras, and answering the same questions over and over again, all the while trying to keep tabs on what was actually happening and how things were going. I knew Wells had it covered, and if I was ever going to do my job as owner, I'd have to tap the brakes on the micromanaging shit, but tonight was too important to let up yet.

By the time I was done talking, or rather bullshitting, with the highest of VIPs, I wanted a moment to take it all in. The flushed cheeks of the newly inebriated matched the vivacious conversations they were having. Rivers of my bow-tied kids weaved in and out of the crowd, trays of cocktails held high above their heads without spilling a splash of booze. The walls, the fucking air vibrated, not just from the music, but from the energy of it all happening. It was all coming together as I'd hoped and expected. What I hadn't anticipated was the rush of pride that came over me, followed by an even stronger wave of…panic.

It was all here. It was all happening. It was the best feeling I'd ever had.

I could lose it all if I fucked up.

Shut the hell up, Marshall. Don't throw that out there.

I wasn't going to put it out in the damn universe either by thinking about it. Everybody knew that shit was like a self-fulfilling prophecy. You think it too much and it happened, especially the negative.

"Hey, Marshall!" someone called.

I turned and the dude—whose name I had no fucking recollection of—from a local restaurant was waving me over. As I made my way toward him, I noticed he was eating one of Alexis's treats.

I reached my hand out to shake his. "Hey! Thanks for stopping by."

"This place looks incredible, and this?" he said, holding out the cupcake, the remnants of the white-colored frosting smeared across the top of his fingers. "Insane."

"Alexis does a killer job with those things. We're a great...
match," I said.

I stumbled on the last word just as my eyes caught Alexis,
standing in front of her dessert table, chatting with people
who came by.

What the hell?

Gone was her pink uniform and hair up in a messy ponytail.
In its place was a skirt suit, and the skirt part? It was short, almost too short, but it was the rest of her that caught me up.
Black stockings, a single seam running up the back, wrapped
around her long legs. Her strawberry-blond hair was longer
than I remembered. It was always up so I never thought much
of it. It hung straight and shiny down over her shoulders, cascading across the matching fitted jacket she wore.

She was smiling.

It didn't look forced, either. It was a genuine grin, the corners of her mouth lifted into a soft curve, as her shiny lips from
gloss or some shit made her appear...soft.

Pretty.

It was all so not Lexie. Yes, she was pretty, stunning even.
Her days in the corporate world always had her in similar out-
fits, with a perfectly made-up face. This was different.

This was Alexis.

A few of the puzzle pieces that were Alexis shifted into
place. The whole thing was still a goddamn mess, and I didn't
want to think too much about it, but I was starting to see.

She was different.

I hadn't even noticed that cupcake dude left my side
until I was bumped from behind by someone. Turning to

look, they'd already passed, but by the time my eyes returned to Alexis, I realized she moved fast. Just the amount of time it took me to turn my head and back again was all it took to catch her just as she bent down and squatted, the best she could in a skirt, to retrieve something from under the table. My feet started to move forward to help her, but I stopped.

Dead. In. My. Tracks.

As she moved a box out of the way, scooting farther under the table, her skirt shifted. It shifted *up*. The slit opened slightly across the side of her upper thigh, and what I saw was what made me stop.

The hint of a garter holding up the lace top of her stocking.

I couldn't help but stare. I don't think any man could not have, but when she stood back up, she caught me fixated on her legs. Her hands pushed the skirt back into place as her cheeks flushed in embarrassment. The innocent blush. The sexy garters and stockings. It was too much for me.

The energy stirred, the noise level of the crowded bar diminishing to a soft conversation. Something else stirred…in my pants.

As soon as I felt it, I shook myself out of it. A natural male reaction to a very fucking off-limits female.

"What's up?" Wells said, coming up behind me.

"Nothing. Well, everything, obviously, but at the moment, everything's in order."

"Mm-hmm," he said with a shit-eating grin.

"What?" I snapped. "I don't have time for this."

"About half this bar, me included, just caught you sizing

Alexis up. And when I mean half this bar, that included the sizer-upper."

"I don't know what the fuck you're talking about."

He laughed loudly, the howl rising above all the noise surrounding us. "The hell I don't!"

Shit.

"And not that it's a big deal," he continued. "She looks hot tonight—well, every night and day. Whatever. You know what I mean."

Fuck. He went there.

I was pissed because he was right.

I was also relieved because it hopefully explained my reaction to her.

"Please don't tell Phoebe I said that about Alexis being hot," he said.

"Why would Phoebe care? In fact, why would I even tell her anything?"

"Because I'm trying to get something going with her, and I don't want her thinking I'm, like, well, you know."

I shook my head. "No, I don't know, and I don't have time for guessing games tonight."

"Well, like you," he said. "I don't want her to think I'm checking out every girl in a skirt."

"Oh, for shit's sake. I wasn't—"

He made an oinking noise, followed by additional laughter.

"What does that even mean?" I asked.

"We're all pigs. Just remember to keep it under wraps," he said, adjusting his bow tie and turning.

I shook my head and glanced around to see where my next

move should be. My head lifted toward the mezzanine to check it out, but Wells, once again, wasn't finished.

"Oh!" he said, shouting over the music before stepping behind the bar. "Something got delivered for you and it's in the office."

"Okay. I'll check it out later."

A loud crash of breaking glass had me running in the opposite direction to see if everyone was okay and to survey the damage. Luckily it was only a few broken martini glasses after an already-drunk dumbass tried to hug one of my cocktail servers a little too aggressively. That led to me being back in the vortex of the party, pulled in every which direction as I tried to make sure everything else was running smoothly. The line outside was cut by ten p.m. to allow for the ones who had been waiting to get in. While I didn't like the fact we were turning people away, the thought of crowds meandering the streets of downtown San Luis Obispo and seeing the line was so fucking amazing. There was a buzz already, and from what I was seeing, that was going to continue. I was going to make *sure* it continued, even if I had to eat, live, and breathe Ginger. This was my baby now, and nothing was going to stop me from watching her grow.

Before I knew it, midnight had rolled around and the party thinned to a few stragglers. Cleanup began while the staff sat around discussing the night's events while munching on the leftover treats Alexis had brought. I went to the office to retrieve my iPad, to make some notes after I had a quick rundown with my kids, when I noticed a very large gift basket sitting on my desk.

Through the clear cellophane, I could identify several popular Chicago items. I pulled the large blue bow apart and spread open the cellophane. The scents of chocolate and popcorn floated from the basket, and my sense of smell triggered all the memories I had associated with these specific foods.

Vosges Haut-Chocolat and Garrett Popcorn were two of Chicago's (and mine) favorite treats. That combined with Jays potato chips, Salerno Butter Cookies, and even a box of Cracker Jack made me smile. It was all tucked between various Chicago periodicals, but it was what was in the center of the basket that made me really excited: two bottles of single-barrel bourbon from Koval, a distillery based on the North Side of Chicago. While working at WET, I had my pick of tastings from a wide range of often very high-end bourbons, but for whatever reason, maybe because my Chicago blood knew it was made locally, Koval was always my top pick.

A small, plain envelope was taped to the front of one of the bottles, my name written in elegant handwriting across it. I opened it and slipped the folded note card out.

Marshall,

Wish we could be there with you tonight. Couldn't be prouder. Keep working it hard out there, California boy, but make sure you find time to enjoy new favorites in your new town.

Love,
Aaron, Callie, and Delilah

"That's amazing."

I spun around, and Alexis was standing close. Her eyes flickered to the card in my hand before shifting up to me. I attempted to bring it to my chest to hide, but I could tell by the look on her face that she saw it already.

I tossed the card down next to the basket. "Yeah, they are."

She pressed her lips together as she swallowed, forcing out a smile. "I'm sure he's really proud of you. Well, both of them. I'm sure they are both very proud of you."

And this was an impasse I wasn't prepared for. It was going to be a fucked-up thing no matter what. While there were many situations or things I thought might pop up during the time we'd be working together, explaining Callie, Aaron's current live-in girlfriend and really, the only mother Delilah had ever known, to Alexis was something I didn't think I'd ever have to do.

"It's not like I never expected him to be with anyone else, Marshall," she said.

Her eyebrows were lifted, her smile gone. It was hard to know if she was fishing for information, pressing, or if it was the rare form of sincerity coming from her. Again. Fucked either way.

She let out an exaggerated sigh. "Lighten up, will you? It's not like I thought he'd be celibate the rest of his life. I left him."

"He practically was," I mumbled under my breath.

"What was that?"

"Nothing," I said. "Everything seemed to go well tonight, right?"

"Answer my question. What did you say?"

"Just forget it, okay?"

She bit down on her lowered lip as her eyes narrowed at me, egging me on to try and dismiss her. She was, in fact, going to push, and I knew both old Lexie and new Alexis well enough and stubbornness was something they both had in common.

"It took him years to recover," I said with directness. "He was, in fact, celibate. For years. He was a single parent, always putting his daughter first."

I watched as her appearance took on the once-familiar hardness, the pointed, daring stare displayed across her face. She stood taller. Her breathing controlled to the point where it was almost impossible to see the rise and fall of her chest.

"We all have choices, Marshall," she said.

And her tone turned ice-cold.

Unfortunately for her, I was carrying around some serious bitterness about lying to my best friend and for accidentally eyeballing her earlier. How could I've been so stupid?

"No, we all," I said, putting the "all" in air quotes, "don't have choices. If you take off on your husband and baby without even so much as a good-bye, the husband, the father, doesn't have a fucking choice. He has a little person to take care of. He has to help her learn to walk and be a good person. And she is. She is the most dynamic, funny little girl I've ever known. She is everything, absolutely *everything* she is because of Aaron and not because of any DNA she got from you."

I waited to see hurt, some minute sign that I'd gotten through to her. She wasn't around for the aftermath, the destruction that nearly destroyed someone I thought of like a brother, and there was no way I could articulate what that was like to witness. I couldn't imagine what Aaron had felt, but it had to be a level of fucked-up pain like I'd only had a taste of. Even watching it happen was the kind of suffering I could barely swallow.

I waited, but there was nothing from her. No emotion at all. No tears. No downcast eyes. There wasn't even the slightest wavering of her posture to indicate she processed the weight of my words.

"I can't believe I was starting to think you really changed," I said.

"Likewise," she responded, dropping something on the table next to the basket. "I saved you one. I know they're your favorite. By the way, I like the haircut."

I'd completely forgot about my haircut until that moment. In an act of ownership and to show I was responsible, I cut off my shaggy mess of hair in exchange for closely shaved sides and something longer on top.

By the time I glanced to the table, noticing one of her frosted stout brownies, and looked up, her back was already to me. She left without another word, and I knew that when I saw her tomorrow, the harshness of what I'd just said would still be hanging in the air like stale beer and cigarette smoke.

Chapter Six

ALEXIS—

Three things happened at the beginning of the evening.

One: When I walked in and saw Marshall dressed in a fitted, white button-down and ginger-colored bow tie, I reacted. It made my *body* react. It wasn't fleeting, either. I had to consciously shake off the thoughts—his muscular arms and chest pressed against the fabric of his shirt and the faint outline of his tattoos underneath, the way his tall, lean body moved with authority around the bar, respectfully ordering people around while making sure everything was set up properly for the opening. I knew I had to shake whatever response I was having.

Two: My treats were a hit. They were bigger than a hit. While the majority of the customers who came to the opening were locals, and most were familiar with my sweets, there was such excitement surrounding them when they were spotted. The matching up of the different desserts with suggestions of a corresponding cocktail worked out perfectly. Customers would pick up one or the other and instantly be drawn to see how well the complementary item fit. Once the doors were opened for moneymaking, there was no doubt in my mind people would do the pairings when they visited. It came together exactly how Marshall and I hoped it would.

Three: At one point, I was looking for extra mini-chalkboard stands in a box under my table. No doubt my ass was probably hanging out no matter how ladylike I was trying to be, but at five foot ten inches, almost everything was always short on me. As I attempted to pull myself back out from under the table, I sensed someone staring at me. I glanced to my left, and it was Marshall. Marshall was the one staring at me.

It was a moment, and I didn't know what to think.

There was nothing familiar about it, about him, in that moment. The way his eyes fixated on the slit of my skirt before rising up to my eyes. He held them there, and before the intensity made me turn away from the power of his gaze, it was hitting me: It was almost like we were strangers. I wasn't Lexie. He wasn't Marshall. We weren't the two people who knew each other.

But.

I saw him.

Then he saw me.

Then we saw each other.

One thing happened at the end of the evening.

Marshall was a jackass. A pleasant, sincere comment about the gift basket sent from Aaron turned him into a, well, jackass. Something tipped him off, and I wasn't naive enough not to think it wasn't me, but his reaction held nothing back. He went straight for the jugular with his words, wanting and waiting to see me crumble under them.

And I deserved it.

I understood the emotions behind his words, and it was 100 percent justified. I couldn't even find fault with them.

But it was a shame that he'd never see me crumble the way he wanted me to. It would give him his own peace, the place in his heart where I knew I hurt him and others around him he loved, but he'd never see me crack. There was one simple reason for this: Whatever thoughts I inflicted on myself daily, all the things that rolled around my brain day in and day out, were far more vile than anything Marshall or any other person could say to me. Ever.

The brownie was left as a promise of peace. It was all I had. I would allow the anger to come at me at seemingly unexpected times. The residual hurt and his fierce desire to defend Aaron—that *was* something I was prepared for. I had to come to the resolution that if we were going to be working together, I would never let him see all the burdens I carried: I would allow him to think I was strong enough to stand on all of my baggage on my own.

The dark, winding roads were the familiar comfort I needed as I drove home. The breeze from my open windows was chilly but not cold, a balance to try and find my center of reason. While my body was exhausted, my brain was far from it. Marshall's words were what should've been adhering to my thoughts, but they weren't. It was the way that he looked at me earlier.

It was the excitement of the night.

A natural response to a short skirt.

Or was it more?

It felt like more.

I felt more.

As I made the turn down my driveway, I had no idea how to process any of it.

So I decided not to.

What I did decide to do was something I reserved only for occasions when I needed to completely indulge. Being around and taste testing sweets every day led me to add on a few pounds to my average weight for the last ten years. I didn't exercise anymore because I got far more of a workout running Tipsy daily, but I knew that my diet needed to consist of more than sugar. Regularly, I did my best; however, there were times to be conscientious and other times to say screw it instead.

Tonight was a screw-it night and that meant Pizza Rolls and a beer.

My wild and crazy night

I dropped my bag by the front door and flipped the switch to turn on the overhead lights, immediately dimming them. My body, and mind went to a place that only my home gave me. Peace. The tension I had in my neck and shoulders began to dissipate as I kicked off my heels, the coolness of the limestone and hardwood floors a relief to my aching feet.

My home never smelled of anything but baked treats. That aroma always soothed me, not only because it reminded me of home, but also knowing I was doing something with my life that brought me a semblance of joy eased me. I entered the kitchen, switching on the lights in there as well before heading to the refrigerator to retrieve my Pizza Rolls from the freezer.

I leaned over the stove to preheat the oven. Pizza Rolls were fine in the microwave, but baked for exactly eleven minutes resulted in a much more enjoyable roll. Once the oven was ready, I slid a small baking sheet into the oven, with the rolls neatly arranged in rows. With the timer set, I had enough time for a quick email check.

After grabbing my phone, I plopped down on my couch, the plush cushions molding to my body from the years of wear. This couch was the first thing I bought when I moved to Boston, another city I had once loved, after I left Chicago. I stood in the furniture store, alone, and had a panic attack for the first time ever in my life. I had no idea what was happening to me. It was this tingling, burning from the center of my chest and spreading to all my extremities. I tried to breathe it away, taking in all the oxygen I could, but exhaling only gave me a half-second moment of reprieve.

A fear deeper than falling to the bottom of an ocean, or from the highest building, overcame me. Logic was replaced by deception that my brain was feeding me.

I thought, *I'm having a heart attack. The world is crashing down, the earth under my feet shaking. I'm dying.*

In that moment, I was certain I was going to die.

I heard voices asking what was wrong and what they could do.

Talk to me. Be quiet. Don't say a word. Hug me. Don't touch me. Why don't you know what to do? Why don't I?

Let me cry. Tears won't come. I think I'll feel better if I do, but they don't come.

Slice me down the middle. Gut me like a fish and take out whatever is doing this to me.

That attack was one of many that followed in the years after. Medication eased them and they were rare now.

But it took me four times of going back to that same furniture store to be able to choose a couch.

It was the only thing I took from Boston to here.

That couch.

A reminder.

I opened my email app since all my personal and work emails filtered into one and began scrolling through the usual— vendor requests, store ads, and spam. Clicking through, I read or deleted, until I came to the last one and I paused.

And then…impact.

Seeing her email, her name, always hit me in the gut, leaving me briefly paralyzed. *Leslie Matthews.*

Aaron's mother. Delilah's grandmother.

It was always a blessing and a curse to get one of Leslie's emails. I would always be grateful to her for reaching out, especially because there was no telling how angry Aaron would be if he ever found out, but the pain associated with it left me hollow.

Like with everything else, I took it because it was my penance and because I owed it to Leslie.

I owed her everything.

I owed her my life. Literally.

She did something so selfless, so beyond the realm of anything I thought a mother, a grandmother, could be capable of. When I was in the darkest part of my life, the first year of Delilah's life, I thought the only way I could get out was to…make myself…disappear. Permanently.

Aaron thought it was postpartum depression.

I wanted to get as close to his face as I could, scream as loud as I could that it wasn't—it was because I knew I was full of poison and that eventually, if I hadn't already, I'd poison Delilah.

With no family of my own, Leslie was the only one I could talk to. Of course, she never knew the entire truth. No one did, but she recognized it was something different.

She was the one that saved me. I remember the day that she gave me an out.

"Oh, Delilah," Leslie says, hugging Delilah close before sitting her on her lap. "I could just eat you all up."

Leslie's eyes move between Delilah and me. She always does that. She's always looking.

Searching.

But there is still the same answer pouring from my eyes.

I can't.

She nods. "What can I do?" she asks.

I shrug because what can she do?

We sit quietly. I think Delilah is laughing at her stuffed elephant that plays the ABC song, but I can't tell.

"Lexie?" Leslie says after so long I forget she is still there.

My tired eyes move back to hers.

"I believe you," she says. "And I will help you."

Her words cause a cathartic breath to rush through my body. It almost makes me sick to stomach.

It was the first relief I've had.

"Why?" I ask, my voice cracking with shame. "No one does this. You would never do this."

She moves herself to the edge of the couch, placing Delilah on the ground next to her before putting her hand on mine. "You are killing yourself, dear. Little by little. And I know if it isn't fast enough for you, you'll make it there sooner."

She is right.

Ending my life seems logical. I don't want to. It isn't a wanting it all to go away. It is wanting me to go away. It is wanting to save my daughter.

The wolf that chews off its own leg.

"Do you love Aaron?" she asks.

"Yes."

Her eyebrows raise in question.

"Yes," I repeat.

"Do you love him wholly?"

I don't understand what she means.

"Do you love him with everything inside of you?" she asks. "Do you miss him when he's not near? Do you see him as an old man and you as an old woman, together, still in love with him?"

No.

It's an instant reaction, one I have no way to verbalize.

It makes me even more disgusting than I already know I am.

Her grip on my hand tightens. "My dear. You need to find that as well. And you will need to let Aaron find his."

Her tone is so calm, so comforting, like she's wrapping me up in a warm blanket and holding me tight. Why is she doing this?

Again. Like she knows my thoughts, she says, "I'm telling

you this, I'm telling you it's okay because no one else will."

Of course she knows what I'm thinking. She has seen it from the day I found out I was pregnant. I'd asked her to get a manicure with me. I didn't know why, except with no mom, no family, around to confide in, Leslie was the closest thing I had. I didn't even intend to tell her. I just needed her because I couldn't tell Aaron, not for another two weeks.

She has seen me, sees me, and knows what no one else does, what no one else will admit.

I should have never been and should never be a mother. My love for her isn't enough to keep her safe from me. It was as if a gun was pointed at both me and Delilah, and I had no choice but to save her. I'd take the bullet a hundred times over, because while I wasn't capable of being her mother, she was still my daughter.

"They will be okay," she whispers.

I look at her and her eyes are on Delilah. After a moment, they reach mine, and tears are sitting on the edge…for both of us.

"I promise, Lexie," she says. "I will make sure they are fine for as long as I live because I want you to live."

I already knew it was what I needed to do. Ending my life wasn't the answer, because that will only leave Aaron and Delilah with a lifetime of unanswered questions and guilt. I care for both of them too much to do that to them. Leaving them will still bring immense grief, in the immediate future, but it is the lesser of two evils.

Leslie is the voice, the selfless soul, giving me the last bit of courage I need to make the decision.

Leave.

Save them. Save yourself.

"How will you ever tell Aaron?" I ask.

She is startled by my words; her mouth drops open slightly. "I will not, nor will I ever, tell Aaron anything."

I would have to go away, far, far away.

My city, my job, my friends, and what had become my family would be nothing but ashes after I leave it all in flames.

The old Lexie would be left there, too.

"When?" Leslie asks.

Without thinking, as I smile at my daughter, I mutter, "Tomorrow."

I opened the email:

Dear Lexie,

I apologize for it being so long since I've been in touch. I hope things are well for you in California. I always forget where you said you were. Santa Barbara? I hope work is good as well.

Delilah is doing remarkable, of course. Second grade is going well, and in typical fashion, Delilah has situated herself as mayor of the class. She is well-liked by both her teacher and classmates. She's still in dance, and while she's not the best, she certainly has the most personality. Her recital was precious. She was dressed in an adorable chicken costume and danced to "Shake Your Tail Feather." (I attached a few pictures.) She puts it all out there, and you could see her smile all the way to the back of the auditorium.

Another thing she is very into these days is baking, which is such fun. You used to like to bake, didn't you? She's actually quite good and a very good listener. It is one of the few times I can get her to stand still long enough, without her running off to do something else. We made my mother's apple strudel recipe last weekend. Truth be told, she did most of it herself. She was so excited to show Aaron, who even admitted it was *almost* as good as his grandmother's. We have plans to bake many other things together. Aaron's even got her a little embroidered apron and matching hat to wear. It's just darling.

She's healthy. A bad cold last month, but otherwise healthy. She's grown and is at the top of the growth curve for height at 4'3". She has those long legs of yours. She's wanting to cut her hair, but Aaron's afraid she'll lose so much of her curls, and he isn't having it. We've been telling him it's time to let her start growing up and making her own decisions about her appearance. For now, she's still very blond, with those tight ringlet curls past her shoulders now.

Take care, dear. Talk/Email soon,
Leslie

My stomach churned, and a familiar nausea rose throughout my body. The pain, a wound buried so deep within me that it burned whenever Delilah's name was presented to me, never, *ever* wavered. The maternal pull was there, and because of it, I did what was best for her.

It was what a mother does.

It was what I did.

Baking.

My daughter.

Leslie still thought I was working in finance. I never mentioned in my emails back, which were seldom, and she understood why, what I was doing these days. It was basic things. I wasn't capable of any more than that, and she never asked.

She was the only one up until recently who still knew me as Lexie.

I scrolled down slightly and enlarged one of the pictures she sent.

I could only look for a moment, almost peeking through half-closed eyes, because I was never prepared. Ever.

Aaron's eyes.

And that hair. The blond ringlets like Leslie wrote about. There was only one person I'd ever known to have hair that beautiful white blond, with curls that looked like they were made by hand.

Delilah looked so much like her.

It wasn't until the smoke detector went off did I remember the Pizza Rolls. I ran into the kitchen and yanked the oven door open; smoke poured out as I grabbed a pot holder and pulled the pan out. After dropping it on top of the stove, I looked at it—all my neatly placed rolls were burned. They were ruined.

I ruined them all.

Chapter Seven

MARSHALL—

I came in through the back patio entrance to a quiet bar. I loved this time of day, the early afternoon, almost as much as when it was packed. The quiet roar of conversations, the laughter rising above it, and the smiles of the slightly inebriated was a rush, but the empty peacefulness of the bar was a different kind of energy. It was the calm before the storm. It was the teacher preparing before the kids came in for the day.

Three days since opening, and things couldn't be going better. Lines were out the door and down the side of the building to the corner every night. When we opened at three p.m., the crowd began to filter in and ebbed and flowed with the biggest hit coming soon after eight p.m. It was full-on adrenaline. In the bar business, it was always like this. When it was showtime, you hit the ground running, letting the work fuel your energy. It was the only explanation for the fifteen-hour days I was working and still being able to function.

That and coffee.

And the occasional shots of the Koval bourbon that Aaron and Callie sent me—I kept one of the bottles in my office. Yeah. I fully enforced the "no drinking while on the clock" rule with the kids, and for the most part, I followed the same rule. I'd reconsider my stance when one of them was opening and running their own bar.

I stepped across hardwood to the main floor, checking everything out to make sure it was cleaned and set up as instructed to the night crew. For the most part, they were nailing it, but there was always going to be wrinkles to work out, especially in the beginning.

As I walked farther in, just above the rafters that led to the second-floor mezzanine that was still under construction were a few large black feathers. Glancing around, there were several more scattered around on the floor.

"What the fuck?" I said to myself.

I looked at the ceiling, and one of the windows was left open. Something obviously got inside between last night and this morning. Now where the fuck was it?

"Wells!"

"Yeah?" he shouted from the office.

"Why are there feathers all over the floor?"

"Because a pigeon got in last night, and when we were all leaving for the night, we saw it flying around," he called back. "We took care of it."

"What do mean you…took care of it?"

"We took care of it and it's gone."

"Christ, Wells. Where is the goddamn pigeon?"

He emerged from the office, the foam from the latte or

whatever shit he was drinking sticking to his ginger beard. "Don't ask questions you don't want the answer to, boss," he said with a serious business face.

"Fair enough," I said. I was too tired to wonder where the dead pigeon carcass was and how it, in fact, became a carcass. "For further reference, if you don't want me to find out, make sure they know to check all the windows at night and to dispose of all the evidence of it in my bar. Plus, wipe your beard. You have coffee jizz all over it."

"For sure," he said with a quick nod, brushing away the foam remnants. "Anything else?"

"I don't know, is there a dead horse on my desk? The remains of a sacrificed goat or something upstairs?" I snapped.

"Ah. No. Not that I know of."

"Don't be a smart-ass," I said.

He shrugged. "Did you want to double-check the schedule I did for next week?"

"With everything else I have to do, you want me to be double-checking your shit?"

"Ah. No. You told me to. We're using that new software, and you being the control freak micromanager you are, you wanted to see it before I posted it."

"I don't think I did, and furthermore, take your micromanager shit and shove it. That's bullshit."

It wasn't and I knew it. So did he.

"Why are you so cranky today?" Wells asked. "I mean, more so than usual?"

"I'm not cranky," I muttered.

"Yeah. Right. You're jumping at me about everything the

last few days. I get that the opening is a stressful time, but even I have my limits, boss."

I flashed him a dirty look. "You sound like a chick."

"And you sound and are acting like an asshole."

Touché.

"Like I said," Wells said, breaking the silence. "I can't imagine how maddening all of this is. I'm your backup and I feel overwhelmed."

"Fuck. You're right, I'm sorry. And you're more than my backup. You're my backbone and my right hand. I know I don't always act like it, but I'm grateful, man."

His lips twitched as he attempted to conceal a smile. "That's, like, literally the nicest thing I've ever heard you say to me or anyone."

I rolled my eyes. "I'm not a dick. I just talk like one sometimes. You hear how I talk to the kids."

"True, but you've been edgy since opening night. I get it though. Crazy amount of stress."

Yes. It was the bar. It was the hours. It was being pulled in a thousand different directions at once. It was the lack of sleep and not eating well. All of it was enough, but the one thing that overran all of it was how so many of my thoughts were being occupied by Lexie.

Alexis.

I hadn't seen her since the night she left me and the brownie in the office. Phoebe had been making the daily deliveries. I didn't know if that was going to be the norm or if she was keeping a low profile. I didn't blame her if it was the latter. I was beyond harsh with her. It was honest, but even I knew that no matter how much anger I still had for her, the vitriol was fierce. I wouldn't apologize, but I didn't know how to take some of it back without sounding...weak.

We'd have to talk eventually because business was still business. We were getting cleared out of Tipsy Treats by nine at night, and customers were *not* pleased. The ordering, the volume of her sweets, was going to easily double, and I didn't know if she was capable of that.

Yeah. It was all of that stuff. Work, business, me being a dick, but there was something else. Something that rose to the top of all my thoughts, and it made me hate myself a little for allowing it.

She was so goddamn beautiful the other night.

It wasn't only what she was wearing, but it was the... air...around her. How she handled herself with customers and was professional with this added grace. She captivated them, and they responded. Her baking skills were obviously something the locals already knew, but being able to interact with her that first night was the, well, frosting on the cake.

It wasn't the Lexie I once knew.

It was Alexis.

And this was someone new to me, and I couldn't get her out of my fucking mind.

It was driving me mad.

"Fuck. I need In-N-Out Burger," I said, running my hands down my beard roughly.

"Is it even open yet?" Wells asked.

I pulled my phone from my pocket to check the time. "Shit. Not yet, but in about another half hour."

"Didn't you have it yesterday? And like two days before that? You know, Marshall, emotional eating is something you'll have to look into if you're doing it often. I struggled with it myself, and there's—"

"Quit judging me, Wells!" I said. "The only thing that comes close in Chicago is the cheeseburgers at Portillo's and maybe Au Cheval, but neither of them come close to a Double-Double Animal Style."

"Good point. I think I'll join you in on it today. Want me to run out?"

I shook my head in exasperation. "Aren't you listening to me at all? They don't open for another half hour."

"Yeah. I heard you, but by the time I get over there, and you know. We'll get the firsts of the day. It's good to be first…in…something, right?" he asked with a snort-laugh.

He doubled over in a fit of giggles, continuing with his snort fest, and it was obvious to no one but himself that he wasn't funny.

"Jesus," I said. "Just how many times were you dropped on your head as a child?"

"Let me go get my phone and I'll head out to—"

He was cut off by the cheerful, albeit annoying, voice calling out her now trademark "Hellllooooo."

Phoebe always came in the same way, through the front door, announcing her entrance. She floated in with a few of the several boxes she arrived with daily, wearing a smile and twinkle in her eyes for Wells. We had gotten along a lot better since our first meeting, and there was mutual shit talk and banter based on respect.

"Hi Phoebe!" Wells said.

He rushed over to help her, trying to display his He-Man abilities by taking the delicate boxes from her. They paused at the handoff long enough to make googly eyes at each other and stockpile masturbation material for later. Every day I had to watch it was another day I wanted to tell them to start fucking and get it over with already.

However, if they did, it would get them into that whole fraternization thing, and while Phoebe didn't technically work at Ginger, I didn't want the drama.

"Hey, boss," Wells called from where he was standing with Phoebe. "I'm going to help her get all this in. You okay to put the ones in the refrigerator that need to stay cold when we're done bringing it all in?"

"Yeah? Why?"

"We're going to go grab a coffee together," he said, pausing to give me an exaggerated wink.

Phoebe spun around on her toes, twirling her skirt with her hands. These two marched to the beat of their own drummer. I don't think I ever saw two people more perfect for each other.

"You don't have a problem with that, do you?" Wells asked.

There were two problems I had with it.

"Didn't you already drink coffee? Also, you don't want Phoebe to know about the coffee jizz problem," I said.

I held in a smirk at busting his balls in front of a crush, but as I had forgotten, Wells might crumble a tad, but Phoebe would not.

"You're his boss, Marshall," Phoebe said. "Not the jizz police. Not coffee or otherwise."

"Yes!" Wells shouted before they high-fived each other. "Be back in a bit," he said, calling over his shoulder as they headed toward the door, their steps barely under a sprint.

The other problem was the most critical and of the utmost importance.

"What about my fucking cheeseburger?" I shouted as they exited. "Come on! And Phoebe! Tell your boss I need to talk to her!"

* * *

I never got my fucking cheeseburger. Wells was out with Phoebe for over two hours getting "coffee." He was disheveled enough when he returned that my theory that they were keeping their bits to themselves was thrown out the window.

At least someone was getting some.

Not only did I have a completely off-limits, no-fucking-way-in-a-million-years girl running through my mind all the time, but also the fact that I hadn't had sex in so goddamn long was making me antsy and only adding to my grumpiness. A wild, wild roll had me going strong in and out of the bed with a lot of women throughout my twenties, and while there were some meaningful relationships, there wasn't anything super long term.

I had a few standbys that made my bed warm some nights, but since there hadn't been anyone special in my life for a while, those "friends" were enough to keep me moderately sated.

It was hard moving to a new city without knowing a soul,

working the hours I did and not having anyone even on standby. I knew there was apps and shit for that kind of thing, but I didn't want the hassle of all the games that went with it.

Maybe I was over the whole friends-with-benefits thing, anyway.

Like a shot of whiskey, it took the edge off enough to fuck a familiar body, but when there was nothing else there, it never completely filled the void.

Maybe that was why the only pleasure I was getting was from my hand when I wasn't exhausted enough to get myself off, or cheeseburgers.

I was going to gain twenty pounds and be a walking horn-dog.

The afternoon flowed into the night as usual, like a current increasing with intensity the farther it got down stream. I'd try to catch up on something, and another thing would pop up in its place. The bar was getting slammed. Owner or not, if I saw my kids working their asses off and struggling, I was going to hop in and help.

They always thrived when I got behind the bar, sensing my veteran energy and words of encouragement. It always kicked them into high gear at any bar I was managing or, in this case now, owning.

It was still trippy as fuck to think that. *Owner.*

I helped to bring them back around, getting the crowd under a more workable flow, and was finishing up a strawberry margarita with jalapeño-infused vodka for a looker that was giving me some serious eyes.

I told the kids I wasn't going to condone doing it, but if they hooked up with a customer, keep it out of the bar. I wanted all of it, the actual sex and the drama, to stay off my property lines.

In my case, I never dipped my dick in the work pool anymore. It was only asking for trouble. Back in the day, eh. Whatever. Maybe I was older, wiser, or some bullshit like that, but there was an even greater risk now that I was in such a critical position. I was not just the boss. Ginger was mine.

Flirting, though, never hurt anyone. It was win-win. Plus, a little ego stroke was a good way to get through the dry spells without thinking you were a washed-up old man without the ability to land anything that didn't have four legs.

I slid the margarita across the bar to the tall brunette. "Here you go, beautiful," I said.

"Thanks," she said, smiling, her red lips amazing against her white teeth. She brought her drink to her mouth and took a sip while giving me a wink. "Mmmmm," she hummed before putting it down on a cocktail napkin, the edge of the glass stained with her crimson lipstick.

Bartenders always aimed to make a good drink, a great drink, because our entire livelihood depended on it. It didn't matter who the customer was. However, there was something about a beautiful woman enjoying a cocktail that I made that got me going. I wasn't sure if it happened to other bartenders, but it did for me.

"So, how's business?" she asked.

"Great. I'm Marshall," I said, extending a hand. "I'm the owner."

"Ahh. Now I get it," she said.

"What's that?"

"You're not wearing the same thing as the others."

I looked down at my plain, white cotton shirt and jeans, and yes, I definitely didn't fit in. I had ordered Ginger-embroidered white button-downs for management to tell us apart from the employees wearing something similar, but they weren't in yet.

"Caught," I said, grinning. "I wasn't expecting to be helping, but if they need it, that's what I do."

"Not many would. Some would think they were above it."

I shrugged. "I don't think that way."

"What things do you…think," she said, looking me up and down before settling on my mouth, "about, Marshall?"

"Lots of things, beautiful," I said with another wink.

She reached over the bar, running her hand across mine before letting it travel up my arm. "These look like they tell quite a story," she said, referring to my tattoos.

"That they do. In fact—"

I stopped midsentence when the corner of my eye caught the strawberry-blond hair of the girl that shouldn't have been occupying so much of thoughts. Alexis. Through the crowd I couldn't see her face, but I'd know that hair, the slight wave of the hair falling around her face from the bun that twisted onto the crown of her head. When the pack parted, her head, her eyes, were solidly hitting me head-on. Her lips were pressed together tightly, and she looked…angry. The explanation of why rose above the crowd like smoke.

She'd been watching.

She saw me eyeing the brunette.

And then it was her eyes

On mine.

It was the same vibe, the same damn pull that was there since opening night.

Her lips, her expression softened. It was almost a smile the way the corners of her mouth lifted slightly.

It was clichéd as fuck. The only two people in the room. Nothing else. No noises. No anything.

Until…

The sound of rising voices, arguing.

Then glass shattering from somewhere close blew the moment up.

My head jerked to my left as the brunette I was flirting with let out a scream as a man to her right swung at my head security guy, Dave, who must've stepped in when he heard the initial arguing. He didn't even come close to contact, but my body took over when I saw the dude holding a nice chunk of glass in his hand.

And then I don't even remember exactly what happened— that was, what happened after I jumped over the bar to tackle the dude.

It was a mess of bodies, blows to the face, body, and a stinging pain radiating from my stomach downward, but none of it stopped me. By the time I could see through the haze of adrenaline, the dude's hands were free of the glass, his face a mess of blood.

My hearing was the next sense that returned, my name being called, screamed from a voice with such a violent fear I needed to find it. I needed to find her. Was she hurt?

I scrambled across the floor from under the pile of guys and emerged to see chaos, frightened faces, and Wells holding Alexis back. I struggled to pull myself to my feet with uneasy legs, and as I did, glass dude broke one arm free as one of my security guys was trying to move him out.

And he got one perfectly clear, drunken-sized punch to my face in.

Then...darkness.

Chapter Eight

ALEXIS—

It was a level of fear, of utter panic, when I saw Marshall jump over the bar and into a pit of hysteria. Without thought or consideration of the repercussions, I ran toward him, toward the pandemonium, but a pair of arms wrapped around my waist to stop me.

"Marshall!" I screamed.

"Hold up, Alexis," Wells shouted. "Don't. Let them do their thing."

I struggled against his grasp. "No! He could be hurt. Do something!"

"Let them do their thing! They've got it!"

And the moment he said it and I stopped fighting him, I saw that he was right.

I don't know how they knew, but in addition to the two Ginger security guys, another three bouncers from nearby bars did, in fact, handle it. They came in, pulled the fight apart, and had the glass and the douche bag contained in a matter of seconds.

"Is he okay?" I asked.

Just as the words left my mouth, I saw Marshall emerge, his hair and clothes disheveled, blood running down the side of his face.

"No, he's not!" I screamed.

I began to struggle again, unaware of just how hysterical I was getting and what that meant. I didn't care. I needed to get to him.

Wells's grip loosened as Marshall stood, but before I could get to him, the douche bag caught him off guard, and his fist landed squarely in his face with such force Marshall was almost lifted off his feet.

And my heart stopped.

Douche bag was tackled and being dragged out by the time I reached Marshall.

"Oh my God!" I said, dropping to my knees next to him. "What the hell were you thinking?"

But his eyes were glazed over, with no focus. They fluttered shut, and the panic set waves across my body.

"Marshall!" I shouted at him, shaking his shoulders. "Shit!"

Wells was calming the crowd that was now beginning to retreat after watching the show fight, but as soon as he saw Marshall still on the ground, his expression told me he was experiencing the same thing I was.

"Wells," I cried out. "Call an ambulance!"

"Knock it off," Marshall mumbled, coming back around. "I'm fine."

He wasn't fine. Blood covered the side of his face, and the area was swelling rapidly. His "I'm fine" came out more like "Biam phfind" as his hands gripped the side of his waist.

He wasn't fine. He was hurt. Something was wrong.

"I'm serious, Al," he groaned. "Just give me a second to get it together."

Wells knelt down next to us. "Ambulance should be here any minute."

"Fuck that! I said—" Marshall struggled to sit up, but doubled over his side as his attempt failed.

"Will you shut up?" I said. "You're hurt. Don't try and pretend you're not."

"This is my bar and they can't see me all messed up. What the hell happened, anyway?" he asked.

"That asshole saw you talking to his girlfriend, I guess," Wells said. "He started getting loud about wanting to kick your ass, and I radioed to Dave. When he asked him to leave for being a drunk, threatening jackass, he broke the glass and went after him. I think you sort of remember after that, right?"

Marshall's clouded eyes wavered between Wells and myself before lifting to the ceiling. It was obvious he was trying to recall all that went down, but it wasn't connecting . My heart beat against my chest, worry and fear continuing to pump through me. I was always the calm, rational one, but that didn't happen tonight. Just like Marshall jumping across the bar to save what was his, my reaction wasn't that far different. Instinct and a rush of seeing someone you knew, you cared about, hurt, and logic wasn't anywhere in sight.

And I didn't know what that all meant.

There wasn't time to consider it, either. The paramedics arrived moments later, and I didn't know which was worse—the way Marshall was looking, bloodied, bruised, and black-and-blue. Or his mouth that was mumbling about everything that happened.

He swatted the paramedic's hand away that was attempting to check his pupils. "What part of you doesn't understand that I can see fine?"

"Marshall," I hissed. "Let him do his job."

Wells leaned in to me, whispering in my ear. "He isn't right. I can tell. He may have his cocky tone, but not with anyone working for him or anyone in the bar."

I nodded because he was right. The dynamic that was Marshall was something I was still trying to piece together. Six years was a long time to be out of someone's life, but it didn't mean you forgot how that person acted or how they made you feel. Marshall was always somewhat brash, but something else was different now. There was a hardness about him, a rough-around-the-edges thing that had nothing to do with his once clean-cut appearance to tattooed, bearded boy.

One of the paramedics was talking to Wells while two others were now helping Marshall into a chair. I stood up, inserting myself into the conversation between Wells and the paramedic.

"He's going to freak," Wells said to the male paramedic. "But he has no choice, right?"

"What's up?" I asked.

"They want to take him in to the hospital," Wells said.

"Well, then he'll go," I said.

"Yeah, but—" Wells popped and extended his head in Marshall's direction, his eyes opened wide. "Getting carried out of here on a stretcher? He'll lose his mind."

"He's sitting up now, but he needs to have that blow to the face looked at and I'm pretty sure he has at least one broken rib," the paramedic said.

"Shit," I said, looking in Marshall's direction.

He was clearly in pain, but he was also a man. There was no way of telling if the hit in the side didn't do damage or if was "male pain"—that common ailment that inflicts itself on the Y chromosome. The female population was unaware if the inability to handle pain was something that men carried with them in their testosterone or if it was safely tucked away in their penis.

"Someone needs to follow them there," Wells said with raised eyebrows.

Now that would be weird.

"I have to stay here. There's no way we can leave these guys on their own, especially after what went down," he said. "And he knows no one else besides the staff that's here right now."

It wasn't a question, then.

"I'll go with him," I said.

And it was no easy feat.

He bitched and moaned like, well, a bitch the entire time he was talking. When he wasn't talking, he was sulking, which was fine because he wasn't talking.

Three hours in the emergency room, X-rays, along with a physician's once-over, and they released him with pain meds for a bruised and thankfully not broken rib. The blood on the side of his face was from a nasty bump, and his eye was so swollen and black-and-blue that cold compresses were recommended to help. If anything got worse, he'd have to go back.

Or *we'd* have to go back.

"I'll be fine," he said, rising from the hospital bed. "You don't have to stay with me."

I reached him in time to lend a hand, which he didn't take. "I don't mind."

"Well, I do."

He stood for a moment, gathering his bearings while gripping his side. There was no choice. I had to take him home and stay with him. He was so hopped up on pain meds, and with the hit to the head, someone needed to keep an eye on him. With Wells working, still keeping an eye on Ginger, it was me who was on Marshall duty.

"Wait here," I said as we slowly walked to the exit. "I'll bring the car around."

"Don't worry about it," he mumbled.

I stopped and placed my hands on my hips. "Drop the macho shit, Marshall. You got the crap kicked out of you tonight."

"Thanks for reminding me," he snapped. "I was there, and I think you're being a little dramatic."

"How do you figure?"

"I wouldn't say 'got the crap kicked out of me.' I was…surprised, and every dude has been there a time or two."

"I don't really care. In fact, fine. Walk to the car. Crawl if you want. Do you want me to still give you a ride home, or would you like me to find you a broom so you can fly?" I asked.

He tried to stand tall, to assert his stance or whatever, but the pain in his rib stopped him. I winced because he did, and even though he was acting like an immature jackass, it didn't mean I didn't care. We'd been friends, great friends, before I left. It wasn't like I hated him. I never did. Even with us coming together like we have, with all the anger from him and hurt it caused me, thinking of those years wasn't without fond memories.

"What?" he asked.

"What what?"

"You smiled?"

"I did?"

"Yeah."

I was afraid of divulging and had to consider if showing even a little bit of my hand was wise. I wanted to remind him of those times, the times when there was laughter and friendship. That there was a time in which we were part of each other's lives, and even though I left Chicago, left him, it didn't mean I forgot. Over the years, I tried to forget it all, but with him back in my life, seeing how he got hurt tonight, those memories rose.

I wanted to tell him this, but there was still so much indignation that rolled off him. I saw it in his eyes. It scared me that maybe he'd never get over what I did.

But there were moments the last few days, especially tonight, when I saw a fragment of something else behind those eyes.

Desire.

I think he saw it in mine, too.

I wasn't ready to know for sure yet if he was feeling the same.

In fact, I wasn't sure I ever would be. It would be reckless of me to allow any thoughts I had toward him to dictate action. I'd done enough damage, and I wasn't going to inflict any more, especially on Marshall.

"What the hell is the matter with you?" he asked.

I shook my head, releasing my thoughts. "Nothing. Are you ready?"

"I don't know. Are you?" he asked, a tiny glimmer of a smirk emerging.

Who the hell knew?

"I'm never ready but always ready, all at the same time," I said.

"Why doesn't this surprise me?"

It shouldn't.

Things were quiet on the drive back to his house except for when he was giving me directions. My eyes focused on the road, while his stared out the passenger window. At a stoplight, I glanced over at him. Even without the car moving, there was enough of a strong wind to blow his hair around.

That hair.

It still blew my mind.

This was the same guy who probably had his own stake in a hair gel company a decade ago. He was all hard body, perfect hair, and button-downs. Aaron and him were like a page out of a Brooks Brothers catalog.

Now everything was different.

How he looked. My name.

My name. It reminded me of something from earlier.

"Can I ask you a question?" I said.

"Sure," he replied, his eyes still looking out the window.

"You called me Al earlier. Do you remember that?" I asked.

Without turning his head, I couldn't see his expression. His head tilted to the side slightly, and the absence of a response told me he didn't remember.

The light turned green, and I knew his silence meant time was up. "It's all right," I said. "I was just wondering where it came from."

"I fucking hate Alexis," he said, speaking to the wind. His tone was quiet. Simple. And the way he spoke it, I almost didn't hear him because the wind almost swallowed his words.

"You hate me?"

"The name," he said. His head turned, and I snuck a quick glance before bringing my eyes back to the road. "It's the name I hate."

I wasn't sure how to respond to that. He said he hated my name. That wasn't something easy to process. Furthermore, who the hell even says that?

He sighed loudly. "Sorry, but you're Lexie. Do you know how weird it is to call you something else?"

"It's not that different."

"Everything is different."

"Well, I guess a lot can happen in six years."

"Yeah, I get it, but why did you change your name? Aaron wasn't going to try and hunt you down."

"It wasn't Aaron I was afraid of," I said, gripping the steering wheel tighter. "I didn't want anything to do with the old me, with Lexie to hunt me down. It was myself I was afraid of."

Silence again.

"First one on the right," he said, referring to his home in a small three-floor apartment building.

I pulled to a stop in front of it.

"Wait there," I said, putting the car in park. "And I'll help you out."

I opened my door and was about to step out, but Marshall grabbed my hand to stop me. "Hold up a second."

"You okay?"

"No," he answered.

He looked like he wanted to say more, the way his eyebrows drew together and he bit down on his lower lip. With his eyes cast downward, staring at our hands, I couldn't understand what was happening. The only thing I knew was that his hand was still on mine, and every moment that went by, I could feel his grip changing...softening. The tips of his fingers slid between my own as his eyes darted to mine.

And in one expression, it was all right there again.

It was all the heat and curiosity from the night of the opening days ago, and the same from just hours ago. He wasn't just looking at me.

He was staring *into* me.

He licked his bottom lip, his hold growing tighter again. "I need to tell you something," he said. "Or rather, ask you something."

"All right."

"I don't remember calling you Al, but I can see why I did," he said. He shifted in his seat, rounding his body to face me directly. "I like it."

"Okay," I replied with confusion. "Thanks?"

"I think I should call you that. I want to call you that if it's okay?"

"You're asking me permission to call me a nickname of my name?" I asked.

He smirked, and I could swear, even in the darkness, under the blond beard, I saw him blush for the second time ever. "Yes. I'm asking if it's okay if I call you Al, because I can't fucking identify you by either of your other names."

"What do you mean?"

"I knew Lexie. I knew her well, and you're not her anymore. There are parts, and I'm even speaking apart from physical appearance, I see that are familiar, but you're so different. Alexis is this new person you created to run away from Lexie. I think she, or you, whatever, is a hell of a business owner and an amazingly talented baker, but she has such a sadness around her it makes it hard for me to breathe when I'm too close to her."

"And who is Al?"

"Al is the girl I can't stop thinking about, the girl who is getting under my skin and is so off-limits to me it makes my head spin to even go there."

I knew it wasn't my imagination.

He felt it, too.

And he felt exactly how I did.

I was right.

It was wrong.

Or maybe it was drugs talking.

That was a much more logical explanation.

"Marshall," I said softly. "I—"

"Al is the girl who sat with me for hours at the hospital and tried to make me laugh. She's the girl who had always been beautiful, but now I'm beginning to see how beautiful she is in a completely different way. Al is the girl, you are the girl, I think about kissing endlessly."

I wanted him to stop, to tell him it was the drugs, the possible head injury talking. I wanted to tell him when he remembered, *if* he remembered, he would regret it.

But I didn't want him to stop because it may be the only time he would say it.

I was tentative when I asked, "And then what?"

"And then I wake up and know it'll never happen. I can't go where my best friend was before me."

His hand lifted away from mine, and with it what was left of my dignity. A fleeting moment, something that I put a minute amount of hope in, came and went. Maybe it wasn't even hope. It was foolish to even imagine, and as much as his words built me up and then tore me down, they were the truth.

No. It was a moment. We had a few of them. There was a familiarity between us from long ago. It was a natural reaction to something, I didn't know what, and once verbalized, once it hit air, the truth destroyed it.

The truth often did that.

He was already struggling to get out of the car by the time I refocused. "I told you to wait," I snapped. "Do you want to hurt yourself further?"

I flung my car door open, stepped out, and slammed it shut. It was no surprise that by the time I reached Marshall, he was already standing, ignoring my instructions once again.

"Do you have to do the opposite of everything I say?" I asked. "Do you do it just to irritate me?"

I waited for him to argue back with me, but he didn't. He went back to staring like he was in the car, with his hot and cold intentions making me feel like I was losing my mind.

"I have to tell you one more thing, Al," he said.

"Yes?"

"Thank you," he said.

His blue eyes shimmered from the moonlight. It was clichéd and silly that I was even noticing, but it made him appear so handsome. It was another moment—both of us standing under the moon, the sky watching everything that was happening. How many others were standing under the same sky, wondering and waiting and thinking how different their lives could be?

"For what?" I asked, finally responding to him.

"For still understanding me."

* * *

I got him situated on his couch once inside his apartment, complete with him moaning and groaning.

"This is gnarly," he said, trying to tug his shirt off over his head.

I rushed to his side. "Here," I said, assisting him.

He didn't resist, and with minimal amounts of cursing, we had it off. My eyes wandered around his chest, the smoothness of his skin and hard lines of muscles decorated with endless stories. He leaned back against the couch, and I was back on nurse duty.

I hurried off to get him a fresh shirt and pain medication, but when I returned, he was already asleep. He'd gotten himself onto his back, resting his head against a stack of pillows, with his hands folded neatly in front of him.

I didn't know whether to be concerned that he dozed off so quickly or not. Aside from poking him awake or using a mirror under his nose to check his breathing, I concluded I was overreacting. At least, I hoped I was.

Grabbing a blanket from the back of the couch, I laid it across him. I slid to the floor next to him, beyond exhausted myself, resting my head on the cushion of the couch near his face.

"What am I going to do with you?" I whispered to a sleeping Marshall. "Why now? Why you?"

A pain radiated from the center of my chest outward, and I knew what it meant. I lifted my hand and gently brushed it across his hair that had fallen into his face. Instead of retreating after, or perhaps I never should have been doing it at all, my hand hung in the area until I found myself touching his skin. The tips of my fingers lingered above his arm, his chest, before a feather-like touch brushed across them, tracing the lines of his tattoos.

"She's gone, but she's everywhere," read one in a beautiful script in the center of his chest, large enough to extend from shoulder to shoulder. It was flanked by enormous angel wings spreading across his rib cage and inward. It was difficult to make it all out in the dark, but the empty space was filled with flowers, timepieces, and a lion's head.

My eyes focused on his forearm, scattered with dragonflies surrounding a lighthouse reaching from wrist to elbow.

And there was the Superman symbol, brightly colored and appearing to emerge from torn skin on his right shoulder.

So many stories.

I wanted to know them all.

I drifted off to sleep but would startle awake. I'd take a few moments to make sure he was okay, and he was, still asleep in the same position. When I woke, the sun had already shown her face, and I was lying flat on the floor. My back ached as I pushed myself up, tossing off the blanket that had found its way from Marshall to me.

Marshall.

He wasn't on the couch.

And when I checked the rest of the apartment, he was nowhere to be found.

It wasn't until I checked my phone that I saw a text from him.

Marshall: Early start. Didn't want to wake you, even though you looked uncomfortable as fuck. See you later at drop-off.

Four minutes after he sent the first message, another one came through.

Marshall: Thanks for everything. Really.

* * *

I returned home just before Phoebe arrived, and we made the daily cupcakes together as I told her the full details of the night before. Her questions were endless but were a great diversion. I didn't want to think about anything relating to the part of the ending I *wasn't* telling her.

The eyes.

The energy.

Us.

I didn't know if it was all real or not, and that made me frightened so much so that I had to keep my distance.

I had to keep her behind to finish up some other orders and then make some deliveries. It was up to me to do the drop-off at Ginger. By the time I got there, I was a bundle of nerves. I didn't know what to expect.

"Hey," he said, emerging from the office.

He looked like hell, and…not. He'd cleaned up well from the night before, and while he seemed to be standing a tad taller, I could tell he was still hurting from the bruised rib. The swelling around his eye had gone down, but now the entire area was an angry purple color. Even with all that going on, the plain black T-shirt and jeans he was wearing looked anything but.

"Hey," I answered, setting bakery boxes on top of the bar. "How are you feeling?"

"Not bad." He shrugged. "Sorry for taking off this morning. I just, you know. Anyway, what's in here?" he asked, tapping the top of the boxes and looking everywhere but at me.

I was half hurt he wasn't going to say more about leaving without saying good-bye, but the other half was fine with avoiding everything altogether that happened the night before.

"They're chocolate bourbon pecan pie cupcakes with a butter pecan frosting. I have the others in my car."

"Are you fucking kidding me? Chocolate bourbon?"

I smiled. "No, I'm not kidding, and yes, they are that good."

His fingers ran along the top of the box before sliding one under the taped edge. My perfectionist tendency emerged when I wanted to tell him he was going to tear the box, but I held back. The lid flipped up and Marshall's face lit up, as my heart started beating faster.

There was something about seeing a person get so enthusiastic about a creation you made. It always thrilled me, and seeing Marshall do it, after the plethora of treats of mine he'd had, was another level.

"Jesus Christ," he muttered to the insides of the box. "How much will you rage if I eat one?"

"Not at all. I mean, you need to taste to know how to sell right?"

I watched as he lifted one out and carefully peeled back the decorative wrapper before biting into it from top to bottom. His eyes fluttered shut as I heard a soft moan leave his lips.

It was almost indecent to watch.

So, I left him alone with his edible orgasm, which seemed like a good name for some treat I made in the future, and went back to my car to gather up the rest of the boxes. When I returned, he was licking his fingers of the remnants of the butter pecan frosting.

"Al," he said. "Those are...I don't even know. What's a word for more than fucking incredible?"

There was never a time when someone complimented my sweets that I wasn't pleased, but it was the other thing he had said that made my heart skip a beat. He called me Al. I didn't know what it was about it. Maybe it was that he adopted a name only for me, that he was the only one to call me that, but it was endearing.

I smiled. "I think fucking incredible is the right term for it."

"Is this it?" He pointed to additional boxes of beer brownies, margarita doughnuts, and Fireball turnovers I brought in.

"Yeah."

"Awesome. Before you take off, there was one other piece of business I wanted to talk to you about."

Shit. He was going to go there. He was going to bring up last night and what happened in the car. I'd hoped he'd save both of us the embarrassment of reliving it, or maybe it was just me that wanted to be saved from it. I needed to play it cool and not let him see how the whole thing had affected me.

"Oh? What other piece of business?" I asked.

"Well, I assume you were here last night to talk to me, you know, before you saw Monday Night Raw go down, because Phoebe told you I needed to talk to you."

Or maybe it wasn't about the car situation.

"Yes. That's what brought me in. What's up?"

"Tipsy Treats aren't lasting long at all here. Everything is sold out by a couple hours after opening, and while you've been bringing in more than initially contracted for, I think we need to talk about how we can keep the inventory flowing."

"Phoebe and I are stretched as thin as we can be. Keeping up with you guys along with other orders has us at max."

"I get that, and while it's your business, maybe you need to think about hiring another employee."

It wasn't that I hadn't thought about it, but the way Phoebe and I worked together was so perfect. It was hard to find someone like her, and the notion of adding another person into that wasn't a thing I wanted to do. I gripped the end of my hair and started twirling it around my finger as I considered how to handle this. On one hand, it wasn't a bad thing to do for the expansion of the business, but my intention with Tipsy was never to be something bigger than I could handle on my own and with just one other person.

"I see that you're panicking or some other shit," he said. "I'm not trying to tell you what to do or anything, but know we need to come up with some solution."

"How do you know that?"

"How do I know what?"

"That I'm panicking. I'm not."

"You're twirling your hair," he said, pointing to my finger. "You only do that when you're freaking out. And by the way, when did that start? You never used to do that, did you?"

"One, I'm not freaking out or panicking. I'm only thinking. And I don't know when I started doing it. It seems like I've been doing it forever, but I guess not. No one else around me knew me…before."

He ran his hand down and across his beard as he shook his head. "Sorry," he mumbled.

"For what?" I asked.

"For…whatever. I don't know."

We were silent for a few moments before our eyes were back on each other's, and we locked.

Hard.

And the moment was there again.

I took it all in because I knew there would be a time later, when I was alone in bed surrounded by quiet, that I'd want to remember it. I wanted to dissect every single breath, every blink, so I could try and decipher what the hell was happening. What was this thing between us that was growing and deepening despite us trying to avoid it?

"You know, Al," he said in a tone that exuded suggestiveness. "I know I was high as fuck last night, but I can't shake something from last night that keeps coming back to me."

"Yeah?"

"Where were you last night after you left me on the couch?"

"Why does it matter?"

"Because I'm asking you."

"Well, someone had to watch you."

"You were close."

"I was."

"I felt you, smelled you. I wasn't sure if I was imagining it or dreaming. Your hands were in my hair, running across my skin."

"Yes."

His head tilted to the side. "You slept…on the floor? Like where I found you?"

"Yes."

He stepped closer, running his tongue along his lower lip, as his eyes fixated on my mouth. "And why did you do that?"

I could've lied. I *wanted* to lie.

But I'd lived a lifetime of them, and I didn't want to anymore.

"Can you walk me to my car?"

He appeared confused but nodded before following me out the door. No words were exchanged as we crossed the parking lot to my car. It was only the energy.

What had happened.

What was happening now.

There was no way he didn't realize why I asked him to walk me to my car.

Every guy knew.

When we reached it, I paused next to the driver's side door, and there was zero hesitation when he stepped in front of me.

Close.

And then closer.

Almost nose to nose, our heights matched. He was so close I could smell him, the sweetness of the cupcake he'd only just eaten and his cologne. Or maybe it was soap or shampoo. I never asked what he wore or what it was because it seemed like a violation of rules, like I wasn't entitled to know. I did conclude that whatever it was, it worked. It worked on him. It was clean and sexy and the perfect balance between.

I started to panic, turned my head, avoidance being my only defense.

"Why did you want me to walk you to your car?" he whispered, his warm breath of words against my ear.

I shrugged, but I was lying. I'd been alone, so very alone, for so long. Physical contact, conversations that made me think, and mutual intentions were such a distant memory that getting an unexpected breeze of them into my life had me reeling. I wanted him, and it scared me that I was following that. That destruction that would be the follow-through was too overwhelming to consider. I could see the wreck in front of me, and I was walking directly into the devastation.

His fingertips fluttered next to mine, the subtle touch making me shiver from nothing to do with the weather. I knew he was staring without looking and that one small close of the gap between us, one turn of my head, would light the world up in flames. It wasn't what I intended, nor was it what I wanted. Just a walk to my car to keep him next to me a little while longer, but now that lie I told myself was about to give me away.

My eyes continued to focus on the pavement and the orange embers of a discarded cigarette, someone had tossed from the street, next to the toe of my shoe. It seemed strange I was so close, but I didn't destroy it.

"Al?" he muttered.

And then it wasn't about what was right or wrong, or needing or wanting.

It was about me.

It was about him.

Us.

I rotated my head to bring my eyes back to his.

And then there was nothing else to say.

No more questions.

No more answers.

His lips touched mine, so tentative at first to gauge if I would kiss him back. I did, not because I wanted to, but because I *needed* to. We sighed against each other's lips as heat rose all around us. One kiss, and we retreated only slightly, glancing into each other's eyes for reassurance, before our mouths, our lips, were back where we both wanted them to be.

On each other.

My hands wrapped around his neck to bring him even closer, as I was backed up into my car. His body pressed against mine, and with no place for me to run to, I melted. Our lips parted simultaneously, our tongues meeting together with mutual moans. His hands slipped around the small space behind me, gripping the fabric at the back of my uniform dress in his fists, before releasing and moving them up and down.

I tasted what was left of my cupcake creation on his tongue, the hint of bourbon and chocolate, and it made something move inside me.

All I *could* think was this wasn't just a good kiss. This was an amazing kiss—a kiss that I'd remember. It wasn't crazed or rushed, but it wasn't tentative. It was desire and longing coming together in a movie-worthy kiss sequence.

He moved. I moved. Together. Perfectly.

Cars passed by, alarms went off, and the conversations from people walking down the street behind us, going about their lives like they had no idea the world was imploding, were all there.

But I heard nothing.

It was only his hands in my hair, his mouth on my neck, and his panting breath against my skin. My fingers dug into his hair, yanking him closer, but with no room for him to move, he nudged my legs open with his knee and stepped in between them.

He paused for a moment and I startled.

I asked, "Is this okay?" as I continued to stare at his lips.

We were out in the open, outside the bar, for all to see. Any of his employees or people who knew me could've seen.

"Are you okay?" he asked.

A question with a question, and there was no right answer. Logic and reason would bring me to one direction. His pleading eyes that my own had drifted to would lead me to another.

"Yes," I whispered.

I wanted more. I wanted *him*.

All of him.

I wanted his words against my lips and his hands on my bare skin. I wanted to trace the tip of my tongue across every one of his tattoos and know their story. I wanted us to kiss all the bad memories away and remember how good it was to be wanted.

And as I looked at him straight on, feeling him hard against my leg, I knew he wanted the same.

His eyes were closed before our lips met again. Pushed and pulled and back and forth we went, and I didn't want it to stop. My hand fumbled behind me to unlock the car door to get us inside, but as I grasped the handle, he pulled away once again.

He rested his head against my forehead, his chest heaving. "No. Don't," he said. "Not here."

"What? Why?"

"Because I'm not going to fuck you in the bar parking lot, that's why."

I wanted to joke, to tell him I wasn't going to and didn't want to sleep with him, but I knew whatever bullshit line I gave him, he'd see right through. He was so good at that already.

This moment had crossed my mind more times than I could count, but I was still unprepared for where we were at. I needed to remind myself that this was *me* with Marshall, not Lexie with Aaron's best friend.

Him. Me.

Together.

"Do you," I said, turning my head and pressing a kiss to his neck, his stubble tickling my lips, "want to take me somewhere else to fuck me?"

He groaned as my tongue flicked against his skin before he sighed and pushed back. "Yes, I do, but—"

"But what?"

He shrugged and averted his eyes from me. Now it was obvious it was his turn to fight the angel and devil. It was easy to get swept away, to take hold of the moment and let nothing else matter. It was always fleeting, though. The spell broke as soon as reality hit. I didn't blame him, though, because it would've come to me sooner or later. It just happened to him first.

"I get it," I said without waiting for a response.

I shifted around and opened my car door, but Marshall's arm reached across me as his hand slammed it shut.

"I don't think you do," he said. "Would you look at me?"

I glanced over my shoulder without turning completely. "Marshall. I get it. I do. And you're right."

"How do you even know what I was going to say?"

"Because I'm not stupid. We can't. Ever. Or I don't know, maybe we could, but could you imagine?"

"No, I can't, but that is what fucks me up the most."

"What do you mean?"

"I see you, and you look like her. You talk like her. You move like her. Hell, you even smell like her."

I shook my head because while I understood what he was saying, it didn't matter. He'd never be able to look at me and separate the girl who caused so much hurt to his best friend and the girl standing in front of him now.

"You're not her anymore, Al. You're not Lexie. Christ, will you turn around already?"

I complied, folding my arms in front of my chest. "I am still *her*. I always will be. I can change my name, move far away, get a job, whatever. But I'm still Aaron's ex-wife. I'm still the person, the woman, the mother that did all the things you remember. It's me."

"That's not what I meant," he said, brushing his hand against my arm before tugging on one so I'd unfold. "Of course, it's still you, but everything about you is different. You *are* different, and with that you're new to me, but I don't know how to fucking reconcile who you were. I don't know how to separate the two."

He was getting frustrated, kicking some dirt at his feet. I wanted to help him, tell him I understood, because it was the same way for me. I just wasn't sure if I could.

"You know what?" I asked.

"Huh?"

"I haven't dated anyone since I left Aaron."

His eyes opened wide as he tried to conceal a smirk. "Bullshit."

"I'm serious. No one."

"You mean to tell me that you haven't had sex in, I don't know, six or more years?"

"I didn't say sex, Marshall."

His head tilted to the side, processing what I'd said. I knew I could go on to explain that the physical needs associated with loneliness is entirely different than romantic ones. I could help him to understand that sex didn't have to equate love. I was sure he would get that. But I wasn't sure he'd get why.

I patted his chest, willing to stop the moment. It was all so exhausting. "For the record, you've showed more self-restraint than I'm capable of. Thank you," I said.

My car door was flung open, and I slid into the seat before he could say a word.

Chapter Nine

What
The
Fuck
Did
I
Do?

What the holy fucking shit did I do? I kissed her. She kissed me back. We kissed.

And it was so goddamn good. No, not good. It was off-the-charts amazing. There are few times in life when a kiss is so perfect, when the vibe, the flow between two people, is so perfectly in sync that it all comes together in a hot meeting of the lips. In our case, this happened, and it wasn't just hot, it was a…fucking explosion of relentless hunger and desire. And what was left when the dust settled, and we could see what we'd done?

Total carnage.

There was no word strong enough for what an asshole I was. Not only did I let my dick take over for any reasoning my brain had in regards to how this would change the entire dynamic of the delicate relationship Al and I had, but also no doubt she had some sort of feelings for me, too. You can't kiss someone like that, feel the heat rising and not be able to stop it, and not have something hiding behind it.

None of that held a fucking candle to the loathsome betrayal I inflicted on my best friend. I could justify it any way I wanted, but I let what *I* wanted take a front seat to what I knew was right, what I knew was the honorable thing, and dug a knife right into the back of Aaron. The worst part? He didn't even know it. It was just yet another thing I was hiding from him.

His ex-wife. The mother of his daughter. The woman who left them with barely a word, didn't look back, and nearly destroyed him. I had to watch someone who was like a brother to me crawl and claw his way through the wreckage of his life, while still being the best damn dad I'd ever seen. I saw it, and all I could do was watch. Delilah was pure sunshine. No one who knew the truth would ever be able to wrap their mind around the fact that she had a mother that would never know how kick-ass she was. She'd grow up wondering why her mom left her, and she'd have to grapple with it for her entire life. It was really fucking unfair because she didn't deserve it. Neither she nor Aaron deserved any of the grief inflicted on them.

And Al was the one who did it. She was the one who hurt them, and I fucking kissed her.

I did more than kiss her.

I *wanted* her.

Given the chance again, I didn't know if I could tell her no.

I almost fucked her right there. She was going to let it happen, and while there was doubt in my mind that it would've been insane, there was a part of me that was angry at her about it. Granted, I should've fucking known better. Hell, it never should've even been in my brain, either of them, the one in my head and the other in my pants. It didn't matter what was happening between us or why, but it was a place I couldn't go.

And she was so matter-of-fact when she left. It was odd and nothing like I'd ever known any other woman to do when she was rejected. Her face went neutral, almost cold, and she was gone after her remark about my self-restraint. I stood there, watching her car drive off, and then long after her car disappeared. I was so fucking torn up, so confused. Not only did I not know what happened, but I also didn't know how it happened so damn fast. It was anger and bitterness one day and then a shift. I didn't know if it was the night of the opening or if it started before then. Was there always something there? Even when she was with Aaron?

No. No, it wasn't. She was my best friend's girl. She was always hot. I noticed from the first day on the beach. But she was off-limits then.

She was off-limits now.

I ran my hands roughly through my hair in frustration, my fingers digging through the tangled ends.

Her hands were all in it, intertwining her fingers and tugging. I knew why girls got off on that shit when we did it because it felt fucking amazing.

Those same hands that I knew were capable of making delicious cupcakes and cookies were also capable of yanking me gently to her, both with purpose and caution, recalling my rib injury. Her fingers across my skin, the palm of her hand against the side of my face...all of it lit me the hell up, like she'd struck a match and dragged it across every area.

Her soft goddamn lips, the way she sighed against mine, it all seemed orchestrated. It was like it was something composed only for us, but it couldn't have been.

And those fucking eyes. There was so much behind those eyes, even more so than I saw on a daily basis. There was desire and tragedy and so much hidden beneath the blue. I wanted to reach inside and pull it all out of her. I wanted to lay it in front of her so she could see all the things I did, all the wondrous things that rose above all the past bullshit. It was there. I just couldn't reach it yet.

It can't.

I slammed my laptop shut and slid away from my desk in frustration. "Son of a bitch," I muttered.

"Hey," Wells said, entering the office. "How are you feeling? Should you even be here?"

"It's my goddamn bar so I can always be here," I barked. "The real question is what are you doing here? I texted you this morning and told you not to come in until later since I know you were here all night covering for me on your own."

I was being a dick. I knew it and also knew it was misplaced anger.

"Sorry," I mumbled.

"And I can see you are feeling better, considering your cherry disposition is still firmly intact again."

"Smart-ass."

"Back at you," he said. He leaned up against the door, taking a sip from his frosted coffee monstrosity with added chocolate sprinkles. "Seriously. You okay?"

"I'm fine," I said with a sigh. "Thanks for everything last night."

"Man, that was an ugly scene. Everyone was so freaked out, especially Alexis. She get you home all right?"

What did he just say?

"What did you just say?" I asked.

"Thattttt...it was an ugly scene? Did you get home all right?"

"No," I said. "The other part. That everyone was so freaked out, especially Alexis."

His straw made a slurping noise as he sucked the bottom of his drink. "Yeah. She flipped her shit," he said, walking out of the office.

"Like what?" I shouted. "How did she flip her shit?"

"I don't know," he called back. "She just...freaked. When she saw it happen, I had to hold her back because she was trying to get to you. She was screaming your name and stuff."

I didn't remember any of that. I only started to get my bearings and my brain back in order when I got to the hospital. Bits and pieces would return to me about the incident, but mostly there was the recollection that there was no time for reaction, just action. There were vague glimpses of Al's face in those memories, and somewhere inside my mind I could imagine the scared look on her face.

It made my fucking heart ache.

"I guess she doesn't hate you after all," he mumbled, his mouth clearly full of something.

I pushed back from my chair and stood up too quickly, my side reminding me it got kicked good last night. As I peeked around the corner, I saw Wells taking a bite of one of the cupcakes Al had brought.

"What the fuck are you doing?" I shouted. "No wonder we always run out! I'm always catching you sneaking."

He was startled and swallowed what was in his mouth. "There was already one missing so I know you had one, too."

"This is my bar. It's important for me to maintain quality control."

"Yeah, right," he snorted, taking another bite. "Who dropped them off? Was it Phoebe?"

"Can you please wait to talk until after you're done chewing? It's like it's raining chocolate cupcake crumbs in here, you gross bastard."

He leaned over the side of the bar and retrieved a cocktail napkin. "It has to be Alexis," he said, wiping his mouth.

"Why do you say that?"

"Because you're cranky. You know, if I didn't know better, I'd think you two had a thing for each other."

Shit. Shit. Shit.

Be cool. Just play it cool. Avoid and deflect.

"Aren't those cupcakes magic? So good," I said while trying to disguise an automatic grin.

His eyes widened. "And now you're making me wonder."

"About?"

"You and Alexis. You're completely avoiding my previous statement about you two having a thing for each other."

Or I could meet it head-on and try to extinguish any thoughts from that angle.

"That's fucking ridiculous," I said with a fake laugh. "You know who she is to me. She's Aaron's ex-wife. Aaron, my best friend and business partner. That alone makes her the most undesirable woman to me."

And the mother to his child. Their child. The one she left.

Fuck. Why was this so complicated? Why did it have to be her? The first time I've had feelings for a girl in ages, and it was her. I wasn't sure what the hell was in my DNA or if all the drinking years caused brain damage, but I was finding it impossible to wrap my brain around the situation.

"Then why are you two always so...together?" he asked.

I couldn't get into all the nuts and bolts of what went down years ago, even though that was part of it, but there was something more now. Things I wondered, and it irritated me that I didn't know—that I couldn't ask her more.

"I don't know," I said. "There's a lot of history there and a lot I don't know. I'm not sure what she's been up to all these years."

"That's dumb," he said.

"What's so dumb?" I asked.

"I forget how old you are sometimes. You want to know what she's been up to? Use something called the Internet. Inter-net, boss."

He was about to get an ass kicking worse than what I got last night if he didn't change his tune. "I'm aware of what it is, Wells. What's your point?"

"My point is you know her name. Google her. Find her social media. There is a wealth of knowledge out there just waiting for you to snoop through."

"That seems so…" I trailed off, trying to find the right word.

He closed the cupcake box, trying to seal it back up. "I didn't do this," he said, pointing to the ripped box lip. "And yeah, it's totally invasive, but everybody does it. You'll hear chicks talking about it, and every guy will deny doing it, but we do."

"I ripped the box, and this is just so weird. I mean, I'm not that much of an idiot that I didn't know you check stuff out online, but I thought it was after you were dating and shit."

"Oh no. As soon as you know you're interested in someone," he said, raising his eyebrows, a smirk pressing against the sides of his lips. "You start scoping out the situation. But of course, you aren't interested in Alexis, so whatever."

"No, I'm not," I said with firmness. "But—"

"But you want to do it anyway, right? You want to see what she does in her spare time? What dudes she hangs out with look like? Is there a particular one in a lot of pictures and thus means they're close, dating, or banging?"

I didn't consider any of those things because I assumed she wasn't. She said she hadn't dated anyone since Aaron, but was intentionally vague when I asked her about sex.

Maybe there was more about her I didn't know.

"Everybody does it," he sang, walking past me and back into the office.

"Fuck off."

* * *

I sat in my dark apartment, the only light coming from the screen of my laptop on top of my coffee table. The flashing cursor on the Google bar taunting me to enter the Stalker Zone.

What the hell was I doing this for?

I knew why. I wanted to know more about her. I didn't want to admit it, but I did.

"For Christ's sake," I said to the empty space. I picked up my beer and took a long sip.

It wasn't like someone was outside my window, knowing what I was doing.

Wait.

There wasn't some secret software or something that would alert a person when someone was searching their name was there? What if there was an app or shit that notified her, by alarm, someone was hitting up her name all over the interwebs? How would I even explain that?

I grabbed my phone and texted Wells—

Me: There's no way she'll find out I'm creeping on her all over social media and shit, right?

I stared at the phone screen like a pathetic fuck, hoping his response would be swift and reassuring. Luckily, osmosis was a real thing and his message came through.

Wells: How the hell would that even happen?
Me: I don't know! I don't do this shit. I didn't know if there was some alert.
Wells: Ah. No. The Internet snoopers police isn't standing outside your door with their Tasers, ready to drag you out into the middle of downtown and make you wear a scarlet letter.
Me: Fuck off. Why do I even ask you anything ever?
Wells: You're certainly very worried about being found out for someone you're not even interested in.
Dick.
Me: I told you. I'm just curious. I don't want shit to get awkward, since we work together, if she found out.
Wells: Whatever. Go forth and HUNT!

No doubt he was on to me, but I had to keep doing as I had that morning. Deny. Deny. Deny. There was no other way. While it would be nice to confide in someone about all this Al business, there wasn't a chance in hell I'd divulge that to Wells. He had a big mouth, and with him being as into Phoebe as he was, I couldn't risk him slipping something to her. He was too close to Alexis, and he was too close to Aaron by being my right hand.

Aaron.

This was the time I needed him to hear what was going on

with me and give me level advice. He'd always done that for me and vice versa, but that couldn't happen either for obvious reasons. I couldn't even imagine how that conversation would go.

"Hey, Aaron! What's up, buddy? Great. Good to hear. Oh, me? How are things here? They couldn't be better. Ginger has hit the ground running, and lines are out the door every night. It has all come together just like we'd hoped. Plus, as an added bonus, I hired a local baker who makes daily deliveries, in the sexiest like retro waitress dress thing, and she makes liquor-infused mini desserts. And guess what? You'll never guess in your lifetime who it is that makes these treats, the most goddamn delicious sweets I'd ever had? Lexie! Yes! YOUR Lexie! Isn't that a hoot? Are you surprised? Yeah. I didn't tell you because I knew her involvement in the business was a win, and I let my selfishness about making sure Ginger was a hit trump telling you that Lexie was aiding in that. You know, she goes by Alexis now, but I hate that so I call her Al. By the way, I'm totally hot for her and kissed her and really would like to have sex with her, and maybe more. I know, right? I agree—I'm a total jerkoff who has no moral compass and who obviously has brain damage from all those years of drinking to have even taken it this far."

I was being optimistic about how well that call would go. It wasn't going to happen. Ever.

Which was why as I typed in her name into the search tab,

I was more conflicted than ever. I was indulging, allowing myself to dip my toe into dangerous waters, by seeking out more information about her. Sure, I could pass it off as being nosy or some other bullshit, but what was the point in lying to myself.

So I typed in "Alexis Bell" and hit search.

The results came back, and I started scrolling through to see if any of it was about Al. Her name appeared in a few articles about Tipsy Treats, and there was a simple website for it as well. But I couldn't find photos of her or any other information.

I dug deeper and deeper, feeling more and more like a creep the further I went. It was like I was sneaking through her attic or, even worse, her underwear drawer, looking for answers. To what questions? I didn't have a fucking idea.

I rubbed my eyes, remembering as soon as I did it that I'd been knocked out in one of those eyes twenty-four hours ago. Pain radiated across my entire eye socket and into my cheek until it dulled to a burn.

I wasn't getting anywhere. She had wanted to stay under the radar, and she had done that. She had done it well. Even when I searched under Lexie Matthews, a few things popped up, mostly career related, but even that ended abruptly six years ago. How does one not have any social media or Internet information out there on them? I wasn't as savvy as most with the whole Facebook, Snapchat, or whatever everyone was using to keep tabs on others 24-7, but I wasn't ignorant to it, either. Photos got posted every day of others without them even knowing it. With no idea about her family, either, to try and sneak through that way, I thought I'd hit a dead end. Then, it came to me. The one person in her life and who was probably on social media.

Phoebe.

But I didn't know her last name. However, I knew someone that did.

Me: Hey. What's Phoebe's last name?

Wells: Why?

Me: Because of course, I can't find shit on Alexis, and I bet Phoebe might be the only link where I can.

Wells: Williams. And do me a favor? If you find out any dirt on her, pass it along my way?

Me: Like what kind of dirt?

Wells: You know, like ex-boyfriends (or even ex-husband she has neglected to mention!) still sniffing around. Risqué or excessive partying or duck lip photos. Questionable political views. Overly vague status updates.

Me: Why does any of that, aside from the dude stuff, even matter?

Wells: It speaks to character. Plus, it's annoying.

I shook my head at the phone because all of it was so ridiculous. Maybe it was a twentysomething thing. These were things that were important to them—status updates and duck lip photos. Here I was trying to figure out if the girl who had been married to my best friend, abandoned her daughter, and was once one of my friends had done a one-eighty since then. Maybe *that* was a thirtysomething thing.

I didn't even want to consider what the fortysomething thing was. What a fucking shitshow that must be.

Me: I thought everyone was snooping on everyone? Don't you know all this stuff about Phoebe already since you're interested in her?
Wells: You never know when truths may rise to the surface.

Whatever, I thought, as I tossed my phone to the side and typed in "Phoebe Williams San Luis Obispo." I hit search and, as I expected, jackpot.

Every social media and reference a twentysomething girl would be on popped up. Clicking on her Facebook link, it opened to her page, her profile picture of a smiling Phoebe, with a New Year's Eve tiara on her head. I scrolled down her page but a lot of it was hidden, probably because of her privacy settings or whatever.

One photo that was in an album was linked to an Instagram account, so I clicked on it to see where it led me.

And it led me to right where I wanted to be. An unlocked, solidly stuffed with photos, Phoebe Instagram account. I picked up my beer and took a sip as I began to scroll through, looking for any sign of Al. My eyes scanned rapidly, knowing if she was there somewhere, I would catch her. As I took another long swig from the bottle, I saw it. I saw her, and I almost choked on the beer I was swallowing.

What the fuck? Who the hell is that?

I scrolled through the next several photos of Phoebe, Al, and others at some sort of a party. Al was mostly background in some, but there was one shot of her and Phoebe together, Al's long hair curled into glossy twists and her lips a shiny pale pink, appearing to be having a good time. It was nice to see her having fun for perhaps one night, but it was the next photo that had me seeing red.

Al and some…dude…her arms wrapped around his waist, as he kissed the side of her face.

She was smiling, a bright, strong grin.

His hand was resting on her lower back, dangerously close to her ass.

Asshole probably tried to cop a feel right after the picture was taken.

I had no idea why this angered me so much, why a blaze of rage was bubbling up inside of me.

Stupid fuckbag Marshall. Of course you know why.

She said she hadn't dated since Aaron, but it was evident by the photo there was something—and by something, I concluded probably boning—going on between them.

I recalled her saying no, she hadn't dated, but that it didn't mean she hadn't had sex or some variation of that. If sex had happened, was happening, this was probably the guy.

Or at least one of them.

I didn't begrudge or judge any woman out to get hers in the sack. In fact, I found it downright sexy. The double standard between men and women's sexual behaviors was fucking archaic, and a woman going after what she wanted, fulfilling her own desires was kick-ass.

However.

That was where the double standard ended.

No guy wants the girl he was interested in to be with other guys, even if it's assumed he was with other girls.

And if a man was truly interested in pursuing something more with a lady?

Not only did he not want her sleeping with anyone else, he didn't even want her *looking* at anyone else.

I wasn't sleeping with Al, nor could I indulge in anything further with her. It didn't stop me from reeling with jealousy, though, my desire to make her my own, to claim every inch of her body with a trace of my tongue and make her mind think of nothing else but me.

There was right and there was wrong.

Angel and devil.

You never knew what truths would rise to the surface was right, Wells.

Chapter Ten

ALEXIS—

Marshall: Can I see you? Ginger at eleven?

The message came through long after I was asleep at 1:48 a.m. It was an odd time to be texting me, but then again, what wasn't screwed up with what was going on between us?

It was barely 5:30 a.m., and I was doing my morning ritual outside on the porch swing, waiting for the sun to rise. Considering how late it was when he texted me, my guess was he was still asleep and it was far too early for me to respond. However, he didn't seem to have any second thoughts about reaching out to me in the middle of the night. This could've occurred for two reasons.

One: Something was urgent. Something had happened, and he needed to speak to me about it immediately. While that wouldn't explain why he wanted to wait until eleven a.m. at Ginger to do it, perhaps there was a reason behind that as well. The uncertainty made me anxious…fearful. He was my only tie to my old life besides Leslie. I'd often wondered if she would reach out to me if something happened to any of them, and if she had, what would I do? My face appearing during a tragedy would only further whatever pain they were going through. The flip side: If I was made aware and did nothing, how would that appear to them? How would it affect me? These were those nuggets of disconnect that were never part of the equation, were never even a thought when I had to make the decision to leave. All the what-ifs came later. They still came, but I had no choice but to swallow them as they arrived. I'd given up any right to a decision when I left them.

Two: Marshall was just an inconsiderate asshole whose emotions came at him like a firing range, and instead of thinking through them, he had an immediate reaction.

I was leaning more toward reason two, to be honest.

I texted back.

Me: I'll be there.

I sat back and swung, but there wasn't much of a sunrise. Dark, ominous clouds lined the sky, blocking the day from making its full appearance. The wind kicked in, and I knew something was happening.

A storm was coming.

* * *

It was ten minutes before eleven a.m., our agreed-upon time, but I was nervous and couldn't stand waiting around any longer. Plus, I was driving Phoebe up the wall, and she all but kicked me out of my own house.

The sky had grown even more threatening, a late-morning darkness that was so unusual to see. It looked like any moment everything it was holding back would be unleashed. I wondered what it was waiting for.

Marshall's car was the only one parked in the small lot that backed up to the alley of Ginger. That meant he was alone and that Wells wasn't in yet, either. We were going to be alone. I had no choice but to assume he wanted it that way.

I entered through the unlocked back door, careful to close it behind me, before making my way through the quiet, empty bar. My fingertips ran across the length of the marble bar, everything shiny and untainted. I glanced into the office and saw him sitting there, his eyes concentrated on the screen of his laptop in front of him.

I watched him for several moments, taking in the handsomeness of his face, his strong jawline still visible from underneath his neatly trimmed beard. His tattoos, streaming from under his fitted, white cotton T-shirt, were a wash of colors and stories that even though I got a glimpse at the other night, I still wanted to know more.

"Al?"

I jumped, startled and embarrassed at being caught gawking at him. I didn't even want to know how long I was doing it or how long he noticed I was doing it.

"Hey," I said. "Sorry."

A slow grin materialized. "What do you have to be sorry for?"

"I was...staring."

"Yeah, I noticed. I certainly don't think it's anything to be sorry for, though," he said. He leaned back in his chair and bounced against it. "Although there are other things you might be sorry for."

"Really? I can't imagine I'm sorry for anything else, but I'm sure you'll tell me what I did wrong."

He let out an exaggerated breath and stood up slowly, his hand moving to his bruised rib's side. "I don't want to start today with the bickering or whatever," he said.

"Neither do I," I said. I attempted my best flippant tone, even though my brain and heart were telling me there was something to be concerned about. "But you asked me to come here, so I'd appreciate it if you'd just come out and say whatever it is you have to say."

"Why do you always have to do that?"

"Do what?"

"That," he said, waving his hand up and down my body. "Challenge me. You always take whatever I say to immediate defense, like you have something to prove."

He was 100 percent correct, but I wasn't going to readily admit that. It would be like handing him a piece of my dignity and letting him play catch with it. It was one of the only things I still had, and even with all the chemistry floating between us, I couldn't let my guard completely down. There was no telling when anger would rise to the surface with him, in regards to me. There was no choice but to always be on defense.

Also, he was one hell of a hypocrite.

"And you don't think you do the same to me?" I asked. "Nothing is ever said or done without you coming back swinging at me."

His jaw tightened. "Listen, Al. I'm doing the best I can with all of this, okay?"

"So am I."

"Are you? Why did you kiss me yesterday?"

My jaw dropped down from shock. Was he kidding me with this?

"Um," I said. "I seem to recall *you* kissing me."

"That was only after you wanted me to walk you to your car, and then…other stuff."

"Do you seriously want to argue about who kissed who first? The fact is we were both there, and I'll take half the blame. There is obvious regret, so let's just leave it at that, okay?"

I knew it was wrong, but I didn't regret the kiss. Regret meant you wished it had never happened, that it was a disappointment. I felt neither of those things.

He, though, appeared full of regret, and disappointment, and both were pointed toward me.

I understand, though. How could I not?

"How about we just discuss what I asked you to come here for, okay?" he asked, his face shifting back into a neutral expression.

"Fine."

"I was considering our talk yesterday, about how to increase the inventory of Tipsy into here," he said.

"Good. I was considering it as well."

"Oh? And what are your thoughts?"

"My thoughts are that I do two drop-offs a day instead of one," I said. "Phoebe can do one, and I can do the other. We can uptake the inventory a bit, but spreading it out like that will hit the right-after-work crowd, and then the second one will hit late-night people."

He ran his hand down and across his beard while staring at the floor. "Huh."

"What?"

He began to smile again, shifting his eyes to mine before the grin disappeared. "I was actually thinking the same thing."

"Well, how about that," I chuckled. "We can agree on something together and come to the same conclusion independent of each other."

It could've been so simple. *We* could've been so simple.

Regular.

Boy and girl meet. They do the dance, play the required games, and then give in.

But we weren't simple.

A lifetime of baggage followed me wherever I went, and I was going to be damaged for the rest of my life because of it. He only saw a piece or two of that baggage, but he had no idea of all that I carried before he even knew me.

And I didn't think he realized that Lexie died when she left Chicago. That the girl he knew, the investment banker with meticulous plans for her future, a sharp, ice-cold demeanor, and the picture-perfect boyfriend, was dead.

Alexis rose from it, and while I wasn't unhappy, I knew the

part of myself I closed off to the world was the same thing I wanted, I needed, so desperately.

Love.

But whoever could? Who could ever love, respect, and accept a woman who gave up her daughter? The woman who ran away from her family, but also ran away from her other family before that? Who could ever comprehend why I had to do any of it?

"Why do you always look so fucking sad?" he asked, taking a step toward me. "You go off into these places, and I watch your eyes and they're moving everywhere. It's like you're searching, but then you'll lift them to the sky and the sadness recedes a little."

"I'm not sad. I'm just—"

He stepped in closer again. "You're just what?"

"I'm wondering how I can look at you and see so many things I never saw before."

"Are you ready for me to blow your mind?"

"I don't know. Am I?"

"I think we agree on something again."

"We do?"

"Yes. Because I've been wondering—fuck, more than wondering—it's more like obsessing about how I know how much pain you caused, that I saw it, but knowing that isn't who you are anymore."

I didn't know how to process what he'd said. He did see Alexis now, but with the face that matches all the pain and betrayal, could he see past that? Did I even want him to?

He took one more step closer, closing in on my personal space. "There you go again. Sad eyes."

I needed out. I needed to get away from him and from him seeing what was under my skin, how he was affecting me. It was dangerous.

"Was there anything else you needed to discuss?" I asked.

"Yes," he said, his eyes running up and down my body. When he reached my face again, he sighed, a soft exhale of breath from his parted lips. "I want to know why you lied to me."

"Lied? About what?"

"Well," he said, clearing his throat, his demeanor changing to something nervous. "In doing some research into employee social media behavior, I came across Phoebe's."

"Okay. So what?"

"And I looked through her Instagram photos."

"Okay again. So what?"

"Let me fucking finish," he snapped. "Jesus. Give me time in between breaths to form my thoughts."

I rolled my eyes before pretending I was zipping up my lips by running my fingers across them.

"Thank you," he said. "My observation was that by casually scrolling through I came across a few photos of you. Upon further inspection at said photos, I noticed you were with a gentleman and that you looked…happy."

He spit out "happy" like it was from the bad part of an apple. Here he was sapping about how I always looked sad, but then criticizing me when I appeared happy.

"Are you getting to the point?" I asked.

"The thing is, Al. You said you hadn't dated anyone since Aaron, correct?"

"Yes. That's true."

"You also said that didn't mean sex, right?"

I saw the train coming and knew right where this was going. Marshall was the conductor, and he was going to stop and unload it all right at me.

"Correct," I replied.

"So you haven't dated anyone?"

"Yes! That is what I said, and if that was what you were implying I was lying about then…"

His eyes narrowed at me, and he closed the small gap between us. "One more question, Al. Are you still sleeping with him?"

"Who?"

"The asshole in the photos," he said. "Who the hell still wears Ed Hardy T-shirts and doesn't know they're walking around proclaiming their douche bag status?"

"I have no way of even answering this when I don't know what photo or—"

"Who is he?"

The delivery of the question was stern, demanding. My gut reaction would be to tell him or any man who used that tone with me to go screw themselves.

So why didn't I?

Why was it so hot he was getting into my personal business?

His jaw was clenched so tight a vein was protruding from the side of his neck as his chest rose and fell with rapid breathing. This wasn't only him meddling in my private life.

He was jealous.

He was crazy, senseless jealous.

And it was hot as *hell*.

I scanned my brain for a time when I was out with Phoebe, photos were taken, and there would've been some with me and a guy. There was not a lot of recollections to choose from because it was something I normally never did.

"Oh!" I said when it came to me. "It was her birthday party last year. She begged and pleaded for me to come, said it was the only gift she wanted. As you can imagine, she lays it on pretty thick in the guilt department. So, I did for once."

"And?"

"And what? That was what night that was."

"I didn't ask you what night it was. I asked you who the tool was with his hand almost on your ass?"

"Why do you even care?"

That stopped him in his tracks, and he retreated, both physically and emotionally. It seemed like he realized he was legitimately being insane and acting like a possessive boyfriend.

I wasn't going to let him off that easy.

"I asked you a question now. Why do you care?"

"You fucking know why I care, Al."

I did?

I did.

Shit.

I didn't know what to say. I didn't even know where to look or what to do because he had confronted it head-on. He was leaving it up to me to decipher, but he knew. He *knew* I knew because I felt the same way.

A loud crash of thunder hit close and made us both startle. It was a relief, a distraction from the intense volley of energy between us. It also was the perfect out.

"I better go," I said.

I didn't wait for him to stop me or ask any more questions. My feet moved quickly to the door, and even though I didn't look, I could sense him right behind me.

Just before pushing my way out the door, I stopped.

"Shit," I said, looking up at the sky.

The dark clouds that had circled all morning had unleashed all their angry fury in the form of buckets of rain. Steam rose from the street after being heated by the blazing midmorning heat.

It was going to be difficult to make an easy getaway.

"Where are you parked?" he asked, sticking his head out a bit to see how badly it was coming down.

I pointed toward my car. "Over there," I said pointing to the opposite side of the parking lot."

He leaned back against the doorframe. "I think this is going to continue for a while. You want to wait it out?"

I glanced at him, his blue eyes tinged red from his obvious lack of sleep. The black-and-blue remnants from his eye injury were fading, yellowing around the edges. I wanted to run my finger across the bruised flesh and allow him to feel my touch, know how much I cared.

"No," I said. "I don't."

I did want to stay with him, but I wouldn't. Things were shifting, and I didn't want to stumble. I knew he didn't, either. The kiss that had happened pushed it further than it should've ever gone. He was the one with all the restraint then. Now, I needed to be.

He had far more to lose than I did at this point. I'd already lost or abandoned everything I'd had.

"I'm closer." He jutted out his chin. "I can drive you to your car if you're game."

"Game for what?"

"Getting a little…wet," he said with a smirk.

"Really, Marshall," I said, rolling my eyes. I stepped forward, the torrential rain past the doorway was soaking my feet straight through my socks and shoes.

He stepped up next to me, shoulder to shoulder our heights matched. Just like I had noticed when we kissed or maybe even before then. Our heads turned toward the other at the same moment, the powerful thunder vibrating the ground beneath us.

I didn't want to run, but with the rain, I had no choice, right?

There were always choices. Right or wrong.

"Do you mind?" I asked.

His eyes narrowed, seemingly almost confused by my question, like he was wondering what I was asking. A ride to the car? Something else?

He turned his body, stepping up closer. "I don't mind at all, Al."

Everything about this moment was wrong. Everything except the rain and us.

He turned and retrieved his keys from his back pocket, locking the doors to Ginger.

When he turned back around, his eyes looked me up and down. "Ready?" he asked as we moved forward, the rain continuing to flood everything around us.

"I'm ready."

He pressed a button on his key fob. "See those lights?" he asked, pointing to the only illumination in the dark lot. "That's me. Despite what the movie told you, run toward the light."

I didn't have time to think before his hand gripped mine and we took off. The deluge poured down on us, soaking our hair, our clothes and everything else in mere moments. Strong winds whipped the rain around, stinging the skin and making it impossible to see anything but the glow of his headlights guiding us. He never let go, tightly tangled fingers wrapped around mine, until we raced to our respective sides.

"Shit," Marshall laughed as we slammed our doors shut.

"Right?"

We looked at each other, and there was nothing else to do but join Marshall in laughter. There wasn't an inch of us that wasn't wet; leftover rain ran in streams down our skin and fell in droplets from the ends of our hair.

"Do you need a paper towel?" he asked, reaching into the backseat with one hand and starting the car with the other.

I shook my head. "I don't think that'll even help."

Even though it was still warm outside, I shivered from being soaked through my clothes. Marshall noticed and, without a word, flipped the heat on in the car. The blast from the vent took my chill away, but also made me focus on the fact that he wasn't leaving the parking lot.

"Can I ask you something?" he asked.

"No. No more questions."

He raised his eyebrows, and I knew he didn't understand. I glanced at the window, the rain continuing to pound all around us with such force it was like we were going through a car wash. Marshall shifted in his seat, but my head didn't turn as I felt the heat of him moving closer.

"Al?"

"Yeah?"

"Can I ask you a question?" he asked. "Please?"

I nodded my head, knowing he wouldn't give up until I did.

No way was I going to look at him. There was no budging in that area, though. I knew what was happening, and it was all too much. The rain, the closeness, the intent in his voice. I'd been out of the game a long time, but not long enough to not remember. Desire rose all around us, sending a different kind of shiver across my body, which was easily disguised by the continued warm air.

"Look at me," he demanded, his tone shifting to something almost like a plea, but it held back on desperation.

I should've thrown the door open and run back out in the rain to the safety of my own car. I didn't, though. I knew why I was there. He knew, too, and when there was nothing left for me to avoid, I caved, turning my eyes to his so he could begin to see the truth.

His dark eyelashes, which contrasted with his light hair, blinked rapidly. "The thing is," he said. "I wondered if you'd help me out with something."

"What's that?" I asked.

His body turned toward mine; the only space separating us was the gearshift blocking our bodies. The only noise was from the rain, the thunder off in the distance, and our accelerated breathing.

He licked his bottom lip, staring at my own. "Why are you here?"

Asshole.

He saw it.

He knew.

Anything I'd say would only prolong denying that. He was calling my bluff. It made me uncomfortable, so I inched myself farther back in my seat to gain distance. I didn't like that he was seeing through me, that he knew whatever we were fighting was about to come crashing through the car windows.

"You fucking know why, Marshall," I said, mocking what he'd said to me minutes before.

A tentative smirk while his eyes still on my mouth was all the answer I needed, but he wasn't going to let me off that easy. He was going to open the door and make sure I stepped in all on my own.

"I think you want to find out if we can fog up these windows all on our own," he said.

Holy shit.

Maintain, Alexis. MAIN. TAIN.

"I thought you didn't want to fuck me in a car, Marshall. You always go back on your word?" I scoffed. I was trying to push it back at him, rattle his bones, but it didn't work.

He laughed. "Who said anything about fucking? I just happen to think making out in a car during a thunderstorm is sexy as hell."

"Is that so?"

"Absolutely," he said, reaching his hand to my face. His

thumb ran across my lower lip as his eyes continued to stare at me. "Ever done it, Al?"

I wanted to tell him no and that it sounded hot, a level above hot even.

It would've been *all over* if I did, though.

His blue eyes lazily lifted from my lips to my eyes before he looked at me through his eyelashes. "I can't stop this anymore, and I don't think you can, either."

His face. His mouth. His hands. They were so close I could feel the heat radiating off of him.

Who the hell was I kidding? It was over before I even got in the car.

The words of agreement were on the tip of my tongue, but whatever I'd say wasn't enough. My acknowledgment, my yes, and everything I had to give was thrust upon his lips by my own. I wanted him to feel my want while swallowing the doubts haunting us from the outside world. We were just two people who were so very wrong, in so many ways, to the outside world. Right now, his hands cradling the sides of my face, the way he moaned softly against my mouth, told me the outside world could go to hell.

My heart beat to the rhythm of the rain, making me anxious for more of him.

Kisses got deeper.

Hands got rougher.

Moans got louder.

He bit at the bottom of my lip, tugging, before backing away from me. His fingers ran across my jawline, his eyes following their path before settling on mine.

It was all there. I saw it in his stare, felt it in his touch. It was why there was no wonderment when he flipped the heat to a different direction to defog the windows, and after several moments, he put the car in drive. We passed my car without questioning from either him or myself, because I knew. *We* knew.

No words were said as we traveled the half mile from Ginger to his home. At one point, he moved his hand from the gearshift to mine, slipping them together. It was reassurance, trust, and yearning all wrapped up into the grip we were holding on so tightly to.

The rain continued, harder and with more aggression. It did something to me. It was mysterious, the way a storm was unknown and without direction. It was like the storm, the tornado, circling around Marshall and I. There was no way of deciphering where this would take us and what would be left when it was over. However, like the weather, you couldn't always predict what would happen. Sometimes you had no choice but to stand in the rain and make your body come alive.

And I let that rain rid my body of doubt, as we exited the car, to find what living in the moment meant.

And it wasn't a sprint to his door.

Maybe it was because we were both taking the extra time to be sure the other was, too.

He unlocked the door, me standing close behind him, and he stepped inside. I had barely cleared the threshold when his hand seized mine, yanking me in. My body was pushed up against the wall as our lips crashed together in a mad, mad panic. Cries and whimpers transferred between our lips, our tongues, because of everything that was hiding behind basic sexual greed.

His kisses moved from my lips down across my jaw before he pulled my head to the side, the tip of his tongue running down the length of my neck. Teeth gingerly scratched at my skin, his tongue followed up behind it, easing the area. His hand tugged down the front of my V-neck T-shirt and continued its path, his other hand working my hardened nipple from beneath my shirt.

It was like he was drinking me *all* in.

He paused for a moment, raising his eyes from my chest, his beard tickling my skin, to gaze at me. A wicked grin spread across his face before he licked his lips. "I think I know the answer already, but I still need confirmation. So, let me ask you, are you ready for me?" he asked.

I nodded, unable to answer anything with his lips, the tip of his tongue, skimming across the hollow of my neck, down between my breasts.

"What was that?" he asked. "I didn't hear you."

He nipped at the side of my breast through my bra, and it only furthered my ability to respond to him. I rotated my hips, pushing myself into him, but he eased back. He knew I was trying to find the friction.

"I still don't hear you." He breathed in my air. "Answer me, Al. Answer me or I can't go on."

His hand slid down across my stomach and down.

Down.

Down.

Until the palm of his hand was resting against the seam of my jeans.

"I'm running this show for right now," he said as he began to rub a finger against the area, applying *just* the right amount of pressure. "You'll have your turn, but right now, I need you to listen to me. I need you to *answer* me. I'm not asking you, I'm telling you, Al."

God, he was getting dirty, and while I never was one to take demands either in bed or out of it, the way his eyes were burning right though mine made me want everything he was giving me. It was making me want more.

"Al?" he asked. "Are you not going to answer me?"

I attempted to answer him, but I couldn't even recall what my name was with his fingers pressing directly above, but not on my clit. "What was the question again?" I asked, breathless.

"Are you ready for me?"

"Yes."

"Are you sure?"

I nodded my head, unable to answer him again with even a simple yes.

My body was responding to him because I *wanted* him. However, there was this underlying current, this gentle energy, that always reminded me who Marshall was, who he would always be. Aaron's best friend. I had already done so much damage when I left Aaron, and now, how much more would I cause by being with Marshall?

My thoughts began to take over how good he was making me feel. My breathing began to slow, my body movements halting.

"This is about me and you," he said, clearly sensing my struggle. "And it's no one else's fucking business okay? You and me."

It was a given, but it allowed me to relax a bit more, knowing we were on the same page. He knew what was at stake, and for now we could keep it between us.

"I'm not embarrassed or anything," he said. "It's…"

He had the same concerns I did. Of course he did. I knew his devotion to Aaron. They were practically brothers.

"Trust me," he whispered, his tone bordering on pleading.

His eyes searched mine, and all the answers, all the reassurance I needed was right there.

"Just shut up and go back to kissing me."

I took hold of the back of his hair, fisting it in both of my hands as I rotated my body into him. His hand moved from the front of my jeans to the button at the top. With rapid movement, he undid them and forced the zipper down, before slipping his hand inside.

Inside my underwear.

And his mouth was back on me, moaning against my own.

With his opposite hand, he seized mine and placed it on the front of his own jeans.

"Do you see, do you *feel* what you do to me?"

He was *so, so* hard already.

Chapter Eleven

Marshall—

She was *so, so* wet for me already.

It wasn't from the rain.

It was from *me*.

My finger slid against where she was so turned on for me, and it made my own erection grow. A lot. It was why I wanted her to feel it, to know how goddamn hard she had gotten me already.

None of this was planned.

It was nothing we sought out.

It wasn't anything we even wanted.

Hell. I broke the utmost rule of bro code. It was my best friend's former wife. I'd lay my fucking life down for Aaron, and here I was with her, unable to stop myself. Guilt began to creep in, and I wasn't sure if I could continue.

But I wanted her.

I wanted to taste her skin and swallow her words. I wanted to undress her soul and erase the sadness from her heart.

And I knew she was feeling similarly. I could tell by her hesitation at the exact time I did, and in that moment, I knew it was only her and me.

How could you turn your back on a moment?

Life was here, for the now, and I'd let enough moments pass by with regret. This one was too intense, too important, for me to walk away from. I wasn't going to do that.

She had gotten under my skin and embedded in my brain. There was no shaking her, no removing myself from what she was doing to me.

The mental, fucking cosmic or some shit, connection was enough to drive me insane. That alone made me want to fucking devour her, but add in how stupid hot she was, how goddamn sexy she was, and I almost fucked her in the car.

She was right, though. I had said I didn't want to fuck her in a car, and I didn't want to do that. I didn't want the cheapness of a backseat screw to dilute what I was feeling for her.

But the way she moaned against my lips simultaneously with my own slid her hands up and across my chest, made me lose my will to apply my finer points of seduction. She had followed me not just to my car and here without question, but to this stage. She was trusting me.

And the way she fucking tasted. I hadn't even gotten to her pussy yet, and I wanted to drink her all in by only getting a sample from her skin.

I stopped making out with her long enough to ask her one final question.

My forehead rested against hers. "Are you sure?"

Her hands ran against the side of my face, her fingertips digging into my beard. "Yes," she mumbled. "Are you?"

"Fuck yes," I said.

I took her hand and guided her to my bedroom, stepping away to get a good look at her all over. "You are so goddamn beautiful," I said, bringing my hands to her damp shirt and lifting it above her head.

Piece by piece, I stripped her down, our eyes never leaving each other. When I was finished, she did the same to my shirt, dropping it to the floor next to her pile of clothes. Her hand ran across my bruised rib with a frown. "I'll be careful," she whispered.

She pressed her lips to mine, running her tongue along my bottom lip until I was pulling her hips against me. I took the opportunity to slide my hands around to her ass, palming it with both hands.

Christ.

She was all smooth and curves everywhere.

Her hands slipped between us and unbuttoned the top of my jeans, sliding them down on my hips. She made use of the minimal space between us and slid her hand down inside my jeans. Once her fingers met my cock, I was done.

Fucking. Done.

My erection stood at full attention, waiting and begging for her to continue her touch. "You don't have to be too careful," I said with a wink.

Her fingers trailed upward again, grazing across my skin, tracing the lines of my tattoos as she studied them. They all told a story, a lesson, and I wanted to tell her every one. Maybe it was the expression I was making, but it was like she read my mind.

"Every one, Marshall. I want to know about every single one of them, and then I want to trace them each with my tongue, my fingers."

Fuck this girl. Like, *fuck*, in a good, amazing way, with the way she brought the sexy.

The room was cast in darkness from the storm still raging outside. It made her features muted, softened in such a way that she seemed delicate.

"Are you just going to stand there staring at me? Or are you going to fuck me, Marshall?" she asked.

But true to form, she leveled me in one sentence, reminding me looks could be very fucking deceiving.

"Get the fuck on my bed, gorgeous," I said, pulling my jeans the rest of the way down before taking her by the hand.

I backed up into the bed, dragging her down on top of me. We tumbled into a tangle, her giggling as her naked body met my almost naked one.

The thunder rolled, both near and far, as our kisses deepened and she rotated her hips against me. I couldn't wait to get inside her, to know every part of her body. I didn't know if this would be our only time together, so I wanted to prolong it for as long as I could.

Or at least until my hard-on held out.

And judging by the way she was moaning against my lips and tugging at the top of my boxers, she wasn't going to hold out much longer, either.

She straddled my lap, flipping her hair over her shoulders, as she looked down at me.

She kissed her way down my chest, pausing a moment to

look up at me through her eyelashes. Her finger lowered the top of my boxers completely, my dick springing free to meet her.

While still gazing at me, the tip of her tongue emerged from between her lips and met the top of my cock.

And that alone almost made me fucking come.

She hummed against me before bringing her mouth deeper and deeper. "Mmmm, Marshall," she said, still with eyes tightly on mine.

"Fuck," I muttered. "You feel so good."

She scooted back, releasing me for a moment so she could slide the rest of my boxers off. Once she did and tossed them to the floor, she eased herself back up, carefully straddling my waist.

"Is this okay?" she asked.

"Are you fucking kidding me?"

"No," she giggled, moving her very wet pussy up and down my dick. "I was worried about your rib."

I lifted her by the waist, rolled her to the side and underneath me. "It's fine. It was only bruised, but I'd break three ribs for the chance to fuck you," I said, looking down at her.

"That's a mighty bold statement. Broken ribs for the chance to...fuck...me?"

"I love the way you say *fuck*," I said, rubbing the head of my cock against her opening. I brought my mouth down to her breasts, running my tongue around the tip of her nipple.

She started to squirm again, getting herself closer and closer to bringing me inside of her. It was good she wanted to wait, too, because I wasn't sure how long I'd last. It had been a long,

long time since I'd had sex, and this was a girl I'd wanted very, *very* badly.

"It's the rain," she whispered. Her hands ran down the side of my beard before lacing her fingers behind my neck.

My head turned away, reluctantly, from her tits. "The rain?"

She nodded. "It does something to me. This kind does, the violent thunderstorms."

The fucking rain turned her on.

Why did that turn *me* on knowing that?

I reached above her head, above the headboard, and cracked the window a slight amount. It was enough to let the coolness of the front coming in to filter through, but not enough for the rain to get on us. Plus, it gave her a bit more of what she wanted.

"How's that?" I asked, moving my way back down, running my lips across the side of her jaw.

My tongue. My kisses on the hollow of her neck.

Down between her breasts, my hands all over them, my fingers rolling her nipples across my fingertips until my mouth replaced them.

And she repeated my name over and over.

And over.

I ran my nose across and down her stomach.

My lips on her hips.

Down.

Down.

Down.

One taste of her pussy and it was…extraordinary.

And she liked it.

A lot.

Shout-outs to God, Jesus, and several other holy grails shit came from her mouth.

So, I worked out how she liked it more and then added my finger in addition to my mouth.

She came so hard against me her legs shook as she pulled my hair.

"That," she mumbled after. "Is perfect. *That* is how it is."

I kissed her just above her clit, smiling against her skin.

"Now get inside me, Jones," she said.

"Awfully bossy in bed aren't you, Bell?" I said, positioning myself above to give her what she asked for. "You could say please, you know?"

"I'm always the boss, but I'm willing to give a little to have you give me what I want. So, please, Marshall, get inside me."

"Do you want me to put a condom on?" I asked.

She shook her head. "I have an IUD."

"Good girl," I said, pushing myself into her, both of us gasping at how fucking good it was.

It was as she said...perfect.

Moving in and out of her as she gripped my shoulders, running her hands along my face, was sexy and...something else...all together. It made my heart beat faster.

The chilling breeze traveling in, cooling off our sweaty bodies.

I had to believe I was giving as much as I was getting, that the emptiness that echoed through my body, vibrated against my bones on the daily, was filling a part of her. It wasn't just the fucking. We both could do that with anyone. It was this vibe, the insane energy, passing back and forth between us. I'd push deeper and deeper into her as her fingertips and her nails ran up and down my back, and I fucking knew this was something I'd never had before.

Our eyes were closed, and then they were open. Moving above her, and then she above me, her long hair falling across her damp forehead, her breasts. Back and forth. Giving and taking.

And when we came, it all seemed to fit. It all seemed to be right.

It all made sense.

It was like we'd said—her and I. Me and her. Just us.

When we were done, she tucked herself into my side, and I was closer to her than when we were having sex.

And that scared the fucking shit out of me.

She was where she belonged.

* * *

The sun was streaming through the gaps in the curtains, the only hint that morning had come. We had spent the entire previous day in bed. There was sex, talking, food breaks and more sex. The outside world, the place where nothing made sense, was closed off to us. For that day, it was only about two people who couldn't get enough of each other.

Al's body was wrapped up next to mine, warm and peaceful, in almost the same position as when we fell asleep. There was a slight chill in the air, but gratefully, I'd remembered to shut the window after our romp.

I moved myself with a slight turn, rearranging my body to a more comfortable position. My side ached, my bruised rib taking a neglectful beating the night before.

Did I give a fuck?

No. Fucking. Way.

Every moment was worth it.

My fingers twirled around her hair as I watched her sleep. It was, *I* was, a damn cliché—a schmoopy, feeling-filled dumbass. I'd make fun of any dude who exhibited such a pathetic act. However, I didn't care.

She sighed against my bare chest, and that hint of a noise, similar to the ones she'd made the night before, brought my normal morning wood to full-on attention.

I didn't want to wake her, but I knew I'd have to soon. It was after seven a.m., and she was usually working the baked goods train by this time. Plus, if I waited much longer, she might be in such a rush to leave I'd have to take morning wood into my own hands.

Please hurry and wake the fuck up, Al.

My phone vibrated on the nightstand next to my bed, making a loud noise as it echoed across the wood surface. I snatched it up and looked at who was calling.

Aaron.

Shit. Shit. Shit.

I immediately wanted to take back my thoughts from moments ago about not giving a fuck. I did give a fuck…about him.

An aching body was no match for the explosion of guilt that impaled my heart. Reality was calling me, and there was no hiding from it.

I slid myself out from under Al as swiftly and carefully as possible before racing out of the room, but before I could answer, the call ended.

"Son of a bitch," I hissed at the phone, at him, and at me.

My heart was pounding the beat of what seemed like a hundred drummers. Christ. Of all the moments, it was now he called?

The phone began to buzz in my hand again, a picture of Aaron, Callie, and Delilah popping up on the front.

I have to change that. If Al saw… I don't know. I really didn't know how she'd react. She hadn't seen them in so long. I didn't know if it would hurt her, upset her, or if she would even care at all. Any number of reactions gave me cause for concern.

"Hey," I answered, speaking in a low tone. "Two hours behind. Two fucking hours behind you."

"I know. I know. I'm sorry. It was Delilah," Aaron said. "She had asked last night if she could call you. Callie said yes. She obviously didn't mean at seven in the morning after snatching my phone when I wasn't looking. Can you believe she's asking for her own cell phone already? It's ridiculous. Anyway, she's leaving in a few for school, so I told her I'd call you back, apologize, and tell you she needs to talk to you later."

I made my way to the kitchen, the room furthest from the bedroom, so I could be as out of Al's earshot as possible.

"Everything okay?" I whispered.

"Oh yeah," he said. "She read a book, a fairly advanced one, too. It's a level three in the series, which means it's for independent readers, up to the fifth grade, but since Delilah is second grade, it's pretty impressive that she read the whole thing. I don't know if I ever told you, or if you knew, but a seven-year-old who won't be eight until May is a young second grader, and for her to a read a book about—"

"That's great, Aaron," I said, cutting him off. "Have her call me after school."

"She was just so excited about the Superman book she couldn't wait to tell you, but I'll have her call you later."

Superman.

That sweet, sweet little superhero girl of mine.

"Yes. Please do. I haven't talked to my Nutter Butter in a few weeks," I said.

"Everything else cool? Ginger still making its way up?"

"For sure. Better than we could've imagined."

"Why are you whispering?" he asked. After a moment's pause he let a loud laugh, followed by an "ahhhh."

"What?"

"You have a girl there. Sorry to have interrupted the morning-after plans. I'll let you get back to her, but I got to know. A one-nighter or a special one."

"A special one, I think."

"That makes me happy for you, man. For real. Okay, I gotta run. Talk soon."

The call ended, and I was glad I was leaning against my kitchen counter. My head was cloudy, my vision muted, from whatever the hell that call did to me. I made my way down the hallway, shaking it all out of me as I did.

I stepped back into the bedroom, leaning against the door-frame. She was awake, her hair in a wavy mess across the front of her naked body, staring off in a different direction.

The conflict in my heart, over the girl I had no doubt started to have feelings for in my bed and my best friend who I loved already, made my chest burn. Aaron's trust in me. His loyalty. Delilah's voice of unconditional love. Her innocence.

They had been my saviors.

Looking at Al, knowing what was happening, it was if she was gradually taking their place. I couldn't think it terms of logic, what I believed to be right and wrong, because as she slipped into her purpose in my life, there was no way to rationalize it.

I couldn't choose between them.

It was too fucking late.

"Who were you talking to?" she asked, her voice shrouded in sleep.

There were always choices.

The heart always won.

That fucked-up, delusional heart.

"No one," I responded. "It was…no one."

Chapter Twelve

Where the hell have you been?" Phoebe screamed as I pulled up into the driveway. She came barreling out of the house so fast my screen door hit the side of the house.

Where have I been? Where have I been? Where have I been?

I wasn't getting dropped off at my car downtown by Marshall after we spent the entire day before in his bed.

"Sorry," I said, putting my car in park. "Just had to take care of something."

"I was worried to death! I get here, had to use my key, which I never have to do, and you were nowhere to be found. The lights were all off still, and the coffee wasn't going like normal."

I exited my car with my tail between my legs for not being a responsible boss and business owner, but also for feeling like I was getting the third degree from my mother.

"Well," she said, blocking my way through the door. "What do you have to say for yourself?"

She even had the "mom voice" down pat. It was impressive.

"Like I said, I was taking care of something. I was a little loopy this morning," I said.

I attempted to step around her again, but she stood her ground. She narrowed her eyes as she brought her face closer to mine. Phoebe was never afraid to look people in the eyes. It was often uncomfortable for others because so few people did this, *really* looked people straight on in the eyes, but she claimed she could see the truth behind them. I hid from the truth. She'd say, "If you know someone can see the truth, why would you hide from it?"

I let her have her once-over, and when she was satisfied, she backed away, letting me through.

"Did you start the peanut butter cookies yet?" I asked her.

I headed toward the kitchen and saw several piecrusts rolled out.

There was my answer.

"Ah no," she said. "It's Thursday. I did the brownies and cookies yesterday for today. Plus, it's hot butter rum mini apple pies today."

I grabbed an apron from the back of the walk-in pantry door, swearing under my breath. She was right, but I mixed it up; since the peanut butter cookies with raspberry Chambord filling were such a hit last week, I wanted to do them today, too.

"Sorry," I mumbled, tying the apron my waist. "The peanut butter raspberry cookies were up today, too, so I was going to do those instead of the pies, but I guess I forgot to tell you and mark it down. But since you already started the crust, we'll just do both."

She shrugged and went back to the floured surface she was rolling the dough out on. "Weird," she muttered.

"What?"

"I've never known you to forget a menu change. You said you were a bit loopy this morning, and I guess you weren't kidding."

"I guess," I said, grabbing a large bag of sugar from the pantry.

"If I didn't know better, I'd think you got laid."

The sugar fumbled from my shaken arms as I heard what she said. My nerves took over, and in an attempt to avert a panic attack, I lost all sense, dropping the bag of sugar on my foot.

"Fuck," I shouted. I immediately followed it up with an "I'm sorry" for cursing.

"Yup," she said, smiling as she started to cut the pastry crust into rounds. "Fucking was exactly what I was thinking, too."

That girl and her "eyes on eyes" truths.

I would admit nothing. I couldn't.

We were under too much of a time crunch to banter about the state of my sex life, so we worked quietly until I knew I couldn't put off the inevitable.

With the late start of what needed to go out today, the deliveries were going to be off as well, especially to Ginger. I didn't want what happened between Marshall and I to interfere with the business relationship we had. An already fragile dynamic could break at any moment, especially after yesterday's shenanigans. Unfortunately, I didn't have a choice. I'd have to let him know.

I pulled my phone from my back pocket and texted him.

Me: Hey. I got a late start this morning. Well, obviously. You were there. Oh. By the way, thanks for dropping me off at Ginger. Speaking of which, I'll be or Phoebe will be in around four instead of the usual. I messed up with a menu change, and that's all on me. I apologize. So, yeah, it'll probably be me dropping off. Phoebe has to do the other deliveries. Is it okay if I not start the two-a-day deliveries until next week? We never did discuss when that would start because, well, you know. Anywho, it'll probably be me dropping off. I think. Yeah. I already said that. Typed. Unless it's weird now if I came in? So. Thanks. For understanding. About the deliveries. And thanks for last night. It was fun.

I hit send, and it was a second too late that it occurred to me what an idiot I was. The text was not only confusing, but also poorly written, unprofessional, and completely flippant for someone I had sex, really, *really* amazing sex with the night before.

Marshall: No problem.

Okay. Maybe I wasn't flippant enough for it to be considered that because his response nailed it. That was it? No problem? It was almost disrespectful, and I could sense Lexie, the old me, emerging. My reaction would've been swift, sharp, and overreactive. I gave myself a moment to process it all and put myself in his position. If I had gotten a text like the one I sent to him, I would've replied in the same way he did.

Shit. I needed to smooth this all over, but how?

* * *

Ginger was already starting to fill in with the after-work crowd when I arrived at four. It wasn't an ideal time to be making the drop-offs, but we had busted our butts to get it all done.

"Hey, Alexis," Wells said from behind the bar, giving me a nod. "Need a hand?"

My arms were full of a few things I brought as peace offerings for Marshall and only a couple of pastry boxes. The rest were in my car.

I nodded. "Do you mind? My car is open, and they are in back."

"No problem," he said.

"Is Marshall in his office?" I asked.

"Yeah. Want me to tell him you're here?"

"No, I'll go check in with him after I drop these off in the kitchen," I said.

"Cool," he said.

I walked the pastry boxes to the back and placed them in the dessert area—which really was just my area. A member of the kitchen staff would set them up on trays, and when the orders came through, they'd plate them for customers.

After I rounded my way to Marshall's office, I knocked on the closed door.

"Yeah?" he called.

I opened the door a crack. "Do you have a minute?"

"I do," he said. "Come in and close the door."

I did and set the shopping bag down on the floor next to the door. He was wearing a white button-down, GINGER written above the pocket in white lettering, and dark pants. It was something different from his usual jeans and T-shirts, but it worked.

I didn't know what it was, but he looked *hot*.

When the moment passed, there was something floating in the air that deflated my desire of wanting to jump his bones.

Awkward silence.

The kind of quiet that occurred when you're seeing the person you had sex with the night before, and you both are unsure about how the other is feeling.

"How's everything?" he asked finally.

"Good," I said. "Well, busy. You know, late start and all, but it's good."

"Yeah. Sorry about that," he said, leaning back in his chair. His shirt stretched against his strong chest as he did, and my brain took a straight shot to the night before, recalling my hands all over that chest. The smoothness of his skin, the hard dips and curves, and the tattoos that decorated it all. My fingers were all over the chest, my hands pushing against the taut muscles as he moved in and out above me.

"Well, I...," I mumbled, as I picked up the shopping bag. "I wanted to apologize for being late and assure you it wouldn't happen again."

I carried the bag over to him and set it down at his feet. He cranked his head to look inside, tilting his head in confusion.

"What's all this?" he asked.

I leaned over and picked the first bag out of it. "I know things have been crazy since you moved here, and considering you're a guy, you probably eat crap all the time, so I went to a few of my favorite places in town for some lunch. I guess dinner now, huh? Whatever."

"Are you kidding me?"

"No," I said, placing the first items on his desk. "These are my two favorite sandwiches from High Street Deli. One is an Italian sub, better than any you can get in Chicago, and this other one"—I poked the top of the wrapped sandwich—"is incredible. It's called the Highzenburger. It's a meatloaf sandwich on a brioche bun with bacon and cheddar and this amazing chipotle mayo. So good."

I paused as his mouth gaped open. His reaction was understandable because Highzenburger was even better than it sounded.

"Anyway," I continued, digging back into the bag. "This next thing is so, so good, and I'm not even sure if you like seafood. I couldn't remember, but I took a chance," I said, setting down a white soup cup and a massive hunk of bread. "This is the clam chowder from Splash Café. It's the best I've ever had. Even when I lived in Boston for a while after I left Chicago, it wasn't ever as good as Splash. Oh, and a sourdough bread bowl because...yum."

"Al...I...I," he stuttered.

"I know. It all looks so good, right? I have one more thing, though. For a while, indulging in the things from this place felt like I was cheating on myself, but once I got over the fact that bakers need treats aside from their own a time or two, I was hooked."

I took some care removing the brown bakery box, the final thing in the bag, and placed it with the others. "These," I said, flipping open the top, "are some of the best from SLO Donut Company. Now, I don't ever claim anything I make is the most delicious or best. I leave that up to the customers. However, I don't think it's a jab at my treats to say these are another level good. Maple bacon and frosted animal crackers–topped doughnuts, bear claws, apple fritter, and oh my God…doffles."

"Ah. What-els?" he asked.

"Doffles," I repeated. I pulled the triangle-shaped delight out of the box. "It's a doughnut waffle, and I can't even think after having one."

I took a bite of the chocolate doffle, with chocolate glaze and colored sprinkles, and moaned softly with how good it was. After a wipe of the fallen sprinkles from my lips, I placed the rest of the doffle back in the box. I brushed off my hands, and a few sprinkles landed on his desk.

"Do you ever wonder about the people who make sprinkles?" I asked, staring at the sprinkle of sprinkles. "There are people that work in a sprinkle factory. I wonder what their life is like, you know? Like is it like glitter and they leave a trail of it wherever they go? Do they find sprinkles scattered around their home? I'm sure it gets annoying, but I don't know. They don't taste like much of anything, but colored sugar on top of sugar makes me happy."

When my focus moved back to Marshall, he was once again slack-jawed. This was understandable. I was babbling about sprinkle factories after shoving half of a doffle that I brought for him into my mouth.

"All right," I said. "That's all. I hope you—"

He stood up, placing himself close in front of me. Very

close. I could smell the now-familiar scent of his soap and his home. His home smelled like him, and it wasn't a fragrance. It was something that was all over my clothes this morning, and when I took them off to shower, catching the scent, *his* scent, gave me goose bumps all over my body.

His eyes lifted up to mine, and a casual grin emerged in a way only a man who knew how damn sexy he was could. "There was a lot of thought put into this, Al. Are you sure it isn't more than just a business apology?"

The way he phrased it, the way he was looking at me, gave me a hint to what he was getting at. I wasn't going to let him know that, though.

"I'm not sure what you're presuming," I said.

"What I'm presuming is this isn't only a professional peace offering, but rather a thank-you-for-fucking-my-brains-out-yesterday-gift."

Oh, God.

Oh.

My.

God.

He stepped closer, invading whatever space was left between us. "You have a little chocolate left right here," he said, tapping the edge of my lower lip.

With a boldness I hadn't been prepared for, with an unlocked door and the world on the other side of us to see, he took my face in both of his hands before using the tip of his tongue to run along my bottom lip. He moved back and forth, removing whatever was left of the chocolate I'd left behind, before kissing me. And by the time he slipped his tongue in to meet mine, the world could've been exploding and I wouldn't have cared.

After several moments—or maybe it was a hundred, I couldn't tell—his lips and himself, had pulled back. "You leave a little sugar everywhere, don't you?"

My head and thoughts clouded from his kisses and words. I ran the tip of my index finger over the faded yellow edge of his bruised eye. "This is getting better," I said.

"Yes, it is," he said, winking. "It's *all* getting better."

I patted his chest and turned away from him, both uncomfortable and turned on by his flirty, forward ways. I knew what I wanted, why I was there bringing him all the things, but it still didn't make it right. The fight occurring between my brain and my heart was fierce, and just when I thought I had conceded to one, the other came out swinging.

It was such a powerful dynamic between us, a blending of two people who could bring such catastrophe to others around them. I didn't know how something that felt so right could be so wrong.

"What's going on in there?" he asked.

With my thoughts, I had drifted both emotionally and physically away from him, leaving him still standing in the same spot. He could see, sense all of it, and I didn't have an answer for him.

"What is it, Al?"

I shrugged. "What is this?" I asked. "Last night. Now. What are we doing?"

"Your guess is as good as mine, but I do know last night was fucking amazing."

"It was. The sex, you, it was great," I said.

He recoiled slightly, whatever hint of a smile he still had post-makeout gone. "Great, huh? The sex was great?"

"Well, yeah. I was agreeing with you."

"And there wasn't more than that there with you, with us?"

"Like what? It was great sex. We've had this intense chemistry, and we gave into it, right?"

I could see anger rising through him, but I didn't know why. There was no way he was feeling all the emotions, all the conflict, like I was.

"Do you think that was just sex?" he asked. "You think that was the only thing I wanted from you?"

A muscle in his jaw twitched in anger, his flamed red cheeks visible under his beard. He folded his arms across his chest, waiting for my response.

"I don't know," I said.

"You don't fucking know?" he shouted.

"Don't yell at me, Marshall."

He blew out a strong breath and raised his hand up. "Sorry," he said. "I'm sorry I yelled, but I can't fucking believe you just said that."

"So what? That I didn't know if it was just sex? I don't know. I don't think you do, either."

"I do know!" he said, his voice rising again. "It wasn't or at least it wasn't for me."

I was so confused because this was *not* how it was supposed to work. Not only was it not supposed to be this way for us, getting all the emotional strings tied into sex, but it wasn't supposed to be what *guys* did. It was what *I* was doing, but trying *my* hardest not to.

Then it hit me.

Marshall was acting like a girl.

A small giggle escaped from me, but when I tried to hide it, it came out as a snort. Of course, this only made any laughter I was trying to hide become more apparent.

"What?" he snapped. "What is so damn funny? Are you...laughing at me?"

I waved my hand around while I settled my snickers. "No. Well, yes."

"You're acting so immature, Al. It's nothing I would expect from you."

Laughter emerged again. What was happening to him?

"Screw you, Al," he said, plopping himself down hard in his chair.

"Hold up," I said. "Sorry I laughed. It was that I was thinking—"

"Is this a fucking joke to you? Do you think I'm taking this lightly? I'm not."

"Neither am I."

"You could've fooled me."

"Of course, I don't think this is a joke, Marshall," I said, my own anger rising. "Do you think I go around sleeping with every guy that tries? I don't. In fact, I think I made that clear to you."

"Actually, you didn't make anything clear. You said you hadn't dated."

"And I haven't."

"So what were you doing with me?"

"Marshall. Come on. Don't."

"Don't what? Ask you these questions? Make you fucking realize everything I have to lose? Have you even thought for a second what Aaron finding out would do to me? It will kill me if I hurt him. And not only that, Ginger would be finished."

My jaw dropped open because I couldn't believe he thought this about me, that he thought I hadn't been over and over these things in my mind.

"That," I said, pointing at him, "is bullshit."

"Is it?"

"Yes, it is. You don't think I agonized over this? You don't think I've laid awake at night feeling awful that I'd been inadvertently inserted into not only your life, but Aaron's? That if he knew, not only about us working together, but now sleeping together, it would cause him pain all over again?"

"Exactly! We are both putting it on the line, both with the interest of Aaron and Delilah in mind, but you still think what we did, what happened was only about sex? That doesn't even make sense."

It didn't make sense. It wasn't what was running through my brain, making my body shake when I thought it all out. I was terrified, with a bottomless fear that was so dark it made my stomach hurt considering it. The truth rendered me paralyzed.

"What is it, Al? You have sad face," he said, his words gentle. "Look, if I was too hard on you, I get it. This is super overwhelming."

I was reluctant, so scared, to go there with him, but I wanted him to know. He needed to know I was trying. "I want to trust you," I said. "I want to trust you enough to tell you everything."

His head tilted to the side. "I want to trust you, too," he said.

"But you don't, do you?"

His silence was all the answer I needed. He didn't, and why should he? You couldn't trust someone who you saw destroy lives. If he did know everything, like everything-everything, he'd be through with me for sure.

"Hey, come here," he said.

I obeyed him, stepping between his spread legs as he sat. His hands gripped my waist as he looked up at me.

"One step at a time, okay?" he said. "I'm sorry for getting angry and…freaking out like a girl."

The fact he admitted it made me give him a small smile.

I placed my hands on top of his. "And that was what I was laughing at before."

A knock at the door had us both jumping away from each other so fast it gave me flashbacks to high school and trying not to get caught making out with my boyfriend in the basement.

"Sorry to interrupt," Wells said, sticking his head in the office. "Someone puked all over the floor outside the bathrooms."

"For fuck's sake," Marshall said. "Toddlers. People are fucking toddlers sometimes with their vomit. Who gets so wasted this early, anyway?"

I laughed, recalling a certain afternoon when Marshall was the toddler.

"What?" he asked.

"Two words. Big. Star."

His eyes lifted to the ceiling as he tried to piece together what I was referring to. Once I saw the memory surface for him, the way he blushed and ran his hands through his hair, pulling it all back behind his head, I couldn't resist moving from laughter to a full-blown cackling fit.

"Oh, this I got to hear," Wells said, coming in and plopping himself down on one of the chairs in the office.

"Get your ass back out there," Marshall snapped. "They can't be left alone."

"They can for a second. Give me the short version," he said.

"Let me!" I said. "One time Aaron, Marshall, and I went to Big Star, this taco, tequila, and whiskey bar in Chicago, with a hot-spot outdoor patio, on a summer afternoon. Let's just say that Marshall and the mix of both said tequila, tacos, and whiskey didn't sit well with him."

"It could've happen to anyone," Marshall grumbled.

"Yes, Marshall," I said. "Anyone who had four margaritas and one too many bourbon shots to count."

"Gross, man," Wells said. "That's puke worthy only hearing about. What were you thinking?"

"He wasn't," I said, at the same time as Marshall said, "I wasn't."

Marshall shook his head. "Christ, that was rough. I vomited tacos and salsa all over the patio, a packed fucking patio, and if memory serves, which parts are still a bit fuzzy, I thought it was the funniest damn thing ever."

I nodded. "You did think it was the funniest thing ever. What was even funnier was when we tried to wrangle you out of there, you kept shouting, 'I'm fucking Superman,' like a jerk. No one knew if you were trying to say you were, in fact, Superman, or that you were actually fucking Superman. We couldn't go back to Big Star forever after that!"

"Didn't I spend the night on your couch?" he asked.

"Yes," I responded. "After the cab ride to our place where you vomited all over that as well, you spent the night, well, the remainder of the afternoon, too, with us. I thought Aaron was going to lose his lunch, too, that day."

"Yes!" Marshall said. "You made that French toast the next morning! Fuck, you made us a hangover feast with that French toast and eggs and bacon."

"What French toast?" I asked, trying to recall.

"It was banana bread and it had chocolate chips in it. It was all buttered and French toasty, and you put these caramelized bananas on top," he said.

"Ah. Yes, I remember now."

We paused, staring at each other, lost in the moment of remembering a time so long ago. The three of us really were great friends. I'd missed him.

"Sounds like you guys had a lot of good times," Wells said, reminding us he was still in the room. "You want me to clean up the puke, Marshall?"

And Wells was also there to remind us there was a business to run.

"No," Marshall said with a sigh. "I'll do it."

"Are you sure?" Wells asked.

"Neither you or anyone else who works here gets paid enough to do something so disgusting," Marshall said.

"Okay," Wells said, standing, but just before exiting, his

head turned around, narrowing in on Marshall's desk. "Dude. You have High Street here? Oh! And SLO Donuts. Is that Splash Café?"

Marshall moved toward Wells, slapping him on the shoulder. "It's mine. Get the fuck out of here."

"All right. All right," he said, heading toward the door. "You coming, too, Alexis?"

I shot a look with a quick wink in Marshall's direction when Wells was halfway out the door. "Yes. Yes, I'm coming."

Marshall mouthed, "Fuck, you're hot."

"Enjoy puke patrol," I said, following Wells.

"Al?"

"Yeah?" I asked, taking a step back.

"Yes, it's okay if you start the split deliveries starting next week," he said, winking at me.

Chapter Thirteen

I said one step at a time, and that was how we were fucking riding this out. It was the only way it could be. It was a trip, a ride so out of control the only thing I could see ahead was that there was no way this would end well. This was the reason delving into the "where is this going" was a moot point. Thinking too far ahead, trying to predict where it was going, only led to a plethora of convoluted bullshit that took us away from what it was all about.

Her and I.

It had been a couple of weeks since our first night together, and there were several more after that. Our appetite for each other's bodies was off the charts, but the connection, the digging into this cosmic, chemical, or whatever the fuck it was connection was so much more. It was a trip I was not prepared for.

There were two other things I wasn't prepared for.

One: That it would be seventy-five fucking degrees on Halloween. After living in Chicago my whole life, Halloweens were always a battle against the cold and rain. Many trick-ortreating years were ruined by rain, and if it wasn't raining, the dipping temperatures kept our costumes hidden under heavier coats. It sucked, but it was how it was. Not only was San Luis Obispo perfect weather almost every day, but if it did rain, it didn't have the same effect. It was like Al said that first day. Even when it was raining here, it was perfect.

Of course, rain took on an entirely different meaning these days. There had only been a light sprinkling of rain since that first night Al and I made love—*yeah, I said it. So, the fuck what?* Every day I prayed to Mother Nature for an extended, potentially torrential downpour so I could keep Al in bed or other places naked for as long as possible. Who knew rain could have such an effect on a woman's libido?

Two: This town took Halloween really fucking seriously. I had no idea that all the restaurants, bars, and students from Cal Poly would bring their party and costume A game. Wells had put together our Halloween festivity plans, but I didn't realize, until I stepped out of the back office to see one of the biggest crowds Ginger had seen yet, how major it was. These people knew Halloween. It wasn't some run-of-the-mill "I stopped at the drugstore and got a witch's hat, this is my costume" type shit. This was planning and execution to the highest level. Celebrity look-alikes, cartoon characters, vulgar attempts at both, and enough women dressed in costumes close to nothing, but who still looked a step up from the norm in their angel and devil costumes.

I had just checked in with the kids behind the bar and some of the servers when I saw her.

My girl.

She was with Phoebe, who was in a Minnie Mouse costume, and chatting with a few people around her. It was unusual because I knew she liked to lay low, so to see her out on Halloween with such a scene made me wonder. I couldn't tell what she was dressed up as, but her hair was dyed, or maybe it was a wig, red or perhaps it was auburn. I didn't fucking know, but it was different...in a good way. Costumed and with a different hair color, among a sea of people, she still stood out, but it wasn't until the crowd parted and I saw her costume that my heart stopped.

What the *fuck* was she wearing?

It was Halloween and everyone but me was dressed up. The fact that she was here at all shocked me, but I didn't expect her to be dressed as...fuck.

Oh, hell no.

I didn't notice him at first, but it was definitely him.

Him.

The dude that was hanging all over her in Phoebe's Instagram pictures. No fucking way he was here with them...with *her.*

She made her way through the crowd, smiling her sexy grin when she spotted me. "Hey," she said upon reaching me. "It's crazy here tonight, huh?"

How was I not supposed to touch her? Not allowed to bring her into my office, bend her over my desk, and fuck the shit out of her? How would I even get her out of that outfit later? And since when did she wear bright red lipstick? Never since I'd known her did she ever sport a red lip like that.

Or maybe she did but I never noticed.

No. Aaron's girl or not, I would've fucking noticed.

Between the rage pumping through my veins at seeing another dude, *that* dude, so close to her and the insane way she looked, my blood pressure was probably at cardiac arrest levels.

"What's wrong with you?" she shouted over the music.

"I…what are you…who are you…?" I stuttered.

Christ. My girl came in an all-black leather jumpsuit, all fucking shiny and shit. Her tits were sitting right at the top of the lowered—probably too fucking lowered—zipper.

"Black Widow," she said. "Isn't it obvious?"

"Oh, it's really, really obvious, Al," I said, looking her up and down. "*Everything* you have on is very obvious."

Her eyebrows lifted, and I knew what was coming. The eyebrow and next it would be a razor-sharp statement to firmly put me back in my place.

But I wasn't done yet.

"And who the fuck is Fred Flintstone over there," I said, jabbing my finger in his direction. "He looks like a damn idiot."

She turned around to see who I was pointing at. "Who? With Phoebe?"

"Yeah. I saw a picture of you and douche Flintstone looking all close in one of Phoebe's Instagram pictures."

"Marcus. His name is Marcus, and he's Phoebe's brother, you jackass," she said.

Shit.

Damage control.

"Well, he looked like he was getting a little too close to your ass in the pictures, for that matter. I hope he wasn't getting any ideas with you in that outfit."

Her lips drew into a tight line, and I knew I was about to get the wrath I deserved after that last comment. What the hell was I thinking? It was a horrible thing to say, both degrading and inappropriate. It was also—

"How about I shove that misogynistic, cocky remark down your throat so you can choke on it?" she said. "At least I'm being spirited. Your bar owner costume isn't cutting it. And before you roll your pretty little eyes at me in retaliation, don't."

Yes. All of those things. I was all of them and more.

At least I knew it was coming and was ready for the impact.

"Sorry," I said. "That was dicky, even for me."

"Yes, it was. And frankly, I didn't take you as the jealous type," she said. "I never saw you act like that before."

"*Jealous* is a strong word," I said, shifting on my feet.

Okay. So I was jealous. I was jealous of her with *anyone* else. And she was right. I usually wasn't.

That was what was so messed up or maybe right about us. It was all so different.

Additional damage control needed.

I leaned down to whisper in her ear. "I was just surprised, Al," I said, lacing my tone with the sweetness she'd taken to like a bee to honey a time or two. "You look superhot."

She patted my chest. "Save it, lover boy. Honestly, though, you need to represent. Why didn't you dress up?"

I laughed. "What the hell would I've dressed up as? Hawkeye?"

"Oh, hell no. Well, to be honest, I always thought Hawkeye was superhot, but couples' costumes are a level of absurd that I never want to be a part of. Plus, it would be totally obvious."

"How?" I asked. "Two people costumed as two different characters from *The Avengers* doesn't scream couple to me."

"Are you being serious?"

I thought I was, but her twitchy smile, which was she was trying to hide but failing to do so, told me otherwise.

I shrugged. "Does it matter?" I asked.

"Um," she said. "You do know that Black Widow and Hawkeye have been a rumored couple throughout their history, right?"

How the fuck would I know that? I saw the movie once. Plus, I was usually strictly a DC Comics dude. I didn't like to meddle in Marvel.

"And furthermore," she continued. "There was always this banter between them, an underlying sexual tension, but they never acted on it. Well, at least as far as we know, they didn't. But there is quite a history there, and Hawkeye and Black Widow still hold a lot of the secrets."

Jesus. This girl. Superhero knowledge and sexy as hell.

She made me hard just looking at her. I wondered if the red hair was permanent because that was doing a number on me, too.

"Fuck, that's hot," I whispered in her ear. "In fact, there's something else that's superhot. I'm pretty sure there is no way you're wearing any underwear or…anything under that costume."

Her head snapped back. "Wouldn't you like to know?"

"Yes," I said, nodding. "I would like to know. I also would like to know if that hair color is here to stay."

"Do you like it?"

I leaned back into her ear. "I fucking love it. Everything

about what you're doing right now makes me want to peel that leather off of you, drag my hands through that red hair, and fuck you until you come around my cock."

She drew in a sharp breath and was momentarily speechless. Once she registered it all, she pulled back again to look me in the eyes.

This was always how it was with this girl.

Push and pull.

Push and push.

It was always how she was. There was never giving in, never falling prey to the usual art of seduction that worked on most women. She was smart, strong, and totally closed off. There were times I thought I was getting in a little bit with her, but the glimpses were fleeting. For now, I'd pull whatever I could out of my hat because I needed her. I *wanted* her. Immediately.

"Can I show you something in my office?" I asked, shouting over the music. "It's really, really important."

Her head tilted to the side, and she saw right through me. "I'm sure it is, but I don't want to leave Phoebe hanging."

I glanced behind her and saw Phoebe and Wells talking close, very close, and while he was working for the next couple hours, I had no doubt she was going to be on his dick for the rest of the night. After that, she'd for real be on his dick. I needed to seize this moment because it was my own dick I was concerned about.

"She looks just fine to me," I said, pointing in their direction. "In fact, she doesn't seem lonely at all."

She looked around and stepped up into me. "How important is this situation?" she asked.

But before I could answer, she used the very small, unnoticeable space between us to slide her hand across my cock. Words eluded me, but one thought bounced around my head instead.

Good. Fucking feel how hard I am only looking at you, gorgeous.

"I see," she said. "Lead the way."

I turned and pushed my way through the crowd, grabbing her hand as we neared the office door. As soon as the doorknob was in my hand, I opened it and yanked her in behind me, slamming it shut immediately. She was pushed up against the back of it. "Now, I can tell you a little bit more about my…situation," I said, reaching behind her to lock the door.

"Al?"

"What?"

"I like you," I said, placing my hands on opposite sides of her head. She was trapped.

And right where I wanted her to be.

She rolled her eyes, dismissing what I'd said. It was her push back, and I was going to do my thing next.

Push harder.

I smirked at her, biting down on my lower lip and looking up at her through my eyelashes. She would deny it completely, but I always knew when I turned coy motherfucker, she was going to fold.

I saw it in the way her cheeks flushed.

"The thing is, Al," I said, stepping toward her slowly. "I think you like me, too."

"You don't know what you're talking about."

"Oh, I think you do."

"There's no way I'm getting this thing off," she said, putting her hands on the sides of my face. "That can only mean one thing."

I pouted. "No go?"

She shook her head and snapped my head forward, kissing me aggressively. Our bodies pressed against each other while my hands ran across the leather, latex, or whatever the fuck she was wearing. The smoothness, the way I could touch every curve, every dip, of her body, but there was still a barrier, was nothing like I'd ever felt before. It was so goddamn hot.

I had no idea I'd be down with getups like that, but maybe it had less to do with what she was wearing, but that it was *her* wearing it.

I was so pissed I wasn't going to be able to peel it off her.

"Not no go," she mumbled against my lips. She reached a hand to the front of her costume, looking downward and then back up to me as she lowered the zipper. Her back arched as the zipper came farther and farther down before stopping just above her belly button.

"Christ," I hissed.

The way her breasts were pushed up to the top of her bra, how they looked so full and— *Christ.*

"I may not be able to go further than this," she said. "But I can certainly take care of you. I mean, your situation."

She palmed my cock over my pants before fumbling with my belt, my lips dying to hit hers before they were wrapped around my dick. Her fingers were already undoing the button of my pants and working my zipper down when I seized a handful of her hair, tugging her mouth to mine.

Aggressive, passionate kisses passed between us, all lip bites and hair pulling. It was intense as fuck, and just when I thought I'd have to figure out a way to get to her pussy, she sunk to her knees.

And it was a mind-fucking blow jobbing.

I'd been the recipient of some pretty spectacular fellatio encounters over my years. As a whole, I thought women only did them because they felt obligated to. And as a dude, we knew this. We could sense it by the enthusiasm.

Al was *not* one of those girls.

She took to my cock like she fucking *loved* it.

I'd been so ready for her, so turned on before she even started her magic that I couldn't hold off.

"Al, baby...fuck. Now," I growled, not giving a fuck whatsoever if someone on the other side of the door could hear me.

She slowed her mouth and hands that she used in combination and allowed me to come in her mouth. She already knew how I liked it.

She already knew me.

By the time I came down, she was already standing, zipping her costume back up.

"Come over to my place later?" she asked.

"Do I get to be the one to take that costume off you?"

"I wouldn't have it any other way," she said, winking at me. "And for the record, the hair. Permanent."

"Permanent is good, baby."

Chapter Fourteen

It never failed. No matter what, my chocolate chip cookies always sold out the fastest. Recently, I even started sending some to Ginger, and even without the added booze, I've been adding more and more to the daily deliveries. While it seemed like a regular chocolate chip cookie, mine were different. Not only were they huge, the size of my palm, but I also had a secret ingredient: adding in a mixture of pastry flour and bread flour and refrigerating the dough for twenty-four hours before baking. I loved that even with baking nothing was simple.

Nothing was ever as it seemed.

Phoebe and I were working side by side in my kitchen, me scooping out the chocolate chip dough onto a large parchment paper–covered cookie sheet and her frosting the Jack Daniel's honey whiskey cupcakes. I was so proud at how she'd perfected her cupcake frosting swirl, especially since I was particular about how each one was to always be flawless. Yes, the cupcakes ended up in people's mouths, but that was no reason for cupcakes, or any of our treats, to not look like a little piece of art. I loved when people said, "It's almost too pretty to eat!" and then they did.

Marshall commented recently that if he had chosen between one of my treats and a blow job, he wouldn't choose at all. He'd want them both at the same time, so he'd know what it was like to die and go to heaven.

Or hell.

I was sure he said hell because why wouldn't he?

That boy deserved a surprise of a naughty nature. I wasn't sure what, though.

"Let's say, hypothetically, you want to do something to surprise a guy, something beyond the norm, what would you do?" I asked.

"I have a few ideas, but is this for Marshall, hypothetically, of course?"

I stopped, my hand hovering over the cookie sheet with a full scoop of cookie dough. "What did you just say?"

"Oh, please," she said with a snort-laugh. "Like I hadn't figured that out ages ago. I was only waiting for you to admit it to me before I started pressing you for the details."

I was still midscoop, my hands dangling midair. She knew. She wasn't guessing. She knew-knew.

Of course she did. You don't work for someone day in and day out and not start to understand their personalities, their vibes.

Oh, God. How much did she know?

Nothing. She knew nothing except for there was a bit of a thing going on.

Or she knew a little more than that because I had to open my big mouth and ask her for suggestive ways to get a boy excited. She had to know we were having sex.

Or not. Maybe she didn't figure that out. Maybe she thought it was only a flirtation.

"Oh, for shit's sake, lady. This isn't press conference worthy," she said. "So what? You and Marshall are fucking."

"Phoebe!"

"What? Well, aren't you?" she asked, placing her hands on her hips. "And don't lie because I can always tell when you do."

"I...well. Look, it's complicated and it's—"

"God, you're terrible at this," she said, shaking her head and tossing a dish towel over her shoulder. "Okay, I'll put you out of your misery for now because I obviously took you by surprise. However, I'm going to have to insist on details. D-E-T-A-I-L-S. I'm serious. He's one hot, H-O-T piece of ass."

"Phoebe, please. I'm about to die of embarrassment."

"Gather your lady balls, Alexis. There will be a question-and-answer session on his lovemaking abilities, lady-head technique, package size, and assorted other pertinent information in reference to his—"

"Fine!" I said, slapping my hand over her mouth. "I'll tell you. I'll tell you everything, but you can't tell anyone, okay? I need you to promise me. Nod your head if you promise, Phoebe."

She nodded her head as I still had her mouth covered.

"No one," I reiterated. "This is a very sensitive situation."

She nodded again.

I released my hold.

"All right. Back to the initial topic. Why don't you send him like a sexy text or something?" she asked.

I shrugged. "I kind of feel like I do that already, and it always seems so ridiculous."

"Maybe to you."

"What do you mean?"

She sighed, setting down the pastry bag. "You're what? Twenty years older than me? You don't know a thing about men."

"I resent that, Phoebe," I said sharply. "Twenty years is grossly overestimating."

"How old are you, anyway? You always said you hated celebrating your birthday whenever I asked when it was, so I just stopped asking."

She was right. Since Lexie became Alexis, I didn't want to celebrate my birthday at all anymore. In fact, even prior to that, I had issues with it. There was a time when acknowledging my birthday served as a reminder of all the pain I caused others, that because of my actions, others couldn't celebrate birthdays of ones they loved. It seemed selfish, almost cruel to be showered with well wishes and happiness when others would never have that chance again. That, in turn, became selfish to the people around me, who cared about me, and wanted to show me how much I meant to them. It was a vicious circle, and like most things, I came out of it looking like the evil one.

"I'm thirty-four," I said, giving her a little of what she wanted to know, but holding back the rest. "So, you can cool it with old lady crap."

"Lighten up. I never said old lady. In any case, it doesn't

change the fact that you are clueless about what men want."

"Fine, Phoebe. Why don't you tell me what I don't know, okay?"

This ought to be good.

The twentysomething thinking she has them figured out after all I've been through made me press my lips together tightly to keep from giggling.

"Men are visual creatures, Alexis," she said. "Words get misconstrued. I mean, just think about us, for example. Hasn't a guy ever said or texted you something, and it could be something as simple as, 'You look pretty,' and we flip it around into something totally different?"

I was about to argue with her, but then I reconsidered. For as long as I could remember, I thought I was the "antigirl." I could detect bullshit from guys and dissect everything they said down to the molecule. Maybe that wasn't a "me" thing, but rather a girl thing. Maybe I was more of girl than I thought.

"Go on," I said.

"So, get his visual going, and let him know in some way it's only for him."

I thought I understood where she was going, but I didn't understand where it went. Asking her would only further solidify that I had no idea what I was doing, and admitting anything of the kind was more painful than drilling nails into my eyes.

"I can see you aren't following me," she said with a snort. "Take some dirty selfies, and send them to him. Put something in there that is unique to him."

"Okay, I've never sent dirty pictures, for one. And two, what is something unique to him to add in?"

"I can help you with the pictures," she said.

"You can?"

"Don't be so surprised, Alexis. You've been in a time warp or something for years. This is what's happening these days. This is what we do."

"Oh, for shit's sake," I grumbled.

"Oh, shut up," she said. "Lighten up and take your shirt off."

"I will not!"

"Do you want me to help you or not?" she shouted back.

"I…you…I can't even believe we are having this discussion."

"For fuck's sake, Alexis. We're girlfriends. It's what girlfriends do."

"I'm your boss! And you want me to get naked in front of you."

"I never said naked. I said take your shirt off. And what's the big deal. We both have boobs."

It was all so ridiculous, but I knew I needed, I wanted, her help. I wasn't so much embarrassed as I was anxious about giving up control, having her help me settle into a vulnerable position.

"Fine," I said.

I wrapped my arms around the bottom of my T-shirt and began to lift it off.

"Not right here!" she said. "You think we're sending him"—she paused to make air quotes—"Alexis-in-her-natural-habitat photos? No. Plus, he's already done that in his mind, like a thousand different ways, in this kitchen. You want to surprise him. Do something he never expected you to do. He's probably already imagined you baking topless every day."

"I can't even believe I'm doing this," I mumbled.

"Oh, you're going to do it," she said, setting the pastry bag down. "And you're doing it right now."

"Let's finish this stuff first, okay?"

"And lose the enthusiasm? No way."

"Look," I said. "I'm still the boss. We will take the shots, and talk sexting or whatever you call it, when we are done frosting and baking."

She snorted as she picked her pastry bag back up, shaking her head at the cupcakes. "Only here," she said.

"Huh?"

She looked at me and smiled. "Only between girlfriends and only here in this kitchen would we have this discussion. It's pretty awesome."

I returned the smile. "Yeah, it is."

"But before we start back at it," she said. "One thing. I caught a glimpse at that bra, and you're going to need to up that game. My mother has sexier bras than that."

She was right. I was always all about comfort because for so many years, no one was going to be seeing my underwear and bras. Things happened and were still happening so fast with Marshall that when the thought occurred to me, usually right before sex, that I should have something sexier to wear for him, the moment passed.

He didn't seem to mind, though. Although I was savvy enough to know what visual creatures men were and that giving them a little something extra to look at was a turn-on. I caught a glimpse of that from him with my Black Widow costume.

"Phoebe?" I asked.

"Huh?" she said, not looking up from her cupcake swirl work.

"It is Marshall," I said.

Her head turned and she winked at me. "I know. I have known," she said.

"Does Wells?"

"We haven't discussed it," she said. "But he'd have to have the awareness and the brain power of a pea not to have noticed."

Shit.

I was resistant to telling her earlier, but I needed to share this with someone. I didn't have anyone else, and she was my person. At the core of it, as much as I tried to deny it, I was still a girl, a girl that wanted her girlfriend to hear about the man in her life.

"So in that case, no," she said. "He probably doesn't have a clue. I wouldn't worry."

"That's not nice to say. I thought you were in to him."

"I am, but he's still a man. They don't usually pick up on that stuff. And for the record, I don't see what the big deal is, anyway. So what? Alexis from Tipsy Treats and Marshall from Ginger have gotten to know each other in the biblical sense."

I shook my head. "Where do you get this stuff, Phoebe? Biblical sense?"

"How do you *not* know this stuff?"

"I've been out of the game a long, long time, Phoebe. In any case, you know why we can't be open about it," I said.

"I don't know," she said, beginning to drizzle honey on top of the cupcakes. "It just seems like it was so many years ago, and everyone has moved on."

"You can never truly move on from that."

"You're right. Maybe I'm being naive, but I can't help wondering."

"About what?"

She set down the plastic squeeze bottle she was using and wiped her hands on the front of her cherry-printed apron. "How could anyone not be happy if their best friend found love? Maybe you're not giving Aaron enough credit."

It was so simple. Her idealistic notions were one of my favorite things about her.

But she was, in fact, naive.

Some things you never recover from. What I did to Aaron and Delilah was one of those things. Another would be sleeping with Marshall. I couldn't fathom Aaron seeing even a sliver of room for redemption in either.

"It's not love," I said to Phoebe. "And please don't tell anyone. Please?"

"Of course I'm not going to tell anyone. I also am not going to tell you or anyone else that if you want to believe it isn't love and that it's just sex, it's too bad they don't have eyes like I do. It's a love thing. Deal with it," she said. "Can we finish the cookies up, so I can get you sexy photo ready?"

And that is what we did.

No other mention of the *L* word.

It was work and then a photo shoot in my bedroom, which was an experience I never want to have to…experience… again. Mortification didn't even begin to cover it.

"Alexis!" Phoebe would bark at me. "Lift them boobies *up*! No. Not like that. Wrap your arm around your waist and push those suckers to your chin."

Phoebe took the liberty of arranging me in the most contorted positions on the bed. Once I was placed properly and to her liking, she'd hand me my phone to take the picture.

"Why can't you just take it?" I asked, my arm extended in front of me as I was shaped like a pretzel. "Won't it look better?"

She let out an aggravated sigh. "No. I can't just take it, and no, it won't look better. The whole point is for him to think you were sitting here alone, thinking about him, and wanted to send him the sexy pic."

"Whatever," I said. "This all is too much work."

I didn't know what was in store for me until she told me to go into the bathroom.

It turned out, topless and, well, bottomless, in front of a mirror, with my body arched in a supermodel/centerfold type pose was going to be the "the one," according to Phoebe. I wasn't sure, but I was taking her word for it.

The discussion over what three photos to send lasted longer than a jury deliberating a murder trial.

I sent her on her way to make the afternoon drop-off at Ginger as I stared at my phone.

Then there was wine.

And more staring.

Then more wine.

The wine should've begun during the photo session.

Would he like seeing me like this?

Of course, Alexis. What guy wouldn't?

But would he?

There was only one way to find out.

I pulled up his name to text him and attached the first picture.

With my finger shaking, I hit send.

Added the next picture.

Send.

Last picture.

My finger hovered over the send button, knowing this was the one that was the *one*.

You've never been afraid of anything in your life, Alexis.

Except…

But nothing ever like this.

Send.

Then I waited.

Chapter Fifteen

Holy. Shit.

I stood in the middle of my living room, the lights not even turned on since I'd just walked in, when I got the text from her. My eyes and my brain had only begun to register what I was seeing when another came through.

Then another.

Fuck.

The first photo was of Al lying on her bed in little shorts or underwear, I didn't know, and a tank top—a very tight white tank top with no bra. Her erect nipples were clearly visible from under the fabric, and all I could think, all I could hope, was that she was so turned on by taking the picture her nipples responded. I didn't know if there was scientific research to back this theory, or if it was just a dude's way of justifying how tits alerted us we were doing something right.

The second photo was with her top folded down further, the curve of her breasts pushed up, as she laid on her side, smiling this sweetish, sexy smile I'd never seen out of her. I'd seen both: sexy and sweet. Together like that? Never.

"Christ," I said, plopping myself down on my couch as I continued to stare.

I adjusted my eagerly expanding cock because not only did I know what was coming, I didn't know how I was going to respond without coming across as a total sex-crazed buffoon.

The third was…mother of fuck.

I rubbed my hand roughly over my beard and…stared. My girl was facing a mirror, completely nude, her body arched like a fucking Greek goddess or something. Her arm was wrapped around her toned waist, her hand strategically placed to cover her always shaved-bare pussy. I pouted for a nanosecond at not getting to see all of her, but the image was goddamn sexy, so unbelievably hot there was no fucking way I was going to complain about any of it.

How could I've seen her naked so many times, and this was what turned my gears in a whole new way?

I still didn't know how to respond. Maybe she wanted me to act like the sex-crazed buffoon I was trying *not* to be I mean, she wasn't sending me these to *not* get a reaction, right? I was fully reacting. I just didn't know how to tell her that. It wasn't like this was the first time a girl had sent me these kinds of pictures. However, those were always girls I was kind of dating or a friends-with-benefits type of thing. It wasn't the girl I was very much into that I'd known for almost a decade, who was once married to my best friend, and now we worked together almost daily. This was a delicate fucking situation.

God. She was hot.

And she was waiting. She had to be. She was sitting somewhere, maybe even lying in her bed wearing that same outfit or nothing at all, waiting for me to respond.

Be cool, Marshall. Let her take the lead.

Me: Thank you.

There. It was simple and courteous.

Al: Thank you? A girl sends you scantily clad, nude photos and all you have say is "thank you?"

It was…a dumbass fucking response that was going to ruin any chance I had of ever having sex with her again.

Me: No! Oh my God, no! It wasn't all, I was just…still typing! They are amazing.

No, dumbass. They're better than amazing. She is better than amazing.

Me: YOU are better than amazing. I'm fucking speechless, or rather textless, or whatever the fuck it's called if anything. You look so hot. Beautiful. So, so, so, so beautiful. I can't believe you did this. For me.

Okay. That was the best I could do. If it wasn't good enough, I'd have to brush up on my skills—my wooing skills. They didn't get as much use as they did when I was in my twenties, and as the sexy picture thing had definitely taken off these last several years, perhaps my said skills had taken a nosedive.

I waited a few minutes, and without a response, I was starting to panic. What else could I do? Was there something that I was missing?

Wait. Did she want me to reciprocate?

Fuck.

That would entail doing only one type of picture, and while I was sporting some major wood from what she sent, I didn't know if it would stand up to photography.

Do the same rules about the camera adding ten pounds apply to cock shots taken from a mobile phone, but instead of ten pounds you get a few extra inches?

Al: Thank you ;)

Okay. So maybe no exchanges from my side needed. Whew.

Me: I really was surprised. Thank you, baby.
Al: Just HOW surprised, Marshall? Did it…effect you?

Oh, hello, naughty girl. She wanted to play, and I was *all in.*

Me: Hard. The effects were immediate and hard.
Al: Is that so? Elaborate.
Me: I've had the pleasure of lingering over every inch of your body. I've watched you come as you rode my cock. You've pulled my hair as you've come against my mouth as I gave you

head. Getting the pictures? A whole new level. I am so fucking hard, and you're not here for me to show you just how hard.

Al: Thank you for elaborating. ;) Sounds like there is a situation happening over there again.

Me: There definitely is. What are you doing?

Al: Laying around.

Me: How about you get that sexy ass over here and lay around close to me.

There was a pause in correspondence, and I knew she had to be considering it. She better have been considering it since I'm sure it was her intent all along. If that wasn't the case, then I knew I'd reached the pinnacle of cluelessness about women.

Come on, baby.

Come on.

And if you do, bring me a treat.

Al: Be over in twenty.

Yes!

After I decided that it would be fucking rude to ask if she had any cookies or even one of those margarita doughnuts she brought into Ginger yesterday laying around, and if she did, if she could bring one. Or two. Three, tops. I came to my senses, though. She had already been super generous today, and asking any girl to bring you food so you can have a postcoital snack was a level of asshole I didn't want her to view me as.

I used the twenty minutes between her last text and her

arrival to take a quick shower. Even though I wasn't tending bar, the bar funk still radiated around me, attaching itself to my clothes. There never was a day that I didn't have a spilled drink, food, cleaning product from post-vomit cleanup, or regular man funk from doing something at work that needed to be hosed off when I came home.

And let's face it. If I wanted her lingering around my dick, like she so graciously does, smelling nice in all areas I'm sure was appreciated.

I decided to play the art of seduction role and lit some scented candles around the apartment. A few in the living room and several in the bedroom, where I anticipated spending most of our time.

I'd never been in a Bed Bath & Beyond, because as a perpetual bachelor, I never had to, but one of the girls at work told me they had a good selection of the good shit—shit referring to candles. I was sure I came across as a total tool sniffing at all of them, but now I was glad I did. My home already smelled fucking great from the Mango Salsa and Harvest scented candle combination I bought.

Seeing the lights of her car illuminate the pavement outside my house, and then go dark, was a level of excitement akin to fucking Christmas morning. I watched her exit her car, and while I couldn't make out exactly what she wearing, I saw enough to know she was wearing a denim skirt. Outside of working or when she didn't have that sexy uniform on, she was always in jeans. She never wore skirts.

I was a dude. I fucking loved skirts.

Her still red hair blew across her face as she started up the walk to my door, and my heart continued to pound so hard I thought the fucking neighbors would hear it.

They would be hearing something soon, though.

She was a vocal, *very* vocal lady in bed.

I opened the front door and stood waiting for her. She had barely crossed to inside when I slammed it shut and had her pushed up against the back of it. The pictures were a nice appetizer, but her? In the flesh? I was going to fucking devour her.

My eyes focused on her lips as I whispered, "Finally."

"You got a thing for doors, huh, Jones? First your office. Now here?"

Then it was my eyes on her mouth, watching her tongue run along her lower lip, and I knew she was coming for me. It was what she always did before kissing me. I wasn't even sure if she knew she did it, but I noticed. I always did because anticipation rose through my body.

"I couldn't concentrate on anything else after getting those pictures," I said in a low tone, my lips almost touching hers. "Not a fucking thing, Al, and I had a lot of shit to get done."

"Sorry," she whispered.

I brushed our lips together with a gentle shake of my head. "I'm sure you are. In fact, I'm going to make sure I know how sorry you say you are."

Her head tilted back so she could see my expression. "And what is that supposed to mean?"

"It means," I said, sliding my fingers through the back of her hair, clutching it in my hand. "I want you to prove it to me, how sorry you are, because I've been hard for you for so long now. I want you. *All* of you."

Our lips finally connected, and it was hands and tongues and a sexual desire so palpable, I wondered if she felt it running through my veins, through my skin.

My heart pounded more.

Her legs trembled.

She was sorry.

I took her to the bedroom, laid her down, and yes. She was so, so sorry.

When we were done, we laid sated in each other's arms, sleepy from the day and the sex. It was a rare moment of perfection.

Peace.

We sat quiet in it, our fingers brushing against one another's, until I flicked on the television.

Had I known that the one action, in that one perfect moment, would lead to her unraveling, I would've never have done it.

Follow the yellow brick road…

Chapter Sixteen

Alexis—

The waves came crashing through at the most unexpected moments.

I was never ready for the way a memory from a sound, a voice, or smell would floor me.

But buried demons always emerge don't they?

It was *The Wizard of Oz*.

My eyes were half-closed so I couldn't see it, but I heard the music.

And then it was there.

All of it.

Everything I had run from for almost twenty years.

I recalled rolling away from Marshall slowly, him asking me if I was just going to the bathroom.

I might have nodded or maybe not.

My eyes scanned his floor, locating my clothes, as the words to the movie made my panic escalate.

I needed out.

Away.

"What? You're leaving?" he said.

My name, his name for me, "Al?" was the background to the violent screaming in my head, as I put my clothes on with rapid movements.

I shook my head, words nowhere to be found, as I raced from his bedroom.

He called out after me, worry lacing his voice, but I had to get away.

I ran.

And I was almost free, but then his voice was shouting my name over and over again.

The silent street filled with the echoing of his voice, and I still didn't stop.

I crossed the street to my car, the beacon of safety that would rescue me, but he was right behind me.

My hand was on the handle of my car door. I was almost free, but he stopped me.

He caught my arm and he was there, on the darkened street outside his apartment, shirtless, barefoot, and wearing only jeans. I could feel the shift of the earth under my feet and how it was all going to cave in right there to swallow me for good.

Say whatever you need to say to get away. He won't let you leave if you don't.

"I had to leave her," I said. "You know that, right?"

"What? Wha—?" he stammered. "What is wrong? What happened?"

"Delilah!"

"Al. I don't know what you're talking about."

"Don't you understand?" I cried. "I had to do it. I *had* to leave her!"

"I believe you, Al. I know you did, but I still don't understand why you had to," he said, finally piecing together what I was trying to tell him. "What happened? Tell me!"

I pressed the palm of my hand to the center of my eye, the sharpening pain radiating from my brain was overcoming me. I couldn't go there with him. Even if I could explain, it would lead to other questions. He'd want to know why I felt the way I did, why I didn't, I *couldn't* be a mother, no matter how much I loved her.

"I thought we were past this," he whispered. "I thought you trusted me."

"I do," I said, dropping my arms to my sides. "I'm just not sure I trust myself."

"What does that even mean?"

"It means, if I tell you, and I let all of those words out, I don't know who I am anymore. Keeping what I did, who I am, is what keeps me safe. I can trust that…for myself, but if I let that go, then what? It's too terrifying to think about."

"But Al. You're not alone in this anymore. I'm here. Please look at me," he said, bringing my chin forward to face him. "I'm here. I'm not going anywhere. You're not going anywhere. But if we are going to move forward together, I have to understand you. I want to help you."

"I don't need help."

"The fuck you don't. We all do. Do you have any clue how you've begun to heal me?" he asked.

No.

"Haven't I shown you?" he questioned before slapping his hands on his chest. "All of this." He pointed to it. "Every single one tells a story. These are the path to my soul, and I let you view it. So, tell me how you can say I didn't need help, too? Tell me how all the things I held inside began to mend after I knew I loved you."

No.

Please no.

All the things but love.

"Don't say that," I said. "Just don't, Marshall."

He pressed his lips together tightly before asking, "Why not? You don't know that, either? Well, fuck. I should've verbalized it sooner, huh?"

He was pushing.

He was forgetting that I could push back harder.

"It is, it was, just sex. Don't get it confused. That is something a girl does, but I can separate. Maybe you can't."

He laughed, a menacing, angry chuckle I'd never heard before. "That's bullshit and you know it," he said. "You and I *both* know it wasn't just sex. You're only trying to throw what you can at me to try and push me away, but it won't work."

Keep pushing, Alexis. You can break him like you have everyone else.

I shrugged. "I don't know, Marshall. Maybe you were lying all those months ago when you said you didn't want to go where your best friend had already been. Maybe you did want that. Maybe it was some sick fuck fantasy you had in your mind, and I came along for the ride."

It appeared to be working...for a moment. He drew back, moving away from me with a couple stumbled steps before stopping. His eyes went wide before they lowered to the ground. I leaned my back against my car door, waiting for his next move.

His shoulders shook, but I was unsure if it was from laughter or tears. His head snapped up...and laughter. "Oh, Al," he said, shaking his head. "That one stung for a minute, but I know the truth. You won't stop until you get what you want. I'd expect nothing less from you, but this is one fight I won't let you win. So keep the punches coming. Keep hitting me with it because I can take it and I'll still be standing. I'll be standing right here in front of you."

"What don't you get?" I screamed. "It was me or them. I had to choose or I was going to end it all."

"What do you mean end it all? Like...kill yourself? Al, you would never—"

"I almost did! I was so close, Marshall. But if I was going to save them, I was going to need to save myself first."

"Save them from what?"

"Me!"

I was starting to detach.

To break.

The cracks deepened, and as everything turned gray, I knew I couldn't hold out much longer if I didn't get away.

I drew in a deep breath, gathering whatever resolve I had left. "I break everyone I love. I break them, and then they're left in destruction," I said. "I know that seems strange, or I don't know...unbelievable, but it's the truth. You wanted the truth, and I'm giving it to you."

"That's ridiculous. You don't break anything. You're giving me love and everything to me now."

I shook my head. "No. I'm not. And if you think I am, you'll be my next casualty."

I could see the wheels turning, but he was utterly confused. The questions would continue if I didn't end it now.

"And I care too much about you to do that," I said. "I ruin people. I would've ruined Aaron and Delilah, so I left. And now I'm leaving you."

"The *fuck* you are. You still aren't saying anything. You're speaking all in code and some shit."

"That will have to be good enough," I said before I tried to turn around to get in my car.

"What is it?" he shouted, taking hold of my arm and spinning me around. "Fucking find the words. You ran away from Aaron, but I'm not going to let you run away from me."

I yanked my arm away from him, mustering as much strength as I had in my body and heart. "I'm not running away! I'm saving you."

"From what? You?"

"Yes! I'm broken. And I'm not even sad to say that anymore because it's just who I am. I'm broken, and I break everything around me. Anyone who gets close, anyone who loves me, ends up hurt. With Aaron, I thought I could save him, but then Delilah happened and I knew I couldn't save them both. That beautiful piece of my soul, Delilah."

Her name left my lips, and my insides caved. It never, *ever* didn't hurt. It never would. My last thoughts as I neared the end of my life would be of the beautiful baby girl and how I did what was best for her. I didn't know whether that would deliver me to heaven or hell, because who leaves their child?

"Al?" Marshall said in a calming tone. "What?"

Waves of anguish that I'd been able to withstand for decades crashed into me and I had to sit down. Marshall's arms reached out to catch me as I slid down the side of my car to the pavement. I knew if I closed my eyes I could see it, but I didn't want to see it. Every detail of the day that ruined so many lives was burned into my brain and heart. I was branded and the scars that were left were too ugly for anyone to see.

I didn't want him to see any of it, but the words began to spill out like blood, like I was sliced down the middle and torn in two. My eyes went to a small stream of water running from the gutter. It pooled at the end.

Just like the blood.

My eyes stayed there.

Not on him. I couldn't.

Eyes to the destruction.

"She loved the swings at the park so much. I'd promised her after I was done talking on the phone with my boyfriend, we'd walk across the street. If she was extra quiet while I was on the phone, maybe I'd even buy her a sno-cone. Cherry for her and lemon for me. Just like always."

"Al?" Marshall asked again. He joined me on the ground, keeping his distance, but being close enough so I'd know he was there. "Who?"

I didn't answer him. He'd hear everything he ever wanted to know soon enough. Everything.

"She was too quiet, though. I didn't even notice for God

knows how long. The thought occurred to me just as my boyfriend said, 'What movie do you want to see tonight?' The next thought I had was that the tire screeching sound was close."

Too close.

"The cordless phone was thrown to the linoleum floor of the kitchen. My goodness, how I'd pace back and forth, and back and forth, across that ugly butter- and brick-colored floor when I was on the phone. It was a habit. I couldn't see the front door from the kitchen, though. I couldn't hear it open through the mindless, insignificant bullshit I was discussing with my boyfriend."

Marshall's hand rested on my knee as he moved closer.

"Do you have any idea how long it is between the second you realize something and the second it takes for your body, your brain to make the connection? It's so long. It's like a lifetime of choices and decisions and regrets, and it's all right there. A breath doesn't leave you, and I don't think it did for me until I was screaming. Or maybe I wasn't even breathing then, either.

"And that blond hair of hers. You know, Delilah has the same exact hair? The white-blond ringlets. The first time Leslie sent me a picture of her hair longer and I saw it, I couldn't get out of bed for two days. But I saw that blond hair, her curls blowing in the wind as her tiny steps met the middle of street at the same time as the car."

"And then what?" Marshall asked, rubbing my knee.

Even though I told myself I couldn't, shouldn't, my eyes looked at his. "She flew."

She did.

And my screams, my piercing wails, were the music to her descent.

My eyes turned away from him again.

"Sadie. My sweet, sweet Sadie. She loved *The Wizard of Oz*. Rainbows. She loved all things rainbows," I mumbled.

Marshall took my hand from my lap and slid his into it. His grip was tight, almost too tight, but it was no match for the pain radiating through my heart. It never not hurt. Ever.

"Al?" Marshall whispered.

I still couldn't look at him because I knew what I'd see.

Disgust.

Pity.

Horror.

I saw those things every day when I looked at myself in the mirror. I knew if anyone knew the truth—Aaron, Delilah, anyone—they'd see the same when they looked at me. It was why I got so depressed, and ultimately, I had to run. They couldn't ever handle the truth because even I couldn't. And now? I didn't know how to run from Marshall.

It didn't even matter, though. I could run as far away as I could, change my name, and create a new life. There was never any escaping it. I almost thought I did here, but then the poppies came.

"Do you know about the poppies?" I asked.

"Poppies?"

"They come in April. They pop up here in April. Out of all the things to be surrounded by, it had to be poppies."

I must've started crying because Marshall's other hand was

cradling the side of my face. His fingers, on which I could faintly smell the basil and limes that he cut earlier, skimmed across my cheeks to wipe the tears away.

"Let them fall," I said, my voice hoarse from all I'd released.

"Al?" he repeated. "Please."

"Don't ask questions."

"I won't. I promise."

"Because I know what they are. How could I have been so careless? How do you tell parents that you killed their daughter?"

He dropped his hands before crawling across the ground to sit in front of me. My eyes continued to focus elsewhere because I wasn't ready to know my fate. It was sealed the moment the words left my mouth.

"You didn't kill her. It was an accident. A terrible—"

My eyes snapped to his. "I killed her," I shot back. "You can color it any way you want, but that is the truth."

He was on his knees and up in my face so fast I didn't even see him move until he was there. His hands, now holding mine between his, were forcing me to go where I didn't want to—to his eyes.

"It's not the fucking truth, Al," he said sternly. "Listen to me. It was a terrible accident, and maybe no one in your life ever told you, but it wasn't your fault. It was an accident."

I tried to shake my head, forcing my refusal to believe him against his grip. He wouldn't let me, though.

His forehead rested against mine. "Baby, I'm so sorry," he said, his voice cracking. "Fuck. You've been...almost your whole goddamn life...and..."

His hands shook against my skin, tiny tremors of my pain radiating into him. He didn't know what to do with it. I wanted to make it better for him, to take away whatever of my ugliness had adhered itself to him, because I'd ruined so, so many lives with what I did.

My hands brushed against his beard, and I cradled his face in my hands. My lips gingerly touched his, my regret and shame washing across them while my need to replace his disgust of me with desire flowed. He was hesitant, not-not kissing me back, but holding back. This only made me push him harder.

I needed to make something better. I needed to make *him* better.

I stood, nudging him away from me with a gentle push, so I could reposition myself, straddling his lap. With an aggressive grip, I yanked his head back to my mouth, forcing my tongue into his mouth. I knelt to get closer, my knees digging into the hard cement road, as I ground myself against him.

It was reckless, with anyone who could walk by at any time and see us, but it was needed. We *both* needed it.

He was still pulling away, not just physically, but I sensed it in his lips. It wasn't all I had come to know. When my mouth, my kisses, went to his neck and sucked and bit gently, like I knew he liked, there wasn't the same throaty moan I loved. When I wiggled around his lap, he wasn't hard.

"Al," he whispered against my lips. "No."

I shook my head, trying to bring him around, but he repeated, "Stop."

His tone made me still, freeze. When his head backed away, I saw it in his eyes.

He didn't want me anymore.

And there was no chance I could've blamed him.

"I'm sorry," I mumbled as I climbed off his lap.

And I was so grateful that he let me go, even after I heard him scream my name as I peeled out of my parking spot.

I was so grateful he gave me time to cry in the peace of my home.

I cried and wailed for Sadie, my sweet baby sister, and all the guilt I had over my role in what happened.

I screamed through my tears, through the pain, of living a life alone and freed of love as penance for leaving Delilah, even though I know for certain she was in better place because I did.

I sobbed that it still wasn't over. Sadie, Delilah, Aaron, Marshall...they all ran together like spilled watercolors on paper because of my one tragic mistake.

I wept for the girl, the woman, who I was, and am now, that has never felt the weight of guilt lifted until today.

I told Marshall, and there was more I needed to tell him.

I texted him and told him I needed him.

I told him to come to me.

And by the time he did, the tears had stopped.

"I thought I was okay," I began.

He was sitting in front of me on the couch, the crackling of the fireplace the metronome of my declaration.

"I thought I had this," I said. "I was in the safety of my life here, and I thought I had it a long time ago. I thought I was...cured. But all I did was run away and never fix what was wrong with me to begin with. I thought by not being with anyone that I could keep it in check, and I did for a long time.

Then you…the right guy from the wrong time. Or maybe the wrong guy at the right time."

I paused before continuing. "I put it all on the table, Marshall. All of it. Things I never told anyone. Words that have never left my mouth. Not even to Aaron. You caused a crack, and that crack just grew and grew and grew until I split down the middle, and it all came out. It's all there for you to see, and I've never been so scared in all my life. Leaving Aaron? Delilah? I carry that heartbreak, that shame with me no matter where I go. It's crushing, but I always knew in some way I was doing the right thing. I knew Delilah deserved better. Now she has better. And know that gives me the first sense of peace I've known in years. Maybe ever."

The tears began to fall again, a cathartic wave of empathy washing across my soul, my heart.

"But nothing was more scary than bearing my soul to you, Marshall," I said. "My insides. All the ugly, and telling you what I know you've been waiting so long to hear me say—that I want you. I need you. I love you. Because there is truth and power in those words. They can lift you up to the clouds, or they can have you crawling against sinking mud. And for me, they both get intertwined.

"Everything about us is wrong. Who we are, who we were, who we love and loved. But something special, magical, worked between us, and at the end of the day, that is why I opened myself up to you. I couldn't fight it anymore. It just all felt too good to fight against. And I could see the train wreck ahead. The wind was blowing in my hair on that freight train as we sped forward, and I could see the collision coming. I warned you and warned you and warned you. But as hard as I pushed, you pushed back and there was no more fight left in me. The good was just too good. The way you listened to me and understood. The way you saw past my flaws and only focused on my gifts. The way you touched my body, made me come alive from want. So much want I could drink it all up if I could. It was euphoric and I wanted it all.

"With it all, I ignored the rational and the only thing to take its place was irrational. Looking for the wrong. Seeking the bad. Making you see all that was broken. And when that wasn't enough, I created things to make sure I destroyed us. But you know the truth now. You know all of my truths, and there is no way I can comprehend you could want a girl like me—that you *can* want a girl like me. I can't understand how that can be real."

He stood and walked toward me, placing his palms on the sides of my face and leaning his forehead against mine.

Chapter Seventeen

MARSHALL—

You know what you need here, Al?" I asked.

It was morning, and I was still naked in her bed, watching her be naked as she crossed the room. She bent over her dresser, pulling a pair of panties and a bra out.

"What's that?" she asked, tossing the bra on a chair in the corner.

"A dog."

She snorted and shook her head. "No way."

"What?"

"I can't get a dog."

"Can't or don't want to?"

She pulled her panties on over her long, smooth legs before facing the full-length mirror, looking at me in the reflection. "I can't have a dog running around a bakery. I'm in and out of the house entirely too much. Plus, no."

There was something behind her voice, something that told me it was more than that. I didn't want to press, though. We'd hit a stride recently, and I was fucking relishing every moment of it.

I sat up on my elbow, watching her. "You never wear sexy bras or panties," I said.

She looked at me over her shoulder as she hooked the back of her bra. "Nobody has been looking at them for a while," she said, winking. "Back in the day, my lingerie and bra and panty supply rivaled the intimate department at Bloomingdale's."

"Was it for you?"

"Was what for me?"

"Your…supply?"

"Who else do you think was wearing it?" she asked with a mischievous grin, turning around, placing her hands on her hips.

She was so comfortable with her body. She never hid it from me, and that made her so much sexier. I wanted to sit back and ogle her for a moment before getting to the bottom of Underwear Gate.

I didn't know how long I was staring before she said, "Was there something else you wanted to say, Marshall?"

"Ah. Yeah," I said, shaking my head. "I know you were the one wearing them, Al, but did you wear the said previous undergarments for yourself or someone else?"

She dropped her arms to her sides and sighed. "Don't go there," she said, leaning down to pick up the pair of jeans she had on the day before that got tossed across the room during our romp.

"I wasn't fishing and I wasn't talking about Aaron. I just know that some women enjoy wearing such things, and others only do because they know it turns on their man," I said.

She was quiet as she continued getting dressed, annoyance written all over her face.

"Come on, gorgeous. Don't pout," I said, rolling off the bed. I approached her, wrapping my arms around her waist. "This is only me wondering something about you."

Her blue eyes met mine with an unrelenting stare. I knew by now that was what she did when she was searching for her place of trust. Whatever secrets were hidden behind hers, she knew she could find truth behind mine.

It may have been a stupid fucking move on my part, but I let her. It was always all there for her to see, to take, and do with as she wanted. Even something as basic as a conversation about her underwear choices was something she had to have an internal debate about. It was fucking exhausting at times, and it was during those times I just wanted to take her face, kiss her so fiercely, push all I was feeling for her into her so she would continue to let her guard down.

But this was no fucking time to rush or be selfish about shit.

We were moving, growing, and trusting. It was enough… for now.

"It was for me," she said finally. "Everything about me was about absolute perfection back then."

She gave me a quick kiss, returning to buttoning up her shirt. "Inside and out," she said, shaking her head with a bitter laugh. "Everything from my underwear, perfume, even my nail polish color had to be thought out."

"Why?"

"Because it was who I was. If I wasn't presented as completely put together than anyone could assume I was vulnerable. With the career I had, I'd get stepped all over if I portrayed that."

"Yeah, but you weren't walking around in your underwear. No one knew what you were wearing under your power suits," I said.

"You still don't get it. I *knew* it. From under my clothes to under my skin, everything had to be perfection. There was no room for anything else."

I was man enough to admit that as a dude, there were some things associated with women I had no clue about. Periods (and anything related to the female organs including PMS and childbirth); why they wore shoes that were so uncomfortable but were "cute"; telling us everything was "fine" when it clearly so was not and then expecting us, through some magic male ESP shit, to figure out whatever the fuck you're trying to tell us by not telling us what is wrong; and unexpected situations, conversations, that rendered us completely mentally incompetent to understand you.

This was one of those times I didn't have a fucking clue what a female was talking about, but had to nod my head and pretend like I did. If I didn't, if I had pushed and asked more questions, I knew I would have an "everything is fine" problem on my hands.

"It's just one of those things," she said, heading toward the door. "But next time I'm in need of new underwear, I'll keep it in mind that someone is looking at them again. Anything special you like or should I just guess?"

She winked.

My dick twitched against my boxers.

"Black," I said in a low voice. "All black."

* * *

"What the fuck am I doing?" I mumbled to myself.

I stood outside Victoria's Secret, staring inside and probably appearing like a pervert to everyone inside and out. It was what I practically was by standing there, gawking.

All right. I knew I wasn't going to be the first dude to walk into a lingerie store and buy something for his girl. The thing was, I had never done it before. Thirty-four years old and I'd made it this far without having to do it. While maybe the right girl and right situation never was presented, it was now. I wanted to get Al something, something she liked, even though I didn't know exactly what that was.

Or maybe this was a huge mistake, and it would turn into the time I bought my high school girlfriend a stuffed pig animal. She loved pigs, so I thought she'd like it. I got it thrown in my face in the middle of the cafeteria, with the entire school laughing at me. It was humiliating.

I'd come a long way, but I'd still feel like an asshole if I gave Al something sexy and it was misunderstood.

Or maybe she'd love it. She'd be touched I thought to do it, that I'd listened to what she said. She did insinuate that she'd be up for getting new things. She even asked what I liked.

Or maybe…

"Oh?" A salesgirl with long, dark hair the color of black licorice and a plaid skirt so short I was glad she wearing tights popped her head out. "I thought maybe the door was locked or something and that was why you were just standing there."

Or maybe I should get the fuck inside and stop debating with myself to the point of ridiculousness.

"I was browsing through the window," I said.

"Well, you could come in and browse," she replied. Her teeth was super white against her bright pink lips. "We don't bite. I'll even help you if you want."

No. I don't want you to help me because this is already awkward as fuck.

I stepped inside, and while I knew the selection would be vast, I was wholly unprepared. Bras; bra-like things; underwear in a variety of patterns, colors, and shapes; and lingerie, from risqué to modest, lined every inch of the store.

"Fuck," I said under my breath.

"Something for your wife or girlfriend?" the eager salesgirl asked.

I glanced at her name tag—Berry. Her name was Berry.

I wanted to ask her if it was a joke, something of a conversation starter, or if her parents really hated her at birth.

I cleared my throat. "Um, Berry? I'm obviously not here for myself, so—"

She placed her hand on my arm and she gripped me tightly, so tightly I could feel her fingernails digging into me through my hoodie. "We never assume who someone is buying for."

"Then why did you ask if it was for my wife or girlfriend?"

She batted her overly long dark eyelashes at me. "I was curious."

Oh, for shit's sake. This is the last thing I needed. She is flirting.

I gently stepped away as I pretended I was taking in all the choices, creating a foot of space so she'd let go, which she did.

"Do you know her size?"

That would've been good to know, Marshall.

"Do you have, like, comparison charts or something?" I asked.

She looked like I'd asked her if her mother was part horse or something—completely disgusted. "Ah. No."

And like that, whatever vibe she was giving off to me had all but evaporated.

Wasn't she suppose to maintain some level of professionalism even in the midst of my stupidity? I couldn't imagine I was the worst of the worst that came in here?

"Well," I said. "I guess I'll...guess? Can she return it?"

"Sure."

"What size do you wear?" I asked, pointing to her chest.

As soon as the words left my lips, I not only regretted them, I regretted I was even alive.

Disgust from her turned to vile revulsion.

"Sorry," I muttered. "This was inappropriate. Maybe it would be better if I shopped on my own."

"Probablyyyyyyy a good idea," she said.

She was gone with a hair toss before I could even apologize again. After several steps, she stopped and turned. "Sir?"

And now I was sir.

"Yes?"

"It's only underwear," she said. "No need to be so nervous. Men come in here day in and day out, okay?"

"Oh, I know that. It's just—"

"And no matter the size or anything else, I'm sure she'll love whatever you pick out for her."

Mental note: Leave some free shit or something for Ginger for Berry and the girls here to make up for the fact I was an immature asshole.

Her advice was the best kind. It was enough for me to walk that store with my dignity and manlihood intact. There was no shame in the way I tore through the racks and piles of lacy thongs and push-up bras. When I was satisfied I had gone through all options, I ended up heading up to the register, where Berry was ringing up a woman in front of me. Just as I stepped up and put my choices down, she…stepped away.

I deserve that.

Berry stepped away, and from a door behind the register bar a young gentleman with a handlebar mustache appeared, with more tattoos than I had, which was a fuck ton a lot.

This place was as twisted as the town it was housed in. Just when I thought I'd seen it all, something surprised me. And this was coming from a native Chicagoan, a place where the weird and unusual was about as common as raindrops being wet.

"All set?" he asked.

"Yeah," I said.

He laid out my selected items in front of him, one bra, a cutesy polka-dot number with matching boy-short thingies. Imagining her on a rare lazy morning, lounging in it, or in my kitchen like she did sometimes. Imagining coming up behind her, kissing her across the back of her neck as she stood in front of the stove.

Her leaning back against me, my hard dick rubbing up against those shorts, her ass.

My hands wrapping around her waist, running my hands across her smooth skin, her soft stomach, before raising to her breasts.

Her breathing increasing against my touch, my fingertips.

My kisses travel from her neck, her clavicle, along the jugular vein of her neck, her pulse vibrating against my lips.

And then her neck turns, and she licks her lips.

"Mmmm," she hums.

She closes the space between us, pressing her lips to mine. I taste it immediately—whatever was left on her lips—although I didn't know what it was.

The tip of her tongue taunts mine before sliding in against it.

Sweetness.

Sugar.

And she smiles against my lips; a soft giggle emerges before she pulls away.

"You put a little sugar into everything you do, don't you?" I ask her.

She turns completely, pressing a kiss against my chest, as her hand reaches down, her palm running the length of my erection.

"Breakfast here? Or in bed?"

It was almost enough for me to become inappropriately hard in a retail store.

Sales dude cleared his throat loudly. "Sir?"

"Ah. Yeah. Huh? Sorry."

"Do you want me to take the prices off of them?"

"Sure."

He tore off the price tags along the perforated edges of my spank-bank outfit, and then the other I'd picked out, which was the closest thing to dirty-trashy I could find. A lacy black thong with tiny hip straps that wrapped around an almost opened ass back, before tying in a small bow.

Teeth unwrapping that bow.

Fuck.

And a coordinating push-up bra that if my estimating on size was close meant her tits would look fucking amazing in it.

Not that they didn't already.

"Do you want me to put it in box for you?" he asked.

"Yes. Definitely yes, right?"

"It's a nice touch," he said with a smile.

When everything was all neatly packaged up in the box, a satin ribbon wrapped around it, he slipped it into a pink bag and handed it off to me. As I took it, I realized what a huge mistake I'd just made, not with the purchase, but with the bag. And the box inside.

I was manly enough to admit I was a bit of a Neanderthal upon arrival, but I was past that. What I wasn't past was the fact I'd have to walk back to my car, which was parked in front of Ginger, to put the bag in. If I ran into anyone who knew me, how would I explain the lingerie bag?

"Something else?" the dude asked, confused.

"Damn it. This is…uncomfortable, but can I ask you to take it out of the box?"

"Huh?"

"I'm trying to keep it a secret, and if I'm walking back to my car with this, I can't hide it."

He shrugged like he didn't give a fuck and took the bag back from me.

Huh. Maybe there should be more men working here to help the other clueless assholes, like myself.

Once everything was placed back into the shopping bag, I was ready to get the hell out of there before I did anything further to humiliate myself.

Note: Next time. Order online. Overnight this shit.

I headed out the front door, wedging the bag under my bulky gray hoodie for the quick walk around the block to my car. With my arms crossed tightly in front of me, I tried my best to conceal the purchase, without possibly arising suspicion from passersby that I was concealing something concealable…like a weapon or something. It seemed ridiculous, but clearly, I was at that moment.

I made quick steps down to the light, and as soon I turned the corner, to where both Ginger and my car was, I crashed into someone.

"Hey, Marshall!" Wells exclaimed.

Because of course.

"I was wondering where you were," he said. "I saw your car when I got here and figured you went to get coffee. Tried calling your cell a few times because the accountant called and needs to talk to you."

"Okay. Yeah. I'll be inside in a second," I said.

"Also, the dude who's painting the mural called and asked if he can start tomorrow instead of today. I told him calling the morning of, when he is supposed to start, and telling us he won't be around isn't exactly professional. He got a little snippy with me, and now he only wants to talk to you."

The bag began to slip slightly, and I adjusted my arms to keep it in place. I nodded to Wells while I tried to think of an escape plan.

"Great. I'm going to run and get coffee," I said, turning toward the crosswalk.

"One more thing," Wells said, stepping in front of me. While similar in height, his huskiness made him seem enormous compared to me. "Did you tell Courtney that she could switch her shifts this week and next week with Maggie, Brandon, and Miles?"

"Ah. Yeah. I think so. I'll check when I get back in."

"Great because—"

I fiddled a tad too much, and he caught me adjusting my package.

"What's going on?" he asked, his eyes moving up and down from my package to my eyes.

"Nothing," I snapped. "Can you wait until I go get a coffee and get inside before you start dropping all this shit on me?"

"What the hell is wrong with you?" Wells asked.

His eyes narrowed in further, to the bulge under my jacket, the crumpling of the bag under my hoodie. "What are you hiding?"

"Again, nothing," I said, attempting to step around him. "Want anything from Black Horse?"

He blocked me and poked my chest. "You're acting really freakin' weird, and you're totally hiding something here," he said, tapping the bag.

If I told him, I'd have to come clean about Al and me, and I wasn't ready to do that.

"Dude? What is it?" he asked.

He wasn't going to let this go, and judging by the look on his face, he was scared something was really wrong.

"Are you…?" He leaned in close, his hand still on my package, and whispered, "Is it drugs? Are you in trouble?"

"Oh, for shit's sake," I said, slapping his hand away. "Are you insane?"

"All I'm saying is, I've got your back. No matter what."

Telling him anything at that point was going to be better than the road he was traveling down. I was going to give a little of the truth and keep the rest hidden. It'd have to do.

"I'm not hiding drugs, you dumbass. Just," I said, looking around, "come with me to my car."

"You got it, boss," he said, puffing out his chest like a peacock. "Whatever you need."

I walked along the curb, turning my head back to Wells. "Relax. I'm not hiding a severed head under here and not asking you to help me bury the rest of the body."

"I would," he said.

I knew he totally would.

I stepped behind my car and popped the trunk from my key fob. As I lifted it, I moved in as close as I could.

"Come here," I whispered.

With his size, he was able to block anyone from seeing behind him as I pulled my package out of my hoodie. Wells's eyes squinted for a moment before his ginger beard was lifted up high from smiling so large.

"Ohhhhh," he bellowed.

"Shut the hell up!" I tossed the bag in the trunk and slammed it shut. "Christ. So much for discretion."

"Sorry. It was unexpected, man. And for the record, no judgment."

"What do you mean?"

He put his hand on my shoulder and gave it a rough pat. "I get that you want to keep this under wraps, and I swear I'll keep it to myself. There's nothing wrong with kink."

What the hell is he talking about?

Could he have already figured out Al and I?

"Look, Wells—"

"Not another word about it, boss. People are into all their own kinds of stuff. To be honest, you'd be surprised at some of the things I've decided to try, you know, of a *sexual* nature."

Oh God.

Please.

No.

"So," he said. "If wearing women's bras is what you're into, it's not a big deal. I get if you don't want to broadcast it. You're a professional, a business owner, and whatever you do in private is your own thing."

What could I do?

"Thanks," I said. "Coffee?"

"Yeah. The usual," he said.

I stepped around my car, waiting for the traffic to pass, before I ran across for coffee. Perhaps they sold some amnesia-inducing muffin that I could slam down so I could forget this entire morning—well, except for the morning sex with Al—happened.

"Hey, Marshall!" Wells said.

"What?"

"You know you can order all that shit online."

And for once, I had to admit, that motherfucker had me beat.

Except for the fact that when I gave Al the crumpled bag of lingerie later, she was shocked as hell.

"I still can't believe you did this for me," she said, staring at them and commenting for the tenth time. "Thank you again."

We were sitting on her couch, the fireplace going strong, after a long day.

"Yeah, and there was nothing easy about it. In fact, it was a goddamn shitshow. I mean, it was totally worth it, baby, and I'd do it again, but I'm never setting foot in that fucking place again. Plus, I ran into Wells when I was on my way to the car to drop off the bag. I had to let him believe the goods were for myself so he wouldn't figure shit out."

"Can I tell you something without freaking out?"

"I never freak out," I huffed. "I talk and think with passion."

She leaned over and gave me a quick peck. "I know, but still. Don't freak out, okay?"

Shit. She didn't like the stuff I picked out. Or maybe it was the wrong size. Women got touchy about that stuff. They'd get pissy if you got them a size that was too big because then we were implying they were fat. For the record, we aren't fucking implying anything. We just don't know any better. There were times I wanted to pen a letter to the world, with the intended recipients being the female population, and say, "If we are buying you an article of clothing, any article of clothing, be it lingerie, a concert T-shirt, a dress, or even a fucking old lady flowered housedress or some shit, it's because we want to. It's because we want to see you in it. Your body is beautiful, but don't go down the path of self-destruction because I don't know what the fuck the difference is between a size L and a size 8. It all looks the same to us.

"Okay. I won't," I said.

"I think Wells already knows."

"What? How?"

"Because Phoebe knows."

I pinched the bridge of my nose as I processed this. "And *how* does she know?"

"Did I ever tell you how intuitive she was? That she can look at someone in the eye, see so much truth there and if they are lying or not?"

"No, I didn't know that, and I don't care. I want to know how Phoebe found out."

"Well, if you didn't get so crabby, I'd tell you. She figured it out on her own."

She was full of shit, and I was going to prove it.

"Is that so?" I asked. "And how did it come about?"

"Wellllll, she told me."

"*How* did she tell you?"

"I had asked her about taking sexy selfies, and she wondered who they were for, but before I could deny anything, she said she knew it was you."

"And?"

"And what?"

"How did you respond to that?"

"I told her it wasn't."

"So, she doesn't know for sure, then. What's the problem?"

"Because then I did tell her it was true."

"Al!" I said, throwing up my hands. "Come on. Why?"

"Because I'm a girl, and whether you want to admit that or not, I still act like one at times!"

"Baby, I know you're a girl. I know you are *all* girl, but really? What did you say?"

"All I said was that her assumptions were correct. That was it. She swore on her job she wouldn't tell anyone, including Wells, who she believed didn't have clue."

I was so fucking confused.

"So, why would you think that Wells knows now?"

"Because Phoebe is a girl, too, and there is no way she's kept this a secret from him for this long. It's too delicious not to."

My head hurt.

"Look," she said. "I'm not saying to broadcast it. We aren't ready for that, and until we know how to handle things with Aaron, it's best it's kept on the down low. But Wells is around you daily and so is Phoebe, and they're getting closer themselves. Don't you think it would be okay, or even ease a bit of the running around and secret stuff, if he knew?"

I thought back to earlier in the day when Wells caught me

acting funny and with the shopping bag. He was somewhere right now thinking I was wearing Victoria's Secret's best.

She had a point.

"But don't get in to specifics," she said. "Just tell him, whatever, that it's just sex."

Was that what she wanted? I wasn't sure, so I asked.

"Really? Is that what you want me to say?"

She nodded. "Absolutely. It leaves less room for discussion."

It was up to her, and I was completely fine with it.

I pulled my phone from my pocket and called Wells. On the third ring, he answered.

"Hello?"

"Wells? Yeah. Listen. Alexis and I are banging on the regular. The Victoria's Secret bag? It was shit for her. If you tell anyone, you're fucking fired and I will gut you like a fish. See you tomorrow."

Click.

Short and to the point.

I tossed my phone next to me as I slid closer to Al. At least that was done with. No more sneaking, so to speak, at work.

"Okay," she said. "Down to serious business. Which one of these getups do you want me to put on?"

"That depends?"

"On?"

"Will you make me breakfast in the morning wearing whatever I pick?"

She smiled. "Of course."

"Get your sexy ass in the polka-dot number."

Chapter Eighteen

ALEXIS—

We woke to rain on Thanksgiving.

Actually, I was *woken* in the morning by Marshall whispering in my ear, "Baby, it's raining."

And that was all I needed to become alert.

He rolled his body onto mine, and with nowhere to go, and no businesses to attend to on a holiday, we had a long, leisurely lovemaking session. When we were done, there was no rush to get dressed, no missed phone calls that needed to be returned.

It was bliss.

He was playing with my hair, my naked body wrapped around him, when he made a startling proposition. "What would you think if I suggested we blow off Thanksgiving plans at Phoebe's today?"

"Why would we do that?" I asked.

"Because this, what we are doing right now, in this moment, is fucking amazing and I don't want it to stop," he explained.

I giggled. "I agree, but we can't *not* do Thanksgiving."

"Why the hell not? We're adults. If we don't want to fucking shove our faces with turkey and cranberry sauce, we don't have to."

He had a point, but there was one problem.

"I already made the pies," I said. "We can't leave them without the pies."

He rolled his eyes. "We can do a drop and run. Of course, one of those pies is staying here, at your house, because I had to be surrounded by the smell of it and not even get a fucking taste."

"A drop and run?"

"Yeah. I'll drop it on her porch and run."

"Isn't that rude?" I asked.

He shrugged. "A little, but I don't really care."

"And then what? We come back here and stay in bed all day?"

His eyebrows lifted in consideration, and I had no doubt his answer would be, "Fuck yes."

It wasn't.

And it shocked the hell out of me.

"Okay," he said, wrapping his arm around my shoulder. "How about this? We do the drop and run, and then after, we go for drive."

My eyebrows raised. "A drive?"

"Yes, Al. A drive. It's something you do in a car," he replied, mocking me. "We are never out in public as a couple, and I don't know, maybe we take a drive to Santa Barbara or something."

I considered it for several reasons, but mostly because he made a very important point. We were never out in public as a couple. In public, we were Alexis and Marshall—business owners. That was it. Where we were a couple was confined to either his home or mine. The chance to be "normal" for one day was enticing.

Plus, I loved Santa Barbara. When deciding where to move on the central coast, it was between San Luis Obispo and Santa Barbara. SLO won, but it was a close race.

"What do you think, baby?" he asked with eager eyes. "Road trip?"

I gave him a kiss on the side of his face, his beard scratching my lips. "Santa Barbara it is, and I know just the place to go."

* * *

We didn't do the drop and run the way it was intended because I couldn't. I texted Phoebe and let her know both Marshall and myself weren't feeling well after we ate some questionable sushi the night before. I told her I was going to drop off the pies, minus one, but she didn't know that, on her porch, but wanted to be cautious and not stay to visit, in case it wasn't, in fact, food poisoning. She was disappointed but understood.

The normal hour-and-a-half drive to Santa Barbara took us twice as long because we didn't figure in how many people would be on the roads trying to get to their Thanksgiving dinner destinations. I wasn't sure about Marshall, but I didn't mind in the least. By the time we reached our destination, I knew I'd picked the perfect spot to get out of the car and stretch our legs.

Mesa Lane Beach was a lesser-known beach tucked behind a residential area of Santa Barbara that locals frequented. I came across it during my travels and when scouting out properties when I was considering the area. It was practically deserted, only one other car in the small lot, which was unusual for the area.

"You sure about this?" Marshall asked after we stepped out of the car and stretched our legs in the parking lot. "It's a little chilly out today."

"It's like sixty-three degrees out. Did you forget that I'm from Chicago? Wind chills of twenty below run through my veins," I said.

He nodded. "Point taken. I was only making sure."

"Come on," I said, cocking my head forward. "This way."

He followed me across a dirt drive to the top of the stairs that we'd take to get to the beach. I was about to descend, when he grabbed my arm and stopped me.

"Are you fucking kidding me?" he asked.

"What?"

He snorted before running his hands through his hair and shaking his head at me. "That's a lot of fucking steps."

"Yeah," I said. "Two hundred and forty-two steps to be exact. Is that a problem?"

"Yeah, I have a problem." He folded his arms across his chest. "Why the hell would you want to do that?"

"Um. Because the view is incredible."

"You do realize we're going to have to walk back up these stairs, too, right?"

"Do you not want to do it? We don't have to if you don't think you have it in you," I taunted.

And that was what did it. I had *insulted* his maleness by questioning his ability to walk up and down stairs.

"I was surprised, okay?" he snapped. "If I knew we were going hiking or some shit, I would've worn better shoes."

I glanced down at his worn black Converse and began to giggle. "A beach stroll with some stair climbs isn't exactly scaling a mountain, Marshall."

"Don't start, Al," he warned.

"I'm not starting anything. You are the one being a crybaby about it."

"I am not!"

I threw my hands up in frustration. "You are so…"

"What?" he asked. "What am I?"

"Infuriating," I shouted. "If I didn't know better, I'd swear you were trying to ruin today."

"That is completely unfair," he said.

I let out a deep sigh, knowing I had to play nice, even if meant him assuming he was right and I was wrong. I moved back over to him and wrapped my arms around his waist.

"I'm sorry, Marshall," I said sweetly. "You were right. I should've explained better. Do you want to stay, or do you want to do something else? Whatever you want."

"Jesus!" he said, throwing his hands up in the air and startling me. "One minute you're insulting me and getting pissy, the next you're trying to melt me like butter on toast. You're hot and you're cold. It's no and it's yes with you. I can't fucking figure you out sometimes, Al."

I stifled another round of laughs as I backed away from him. "Are you quoting me Katy Perry?"

"That right there," he said, pointing his index finger at me, "was below the belt, Alexis. Katy Perry? Really?"

There was no winning with this guy sometimes, and it drove me nuts. It also completely turned me on.

"How about this?" I said. "We take the beach stroll, see what we can find on the way back home in terms of food before I tuck you back into bed, and let you eat that pumpkin pie you've been waiting so patiently for while I suck your cock?"

His eyes snapped to mine and I knew I had him.

"Lead the way, gorgeous," he said with a smirk.

The walk down the steps to the beach was never the problem. Once you reached the bottom, the incredible view took your breath away. Marshall and I lingered on the beach, strolling the edge of the water, holding hands.

We were us.

There were frequent stops to kiss and watch the tide come in. A soft breeze did chill the air slightly, but to be outside, breathing in the saltwater smell, reawakened my insides. It seemed like it did for Marshall as well. He seemed calmer, more relaxed, and by the time we made our way back to the stairs, I knew I'd made the right choice.

There was something I had wanted to ask him for a while, and I wasn't even sure if this was the right time, but I went with it.

"When are you going to tell Aaron?" I asked as we were about to start the climb.

"Soon," he said. "It's not an easy thing to tell him."

I was relieved in a way that he didn't ask, "Tell Aaron what?" because it meant we were on the same page. But there was also a larger part of me that felt that when he did tell him, Marshall might have to make a choice: Aaron or Me.

"I know it's not," I said.

He ran his hands through his hair. "Fuck. How do I even do that? What the hell do I say?"

"You'll know when you're ready, and I'll be here when you do. No matter what."

I was about to take the first step on the stairs, but he grabbed my hand to pull me back.

"You will?" he asked. "No matter what?"

"Yes."

His hand lifted, brushing a strand of my hair out of my face from the blowing breeze. "Are you sure you're ready for that?"

"Yes. Are you ready?" I asked, my foot on the first step of 242.

He grinned. "Born ready, Al."

It didn't intend for it to be a race, but that was what it turned into. We kept in step the entire time, but the closer we got to the top, he began to lag behind. While I was never one to give in, there was something about reaching the top together that called to me. I paused when I was five steps ahead of him, bending at my waist and faking a cramp.

"You okay?" he asked, breathless, stopping at my side when he reached me.

"Yeah. Stomach cramp," I said. "I just needed a quick break. I'm okay now."

He nodded, and we took the last twenty steps together, landing on the top as one. We paused to catch our breath before he leaned in and gave me a high five.

"Well done," he said. "That was awesome."

"Right? I'm glad you thought so."

He gave me a quick kiss, lingering against my lips after. "Thank you for taking me here," he mumbled. "It was perfect."

"It's going to get even better than perfect when I get you home," I said.

He slapped my ass. "Get in the car, gorgeous. I need to know what will top perfect."

The drive back up the coast wasn't as congested as the way down, which was good, because I knew we were both anxious to get home. Sexual tension and silent innuendo in terms of my hand on his thigh and a brush of his fingers against my cheek filled the time with anticipation. Everything was closed in terms of restaurants and fast-food options. A gas station stop supplied our Thanksgiving dinner meal. As we drove back to my house, we munched on Corn Nuts, Cheetos, beef jerky, and Combos. We didn't get the Honey Buns and Hostess Fruit Pies, even though we both wanted to, because we knew the real deal was waiting for us at home.

We pulled into my driveway, but before he got out, I stopped him. "When we get inside," I said, "I want you to go upstairs to my bedroom, take off all your clothes, and wait for me there."

His eyebrows lifted, and his signature smirk emerged. "I see you are the one in charge tonight, huh?"

I leaned over and kissed him before swinging the car door open. "I'm always in charge," I said. "I just let you believe sometimes that you are."

With quick steps, we entered the house, and I watched as he took the stairs two at time to get to the bedroom. While he was getting undressed, I went to the kitchen. The remaining pumpkin pie was sitting on top of my counter, and I intended to put it to good use, just as I'd promised him.

When I entered the bedroom, he was laying naked on top of my comforter, his arm crossed behind his head. "What do you have there?" he asked.

I walked over to him and handed him the plate with the large slice of pie on it. "I always keep my word, Marshall."

He took it from me but hesitated for a moment after. "Fork?"

I shook my head, as I began to undress myself in front of him. "No."

He set the plate down on the nightstand, picking up the pie with his hand. I watched as he was about to bring it to his mouth for a taste, but the vision of me now nude distracted him.

"Baby," he whispered. "That's my beautiful baby."

I climbed up to the edge of the bed, kneeling beside him, as I took his cock in my hand and began stroking it. "Take a bite," I said.

He obeyed. As I watched him swallow the first bite and take another, I lowered my head and took him entirely in my mouth. I sucked and licked and worked him over as he ate something I had made. It was another level of erotic I'd never known, and something that I wouldn't have ever imagined to be so sexy.

He finished his last bite and then gave himself over to me. I swallowed everything he gave to me and his pleasure, knowing I made him so content and fulfilled, was better than any pie I could've had in its place.

I crawled up the rest of the bed, and we got under the covers together where our bodies pressed together as he spooned me.

"Can I ask you a question?" I said, tracing my fingers across the tattoos on his arms.

"Mm-hmm."

"What do they all mean?" I asked. "Your tattoos?"

"Well," he said. "The one across my chest with the angel wings and lion is for my mom. I know you don't know, but she passed away three years ago."

My heart sank as I fought to find words. I'd met Mrs. Jones on a few occasions, and she couldn't have been lovelier. Him and his mom were very close, especially since he was an only child, and I knew his father had died when he was small.

"Marshall," I whispered. "I'm so, so sorry. I know how much she meant to you. I wish I—"

I paused because I didn't want to be insensitive. I didn't want to say what I wanted to say, which was, "I wish I would've known." I did wish that, but these were things about life, birth through death, that I knew I'd miss when I left. It was easy to deny any of it happening when you weren't around to see it.

He kissed the side of my head, his arms wrapping around me tighter. "I know. Thank you."

"Is that when you started getting all the tattoos?"

He sighed as he rested his chin on top of my head. "Yeah. Losing her happened suddenly, a car accident, and it made me realize what I was doing with my life. My dad died of a massive heart attack suddenly, too. Nothing is permanent. This is our one fucking life, Al. I was wasting it."

"Don't say that," I said. "You weren't wasting it. You were a successful trader, living your life fully."

"It wasn't me. I never wanted to be a trader. I didn't know *what* I wanted to do until I got into the bar business. I was just doing what I thought I should, what I thought would make my parents happy."

I understood this.

"I didn't know what it felt like to be content until I started Tipsy. We're lucky, you know?" I said, my fingers running up and down his arm. "Most people will never know that kind of satisfaction."

"Huh," he said. "I never thought about it like that, but you're right. So, the saying 'Even those who are gone are with us as we go on' is from *The Lion King*."

"*The Lion King*?" I asked.

His body stiffened behind me. "Don't knock my love for that movie, Al."

"Since when do you watch Disney movies?"

"Since…" He paused before answering. "Since Delilah."

"Oh. Well, of course because of her." I paused once again, grabbing the end of my hair to twirl it around my finger. "Did you get to watch movies with her a lot?" I asked.

"Yes, a lot. She loved all the princess shit, and I'd sit through it sometimes, but mostly she knew that *The Lion King* was our movie."

My heart swelled because while I'd hoped Aaron would have support outside his family, I don't think I ever thought about Marshall being such a prominent part of that.

"Ah. Let's see," he continued. "I love Superman. Mostly because of my dad, and when he died, it was a part of him I could hold on to. And the dragonflies are a symbol of courage, knowing you can overcome anything."

"Wow," I said. "You haven't gotten to your back pieces, and

I'm already reading your story. Can I ask you one more thing?"

"Absolutely."

"When did your look change? I mean, no offense, but you're not the same clean-cut Marshall of years ago."

He kissed the top of my head. "The tattoos have been a process over the last few years, and the hair? I just decided in the last year to start growing it out until I cut it before the opening."

"But why?"

"Because I finally found some peace. I fought for years against it, but then Ginger was happening and it was the final piece. So that and I decided to stop giving a fuck, that's why," he said.

He punctuated the ending with a laugh, and because he did that, I knew there was an enormous amount of integrity that went along with it. Pride filled me, because while I was away finding the real me, he was doing the same. I rolled over so I could face him.

"So you like them?" he asked. "The tattoos?"

"Very much so."

"I thought you didn't like tattoos," he said.

I tilted my head to the side as I considered his statement. "Why do you say that?"

"Well, I remember when Aaron got the start of his you freaked out."

I laughed. "I think 'freaked out' are strong words. *Surprised* is a more suitable word choice."

"Really? Because Aaron said you flipped your shit, that you were so angry you called him an immature imbecile or something."

I rolled my eyes. "I don't think I said that, but back then, anything is possible. I was shocked. I literally came home from work one day, and he was all, 'Look what I did, babe! Isn't it cool?' He didn't tell me he was doing it. Plus, it was huge."

"Huh," Marshall said. "It's not like you and I ever talked about it. I always thought you hated it, and that's why he never finished it until recently."

"What do you mean he never finished it until recently?"

He shifted uncomfortably. "I mean just that. It wasn't until a couple years ago or something he finished it."

"Why did he wait so long?"

"I dunno. I always thought it was because of you, and then he was so wrapped up with Delilah. It wasn't until—" He trailed off for a moment, pressing his lips together tightly. "Until you know."

I didn't know, and whatever it was he didn't want to elaborate on. That could only mean one thing. It was a girl. It was Aaron's girl. I'd seen her name on the card when they sent the Chicago gift basket of stuff for the bar opening, but I didn't recall her name. There was no reason to dance around it, especially considering what Marshall and I were doing together.

"I'm happy he has someone," I said. "I am. It wasn't love between us, Marshall. I don't know, maybe it was a little, but it was more of a deep friendship. We filled something in each other, but I think we both knew deep down we weren't a forever match."

"Yeah?" he asked, raising his eyebrows. "It doesn't make you feel weird?"

I shrugged. "No, not really. It's like knowing a friend found someone that they fit with."

"She's amazing. She is. And she's so good with Delilah."

I knew it would come at some point, but I didn't know it would be tonight, in this moment. Tears began to burn my eyes, but I pushed them away. I wasn't going to do that—I wasn't going to do the crying thing. It was unfair to Marshall.

It was unfair to me because while many would think me leaving was reprehensible, I knew the truth. I had a choice. A choice to either end my life or to give Aaron and Delilah theirs.

And even though the tears weren't from sadness, but from the place in my heart that I had stored all the hope I had that she would have a real mother, a mother she deserved, I had to maintain my emotions.

"I can't tell you what it means to me to hear that," I whispered.

"Aaron was never going to let anyone in his life that wasn't going to be part of Delilah's, too. Callie balances him, keeps him from being too serious. I've never known him to be happier."

I placed my hand over my heart, the overwhelming gratitude I had that it was going exactly how I'd always hoped.

"Callie is why, the reason, he finished his tattoo, right?"

He nodded. "You know, Aaron. He never does anything a little. It was an act of...professing his love or some shit like that. Callie is short for Calliope, you know, like the steam organs on a carousel? It's that."

What a beautiful gesture.

And something so Aaron.

Chapter Nineteen

MARSHALL—

Al's morning drop-offs were my favorite time of the workday. Wells had started coming in later in the afternoon, so that left me alone at Ginger. I was alone until Alexis showed up.

It was the end of January, the dead of winter back home in Chicago, but the lower sixties in SLO felt downright balmy. I still wasn't used to it, nor did I think I ever would be.

Alexis arrived, and after helping her bring in the treats, I took her hand, guiding her to the bar.

I sat down on one of the barstools and pulled her into me. "Hi," I said. "I missed you."

She patted my chest, as she kissed my temple. "You saw me a few hours ago."

"Still missed you."

My hand slid down from the middle of her back to her ass where I gave it a squeeze before rubbing all across it. The faint outline of her panty line, the fabric of lace I felt underneath made me snap my head back.

"Are you wearing your dirty panties?" I asked.

"Of course not. That's gross. They're clean."

"That's not what I meant, baby," I laughed. "I meant, are you wearing the naughty panties I bought for you?"

She leaned into my side, that mischievous smile that was so goddamn sexy spread across her face. "Perhaps."

I faked a pout. "That's hardly fair," I said.

"Why? They're my panties to do whatever I want with and wear whenever I choose."

"But they were for me to look at you wearing."

"Who said you couldn't? Maybe I had that all planned out for later, along with the bra I'm wearing."

My faux pout turned to dead seriousness. "Don't fucking kid around about that shit, baby. My cock is pressing against my zipper, and a woman has no idea how uncomfortable that is when you're wearing jeans."

She kissed the side of my cheek. "Then maybe the jeans are too tight."

"Maybe," I said, bringing my lips to the side of her neck and kissing her. "You shouldn't make me so crazy turned on all the time, so I'm not walking around with a perpetual hard-on."

I didn't hear the door.

I didn't hear footsteps against the tile floor.

It was Al's eyes.

I saw them when she pulled back from my cheek, and she glanced above my head.

All expression left her face.

Blood drained.

Something was wrong.

I couldn't even turn my head fast before she muttered…

"Aaron."

And it was him.

No one spoke. No one moved.

No one breathed.

He was just…there, stopped midstep.

The fucking universe put on the brakes because there wasn't a sound, not one, in the entire bar.

Or anywhere else.

It was inevitable, but the worlds collided.

Again.

But this time, it was worse. So, so much worse.

And it was no one's fault, but stupid fucking mine.

I'd held on to the enchanted world of Al and me for too long. I took the risk, knowing what the end result would be. It would be this moment.

The only thing I wanted was a little time to prepare.

I didn't deserve to prepare because I knew always I would have to answer to him. I just never wanted to think about it.

Now?

Time was up.

It was up to me.

"Aaron," I said, sliding off the barstool. "Man, I can't believe you're here."

I started to approach him, but every step toward him, he took a step back. I'd never seen this level of shock, this much…unmitigated confusion out of him before. It scared the fuck out of me.

"Aaron," I repeated. "Come into the office, and let's talk."

He stopped his steps again as his head jerked back and forth between Al and I. He was processing or…something. I didn't know. What I did know was that Aaron internalized everything…always. The longer he went without saying anything, the worse it was going to be when he did.

"Hi, Aaron," Al said in a calm, soft tone. "Marshall's right. Let's go talk. I can't imagine what this, what you…you know."

I cranked my head back to shoot her a look to not say another word. This was all on me. I would handle it.

Aaron ran his hands through his hair with force and aggression before lacing his fingers behind his head and diverting his eyes to the floor.

Come on, brother. It's me. This is me. Just look at me and know. I can explain this. I can make you understand. You know me. You know us, you and me. Just talk to me.

His eyes snapped back up, and it was all right there.

We had woken the buried beast.

With his pupils huge and his nostrils flared, he unleashed.

And there wasn't a damn thing I could do except stand there and let the beast eat me alive.

"What the fuck is this?" Aaron asked, every word enunciated and punctuated with rage. "How?"

"That's what I want to talk to you about. So—"

He pulled at his hair again. "This doesn't make sense! Fuck, Marshall. You and…her?" He spat out the word *her* like it was a piece of bad fruit.

The damage was done. There was no point in lying or sugarcoating.

"Yes," I said. "Her and I."

He was breathing so rapidly, panting even. "I feel like this is a dream, like…it can't be real. How can it be real? No. It's not a dream. It's a goddamn nightmare."

"Al lives here in San Luis Obispo," I said. "I didn't know until Ginger opened."

"Well, isn't that a coincidence? Did she move here before or after you got here, and you told her that we were opening a bar here?" he asked.

"Before," both Al and I said simultaneously.

Al, please. Please, baby. Stop.

I stepped forward toward him. "It's not like that, Aaron. Come on, you know me. I didn't know she lived here until she walked through the door."

He shot me a pained look. "I thought I knew you. I thought I knew you better than anyone. And you," he barked in Al's direction. "So, you ran away to the Happiest City in America, huh? What a bunch of bullshit."

A menacing laugh emerged from him, and I was…lost. I didn't know what the fuck to do.

"Aaron?" Al said. "I've lived here for almost five years. I run a bakery called Tipsy Treats out of my home in Arroyo Grande. Marshall and I met again when I came by to meet the owner of Ginger. I had been hired by Wells, who had no idea who I was, to provide desserts and snacks for Ginger. It was a crazy coincidence."

As I imagined, and what Al seemed to have forgotten about Aaron, this—her short synopsis of herself and events—didn't go over well with Aaron. Too much information was thrown at him at once, and when up against any type of battle, Aaron was going to come out swinging.

"Lexie," Aaron said. "I can't—"

"It's Alexis now," she corrected him. "No one calls me Lexie anymore."

Fuck. That was going to do it.

Christ. Why did she have to push him?

"You changed your damn name?" he asked with a lip snarl. "Wow. You took every measure to make sure you weren't found."

She blinked at him, her lids rapidly opening and closing. "Yes," she said simply.

"Aaron?" I said. "Let's go for a walk or my place is close by; we can go there, okay?"

His eyes went back to shifting between Al and I, and I didn't know what else to do. I was helpless. My best friend knew, was standing in front of me, betrayed in the worst way. And on the other side of me was the girl I loved beyond all measure.

A fucking daytime talk show couldn't have written a more fucked-up situation than I was standing in at that moment.

"Where are you staying?" I asked, desperate to get him alone so we could talk it out. "Are the girls with you? Because I'd love—"

"Yes," he roared. "*My* girls are with me. Shit! What the hell am I supposed to tell them?"

I attempted again to step toward him, but he put his hand up, pushing against my chest. "Don't," he shouted. "Don't you fucking dare, Marshall."

He stared into my eyes, anger and rage practically blinding

me. His hand left my chest and went to his side where he balled it up into a fist.

Please hit me. Hit me so you can hurt me. Please, Aaron.

But he didn't, because that was the kind of man he was. He gave us both one last look full of malice and turned to walk away.

"Aaron, please!" I pleaded. "Don't leave before you understand."

Al's arm laced through mine, her coming to my side to stop me from chasing after him.

"Fuck. Fuck. Fuck," I screamed. "This is a fucking nightmare!"

The back door slammed shut, and everything inside me shook. It was the worst kind of hurt I'd ever known, and the real fucked-up part was that whatever Aaron was feeling was ten times worse.

"Let him cool off," Al said in soothing tone. "Remember what a shock it was when we ran into each other here? Well, it's tenfold for him. Plus, seeing us—"

"Fuck, Al! He wasn't supposed to find out like this. A shock? You think it was a shock? It would've been a fucking bullet to my gut if it'd happened to me. Jesus!"

She drew in a deep breath and parted her lips as she exhaled slowly. "Okay. You need to cool off, too. I'm only trying—"

"Why did you have to antagonize him? You knew that would only make it worse! And furthermore, how can you be so calm? You're as cool as can be, aren't you?" I asked, shaking my head. "The Ice Queen is still alive, huh?"

My words gave way to no reaction, and it surprised me. Lexie would've come out swinging. *She was* the Ice Queen.

And like I've had to remind myself so many times before, she wasn't Lexie anymore. She was Al.

"Sorry," I said. "I'm so out of my mind with all of this right now, I don't even know how to process any of it or what to do."

She took my hand and guided me back to the bar. "Sit down," she said.

I did as she said, as she slid into the seat next to me, continuing to hold my hand.

And that was what she did as I let the weight of the shitshow that had just occurred sink in.

It seemed so logical from the outside, so basic. There was no way Aaron was never going to find out. I'd pushed the limits for too long, and now I was going to have to pay the price.

I didn't even know what that fucking meant, either.

Was I going to have to choose between them?

I couldn't.

"Are you okay?" Al whispered.

"No. Not even a fucking little."

She leaned her head against my shoulder. "I'm sorry. I'm so sorry, Marshall."

I shrugged because what could I say? Don't be? No. I couldn't say that.

As if she read my mind, she said, "Don't say I shouldn't be because I am. This wouldn't have happened if it wasn't for me."

She was right. It fucking hurt my insides to admit that to myself, but she was right.

"It's okay to wonder, you know," she said.

"Wonder what?"

"What if we'd never found each other again."

I sighed. "I don't wonder that, Al. I wonder a lot of things, but not that."

"Like what?"

I shook my head. "I don't know."

I didn't know fucking anything in that moment except I needed to get to Aaron and explain.

"I didn't come looking for you," she said.

It wasn't intended to be condescending, but it came across that way, and because of that, it was like she'd poured gasoline on the fire.

"Of course you didn't, but you found me. You walked right through my fucking door and everything around it blew up, Al.

She narrowed her eyes at me. "Then maybe," she spat. "You should go back to hating me like you once did."

I shook my head. "No fucking way. It's too late."

"Why?"

"Why?" I shouted. "Because I fell in love with you, Al. Despite everything, fucking *everything*, I fell in love with you. How the hell does that even happen?"

She shrugged. "I think it doesn't. It's just…something else. Lust masquerading as love?"

"That's bullshit and you know it."

"Do I?"

"Yes. I've never heard a bigger level of bullshit in my life. You can't fake this shit. You can't fake the way you look at me and the way I feel it ache across my entire body. You can't fake chemistry, and that whatever the hell we've both been through over the last seven years created something awesome between us. You can't fake fate, and you can't fake passion, the connection. Love. You can't fake love. And shit, I know you love me. I know you can't say it to me, but it's there and I know."

She shook her head as it hung toward the floor. "It doesn't matter, anyway."

"What doesn't matter? That I know with every single part of me that you love me, too?"

"No. That I thought I loved before you, and it wasn't enough."

"With Aaron I know—"

"No," she said sharply, her head snapping up. "Not Aaron."

I paused before responding because I had no idea what she was talking about. Was there someone before Aaron? Someone I didn't know about?

"Who?" I asked without wanting to know the answer.

Her head tilted to the side, and she grasped at the end of a strand of hair. "A mother's love is supposed to be eternal or something. Oh, Marshall. I did love her, but *I* wasn't enough, I wouldn't ever be able to keep her safe like a mother could. Oh, I loved her so, so much. No. Not loved. Love."

Delilah.

"You did what was right. It was for—"

"The best, I know," she said. "I know that in my head. I do, but my heart always reminds me of something different."

The pain, the palpable agony, radiated off her, and I felt it over my entire body. It hurt me so deeply it wasn't until that moment that I realized just how much pain she must've been in. I had to do something.

There was too much pain, too much regret, on all of us: me, Al, and Aaron. I needed to try and mend it. I had to because I was the one in the center of it all, and I knew where I needed to start.

Aaron.

* * *

It took me until close to ten p.m., calling every hotel I could think of, texting Aaron and Callie repeatedly, to track him down. It was Callie that took pity on me. I wasn't sure why, but I would be grateful for life that she told me what hotel they were at. Before she did, though, I had to promise to leave if he said to and to not be loud because Delilah was asleep. The last message Callie sent to me hit where it should—in my stupid, fucked-up mind.

Callie: You know trust is everything to him. And no matter what or how you explain it, you lied to him…for months. And if that wasn't bad enough, it was with her.

The immense panic that overtook me as I walked through the front door of their hotel and into the lobby was enough to almost make me turn around and run.

But I didn't.

I didn't because while I'd thought Ginger was the most important thing I'd ever done in my life, it didn't hold a fucking candle to what I was going to be doing when I walked into that room.

This was going to change *all* our lives.

Their room was on the third floor, right next to the elevator.

I didn't even have time for more than a couple deep breaths before I was knocking on the door. After a few moments, it opened, and it was Callie.

Her expression was neutral. No usual smile, but no visible anger. It had to be there, though. How could it not?

"Hey," she said as she took pity on me and leaned in for hug.

It was just the gesture I needed to cross inside and be ready to accept whatever was going to come my way.

As I entered, I saw him immediately, sitting in a chair, a glass of Scotch hanging over the side with one of his hands. Callie sat down on the couch beside him, and his hand went to her, resting it on her knee.

"Where did you tell her you were going?" Aaron asked.

It was such a strange first question to ask. I didn't understand why he was asking it, but this wasn't about me. I didn't have any fucking right to question why he would ask anything at all.

I just stood. I stood in front of them because I wanted the brunt of whatever was coming at me to hit me full force.

"She doesn't know I'm here."

Aaron nodded before taking a sip of his Scotch. "How long?"

I took in a deep breath, ready to breathe out honesty. "Since September," I said.

His eyes narrowed at me. "That soon, huh? You work fast."

"Aaron," Callie said, squeezing his hand. "Let him talk. We know you're hurt, beyond hurt, and believe me," she said, flashing me a dirty look, "I am as well, but you know whatever happened, is happening, wasn't done to hurt you on purpose."

"Can I just…say something?" I asked. I pushed my hair out of my face. "Please?"

Aaron sighed deeply, shrugging his shoulders.

"I need you to try to understand," I pleaded. "Separate who she was to you, just for a minute. I'm begging you."

When he didn't object, I continued.

"Have you ever fallen in love with the wrong person?" I asked. "You knew it was wrong, and you fought it and fought it, but it was there. That special fucking thing was *there*, and you couldn't walk away. You knew if you did you'd regret it for the rest of your life?"

Callie raised her brows at him, but he wasn't having it.

"But it wasn't your ex-wife, the mother of your child," Aaron said with a rough tone. "What happened with Callie and I was different."

"He asked you to try and be objective," Callie said. "Just do it."

"Why is everyone ganging up on me?" Aaron asked. "I'm the one who's been lied to."

"No one is ganging up on you, Aaron," Callie said. "But he's asking you to listen, and if you're not going to, then you will start carrying around another very heavy piece of baggage filled with anger and hurt. I don't want that for you. I don't want it for Delilah. So, if you can't deal with this now, that's okay. That's your call, but we're here now. Marshall is here now."

Aaron shook his head before downing the rest of the Scotch in his glass. "What do you want me to say?" he asked, looking at me.

"I want you to say that you know, you *fucking know*, that we are like brothers, and I'd never do shit to hurt you on purpose," I said. "I want you to say that you know I'd lay my fucking life down for you. I want you to ask me to stop seeing her and that you know I will if you asked me to because I would do that. I'd walk away from her, but I want you to say that you know there has to be something really fucking special between her and I that I'd do this to you, and that ultimately, you don't want me to do that. You won't make me choose."

He leaned over, taking both of his hands, after removing one from Callie's grip, and bringing them to his face. His elbows rested on his knees as he pressed the palms of his hands into his eyes.

"I won't make you do that," he muttered. "I've never, *ever* heard you talk or act like this about a woman before."

"Thank you," I said, my voice cracking.

A brief moment of relief washed over me, but I knew there was so much more to overcome.

"I want you to do something for me," Aaron said, his eyes now on mine.

"Anything," I said.

"I want you to set up a time tomorrow morning for her and I to talk," he said. "I don't care how you do it, but I want it to happen."

"Okay. I can do that. I'll make sure."

"Because the thing is, Marshall," he said, "she's caused a lot of heartache, in a lot of lives, and it's time it ended. I need to know why. Once and for all. I want to put this all to bed. For all of us."

Chapter Twenty

I didn't think I could do it.

I told Marshall I wouldn't.

He told me I could and I would.

There was nothing in a handbook to prepare you for sitting across from your ex-husband, the father of your child, both of whom you left. There was no amount of "I'm sorrys" or reasoning to make it rational.

But as Aaron sat across from me at my kitchen table, I knew that I owed him something. I had owed him something even before I left. I wasn't capable of giving him all of it at once, but I would give everything else I had.

I owed it to him. I owed it to Delilah.

And I owed it to others in our lives.

Leslie, Callie, Marshall, and even Abel and Daniel.

All of them deserved a sense of peace, but most of all, I deserved it, too.

"I could never explain during one breakfast why," I said,

twirling my finger around the edge of my hair. "I still don't even understand myself. I'm working on it, though, and I can say this for certain. Knowing what I know from Marshall, you and Delilah are getting everything you deserved. The mom, the girlfriend, and the family you all deserve."

He nodded. "I agree, but I'm sure I don't need to explain that this...thing...between you and Marshall is less about you two being together and more about how I view you."

"I understand that. I do," I said. I pressed my lips together, carefully choosing my words. "But I want it all to end for us now. Today. And I know I have no right to ask you for that or for you to assume I'm asking for you to forgive me. I'm not because you have every right, with every fiber in your body, to hate me."

He sighs. "I don't hate you," he said. "I don't think I ever did. I mean, God! How could I? You gave me her. You gave me Delilah."

Tears filled my eyes. "And that is one part I realized a long time ago. My purpose in her life was to bring her to you and then step aside."

His eyes moved across my face, as he shook his head in disbelief. "God. You seem so...not you, different. You look like the old Lexie, but..."

"Because I am different, Aaron. You can't do what I did, something that others would think is the most reprehensible, disgusting thing like abandon your own daughter, and not have that profoundly change you. But it was the right thing. You know that deep down. Remove the labels and all of the other bullshit, Aaron. I couldn't and I shouldn't have been a mom. You saw it. You knew. And when it got down to the end of it, I had to make a choice. One choice was to end my own life. The other was to leave. You had to have seen how bad it got, how desperate I'd become. It's why I can say now suicide was my only choice for a while."

"Shit, Lex," he whispered, his expression, his voice so full sorrow. "Shit. I knew you were unhappy. I did know that, but I didn't realize it was that bad." He paused before continuing. "You were so…detached. I didn't know what to do. I thought it was everything from postpartum to drug use. And I tried, Lex. I tried so hard to fix it and make it better, make *you* better. And then you were gone. It was all the unanswered questions, that was what killed me. I didn't know if I should've tried harder, and the guilt of that buried me for years. That you didn't trust me to tell me the truth. It all fucking swallowed me…for years."

He was unraveling, and while it frightened me, I was going to be there because I owed it to him to not run away again.

"But like you," he continued, "you don't go through something like that and not come out changed. The anger ate me alive for years, but then Calliope came into our lives three years ago, and I knew what happened between us was all part of some master plan. It took me so long to get there, Lex, and I don't even know if it came full circle until last night, but I realized where I am, where Delilah is, is right where we were destined to be. You and I? It was never there. We both can say that now, but I could never bring myself to regret because…Delilah. You gave me her."

Tears of his own formed in his eyes, and it was enough for

me to release mine because in all my years of knowing him, I'd never seen him cry.

It was all I ever wanted. Them both happy. They were.

And in the ultimate act of empathy, he was telling me he understood why and that he was almost grateful for it.

Maybe it wasn't even "almost." Maybe it just was grateful.

He cleared his throat as he rubbed at his eyes. "I will never not ache or carry around the burden of her not knowing her biological mother. I lie awake at night going over and over in my head how I will explain it all to her because that day will come. I know she'll want answers someday, and I'm sure when she does so much of the hurt and anger I have for you will be there. But she'll never know that. I'll never let her see it because we've had to do what was best with what was given. She'll need to learn that, too."

It was hard to find enough breath to even speak, but when I finally did, it was something I should have told him a long time ago. "You are an amazing man, Aaron. You are an amazing father. You are enough for her to make up for the fact that her mom isn't around."

"But she *does* have a mom," he said. "She has one hell of a mom that...holds the bucket when she vomits, and braids her hair, and is making sure she is a good, decent person. She has helped us both find spirit, and laughter, and a bond so profound, I can't be anything but grateful for that."

Grateful.

"That is...Aaron," I sniffled. "All I wanted for you. For her."

"I'm not going to thank you," he said. "Hell, I don't know if I can even forgive you because I don't think I've processed this entire thing yet, but…it happened for the best."

And there it was.

A painfully beautiful sliver of redemption.

It was like getting oxygen for a time after being without. All my senses seemed to heighten, and my entire body felt weightless. So much was lifted.

And while I knew there was much that I carried, especially about Sadie, that he'd never know, there was one final thing I needed to tell him. Something he had every right to know.

"It was your mom," I muttered after a long silence. "She was the one that helped me."

His eyes squinted at me in confusion at first before his jaw slackened. "Wait," he said, running his hands through his hair. "My mom? She…helped?"

I nodded. "She knew. When the two choices became too much, she helped me. I'm assuming she never told you, and I'm asking you to please don't be angry at her that."

I saw no reason to tell him yet about the emails and letters throughout the years with Delilah updates. That was a conversation I was going to have with Leslie first.

We sat quiet, and it wasn't awkward or painful or anything. It was the building of a reconciliation. There was good, no there was wonderful things between Aaron and I, even aside from Delilah. For the first time in seven years, or maybe ever, I think he knew that, too.

And then I got my answer to all of my questions and all that I wondered, by having Aaron ask me the one question I never thought I'd hear in my lifetime.

"Marshall and Callie, the two outside opinions that mean

more to me than anything, think you should meet her. Do you want that?"

There was only one answer: yes.

"Yes," I whispered. "Yes, I want that, but there is one more thing I need to tell you."

He took a deep breath, preparing himself for whatever else I was going to say. "Go ahead, Lex. Tell me."

"I had a sister. Her name was Sadie and she died."

I didn't wait for him to respond before I began my story. My life story. His eyes were confused at first, but the more I talked, explaining in painfully clear detail, the realization that I was telling the truth began to surface on his face.

He shook his head.

He didn't want to believe it. He *couldn't* believe it.

Why would he? All those years, all that we've been through, and I never told him.

I don't know precisely when the tears came from either of us. And I'm also unsure when his hand took mine and I sat sobbing onto his chest.

"I'm so sorry, Lex," he repeated.

Over and over and over again.

And I believed him.

* * *

I had it all laid out. I agonized for hours about what to make with her. Without knowing a thing about seven-year-olds and not much about Delilah herself, I was torn.

Would she prefer to make cupcakes or brownies? I didn't

do a lot of sugar cookies and such to decorate, but I certainly could. Would she have wanted to do that?

I recalled one of the last emails Leslie sent me and how she mentioned that her and Delilah had made apple strudel together. Maybe Delilah thought cupcakes and cookies were... amateurish. Maybe she was beyond that and was into pastries or breads. I just didn't know.

In some ways, this was the most important day of my life, aside from the day she was born, because for me, she was being *reborn* to me. It was never going to be a mother-daughter relationship. I made that decision a long time ago, and that hadn't changed. What did change was the fact that the guilt I'd held on to for so long because of it was breaking apart. It was crumbling in pieces like a crushed cookie. It could never be put together whole, but you could enjoy what was left.

I was being given a gift, and what I did fear was that I would do something to ruin it.

"What are you doing?" Marshall asked, entering the kitchen.

I shrugged. "Obsessing."

"No shit, Al," he said. He came up behind me, wrapping his arms around my waist before resting his head on my shoulder. "I can't imagine all the thoughts running through your head. I mean, I'm borderline freaking out."

"I know this is enormous, but what, specifically, has you worried?" I asked.

He ran his chin against my shoulder, the fuzz from his beard tickling the side of my face. It was oddly comforting. *He* was comforting. Just his embrace, while so basic, slowed my heart rate. It calmed me. Not completely, but enough to know I could make it through this because he was literally standing right behind me, telling me I could.

"I'm not really worried," he said. "I know this is beyond huge, you know? But I think what's fucking with my head is that it's all come together so amazingly dysfunctional."

I turned to face him, gripping his hips to bring him in close. "Amazingly dysfunctional, huh? That seems apropos, but a bit confusing. Explain, please."

His hands dragged up my arms before he slid them across my face, cradling it in his hands. "Aaron, Delilah, and *you* are the loves of my life."

There were no words, no expression of emotion for me to reply with. There just wasn't any that would fit the beautiful ache in my chest; such a new and powerful feeling was radiating throughout my body. I'd never known real devotion, complete trust, and acceptance, perhaps ever in my life. Marshall was giving that to me, and delivering it to me with such reverence, it made me wonder how I would ever be able to give him back what he was giving me.

I pressed my lips against his with a chaste kiss. "You're my Superman," I said against his lips.

"And you are," he said, grabbing my ass and squeezing it, "my insanely hot woman."

I giggled and pushed him away with a playful shove. "Help me decide what to make with her, please. I don't know what she likes or what she would think is fun or anything."

"Well, I'd deviate from the ones injected with booze."

He couldn't be serious.

"Please tell me you're joking and that you don't think I didn't already know that," I said.

A large grin, the one that made my insides and lady bits ache, spread across his face. "Of course I am. I just like seeing you get all serious and offended."

"You are so twisted and...screwed up," I said.

"Wicked, gorgeous," he said with a wink. "And I have no idea what you should make with her. Whatever it is, she'll have a ball. The both of you will. Promise."

I gripped the end of my hair that was styled in soft waves and twirled it around my finger. As I went through my mind's recipe box, my nerves began to take hold again. What if she didn't like me? What if, for some reason, she figured something out? What if Aaron changed his mind, and it wasn't going to happen at all?

Marshall rummaging through my pantry brought my thoughts back to the moment at hand and not the what-ifs. I knew what he was doing. He was looking for extra treats.

"Just ask," I shouted. "Like I've told you a hundred times before."

"Don't you have any of those doughnuts? The chocolate-glazed ones with the bacon?" he asked.

"The ones with the maple bourbon glaze?"

"Yes!"

"No."

"No, you don't have, or no, I can't have one."

"Both. I don't have any so you can't have any."

"Fuck."

"And watch your mouth when Delilah gets here," I said.

He snort-laughed, emerging from the pantry and closing the door behind him. "You think that girl hasn't heard my filth since birth?"

"Oh, I know she has. I seem to remember you dropping a f-bomb when you first saw her in the hospital after she was born."

"Probably. Shit, I wanted one of those doughnuts. Oh! There it is. Make doughnuts with her."

That was an idea. A simple glazed with maybe a chocolate-dipped top. I had tons of different colors and kinds of sprinkles she might like.

"Hmm," I said. "That's probably a good idea. I hope—"

A knock at the door stopped both my words and heart. Looking toward the screen door, I could see Aaron standing on the opposite side, running his hands through his already messy hair, his brows furrowed together, just like he always did when he was stressed.

I turned to Marshall and almost told him to send Aaron away. My eyes pleaded with him because I couldn't do this, but as soon as I started to process it, it turned. I would do this. I *could* do this.

Marshall pressed his hand into mine and gripped it tightly. "You've been waiting six years for this, Al."

"I've been waiting my whole life for this," I said.

I squeezed his hand before releasing it and went to the door. As I peeked from the side of it to get a look at Delilah before seeing her face-to-face, I didn't see her.

I swung the screen door open, holding it open for Aaron. "Hey," I said, my eyes scanning the area.

"Hey. How are you?" he asked. "I'm a nervous wreck, and I don't even really know why. I mean, I know why, but if I am, I can't imagine what you must be feeling. I just hope that I'm, we, are making the right decision, and all of this is a good thing. I can't imagine it's not. I think it's something we all need, right?"

I smiled. "Yes, Aaron. All of that."

His head turned, and he waved his hand over his head. "Come on, Delilah," he called.

Without hesitation, I stretched out my neck into the direction he was calling.

And there she was.

And I almost crumpled to the ground.

She was sitting on my porch swing, her little legs dangling over the edge, and smiling so brightly that the sun was no match for her.

Her hair was longer than any pictures I'd recently seen. Well past her shoulders, it was still that same white blond, with a gorgeous halo of curls.

I couldn't help but imagine that it's what Sadie would've looked like at her age.

And she was dressed so pretty in a white eyelet sundress and matching sandals.

I think Aaron called to her again, but I couldn't hear a thing because I was too busy watching her. She hopped off the swing and smoothed her skirt down before skipping across my porch toward me.

She was more beautiful than any picture or any dream I ever had.

She reached Aaron and leaned against him. "Hi!" she said.

"Hi there," I said, my voice cracking.

Marshall cleared his throat behind me, and I turned to look at him.

"You got this," he mouthed to me. "I love you, gorgeous."

"Delilah," Aaron said, taking in a deep breath. "This is…my friend Alexis I told you about."

"You're a baker with a real bakery?" she asked.

"I am. Do you want to come in?"

"Yes!" She turned to Aaron. "You can go now, Dad."

She stepped inside as Aaron and I laughed at her boldness.

"A little spitfire, huh?" I whispered to him.

"Just like someone else I know, Lex," he said.

"Uncle Marshall!" she screamed. "You're here, too!"

She ran right to him, and he picked her up like she was a rag doll, her legs swinging about before he wrapped her in a tight hug. "I missed you, Nutter Butter."

"I missed you more," she said.

My past.

My present.

My future.

It was all right there in front of me.

The man who I loved, who saw all my scars and ugly truths and loved me back. If I spent of the rest of my lifetime trying, I could never give him back half of what he's given me.

The little girl who had made me a mother and made me make the most profoundly difficult decision a mother's love could ever know, was in my kitchen.

She was in my life.

And she was hugging the man I loved.

It was all right there because a girl and a boy met on a hot summer day at the beach, flirted their way into a relationship, and formed a real friendship. It wasn't a marriage. It wasn't love. He was my friend then, my very best friend.

But we created a person that was. She was pure love.

I looked at Aaron, and he had the same expression I was probably sporting, tears in his eyes with a small smile, while taking it all in. It was an overwhelming moment. His head turned toward me, and it was then I knew.

He forgave me.

And I'd found my peace.

"Are you going to stay and help us bake?" Delilah asked Marshall as he set her down.

"Nah. Me and your dad are going to head out for a while and let you girls do your thing, but we'll be back in a while, okay?" he said.

Delilah shrugged. "Okay." She turned to me. "Miss Alexis, what are we going to make?"

"What do you think about doughnuts?" I asked.

"Cool!" she said. "I've never made those before!"

"Perfect. Okay. Do you know what is the first thing you do before you start baking?"

"Wash your hands," she said matter-of-factly.

"Yes. So, let's do that over here," I said, heading over to the basin sink.

We washed our hands together, and by the time we turned around, the boys were gone.

Time stood still during those two hours as I got to know Delilah.

Her voice and humor.

Her love of comic books and fear of spiders.

How she bit down on her bottom lip when she concentrated on measuring, and the delight in her smile when she dipped the warm doughnuts in the chocolate glaze.

How I knew she loved her dad endlessly by the way she talked about him, and how sometimes she called Callie "Mom" in conversation.

She was all I hoped she'd be.

We were just beginning to clean up when I heard the screen door slam shut. "Hello!" Marshall called.

"Hi," I said, as the boys began to enter the kitchen. "How was—?"

"Hi, Mom," Delilah said, licking frosting from her fingers. "Look what we did."

Mom.

A brief moment of a burst of sadness and grief washed over me, but then a familiar emotion followed…relief.

A strikingly beautiful woman with long auburn hair and green eyes trailed a step behind Aaron. She held his hand tight as she smiled nervously at me. "Hi," she said in a soft voice to me.

She turned her attention to Delilah. "Those look great, sweetie. You're going to have to teach me now because I've never made doughnuts."

"Sure," Delilah said. "It wasn't hard, and Miss Alexis said I'm a pro, but I told her I already knew that."

There was laughter all around my kitchen at Delilah's modesty, but when it settled, I felt a pull to do something that would seal the day with gratefulness.

I approached Callie and extended my hand. "I'm Alexis Bell."

She took my hand in hers, tears forming in her eyes. "I'm Callie."

We stood holding onto each other's hands before I opened my arms a bit, and she stepped into them. I hugged her, the mother to my child, and didn't know if my heart could even take it.

"Thank you," I whispered into her ear. "Thank you."

"No," she sniffled. She ran her hand down my hair. It was a gentle touch from a girl years my junior, but it was something I hadn't known in years. A mother's touch. "Thank you."

Chapter Twenty-One

MARSHALL—

Out of
Darkness
And sin
Radiates
Beauty
Deep within
Her words
Push you
To see
When you've
Never seen
Touch what
You've never
Felt
Live when
You've never
Lived.

—R. A. Knipe

The poppies came and everything was different. I didn't know until it happened, but it seemed everyone in town knew they were coming. Never one to pay much attention to the wildflower patterns of any area, I brushed it off.

But then they happened, seemingly overnight.

Funny how things worked out that way.

The green lush hills of San Luis Obispo sprout an array of wildflowers in March, and it's specifically when the poppies came. You could see the poppies along Shell Creek Road, with vineyards surrounding them, turning the landscape this fucking insane color orange, like the color of orange soda or the tips of the fall leaves in Chicago. The hills were covered in them, leaving people only a glimpse of the green that was usually there.

There was something about those poppies, though.

Maybe it was the whole *Wizard of Oz* thing, and Dorothy attempting to get to the Great and Powerful Oz. It was such a long-ass journey for her. She had to face her fears, loneliness, and regret, but she never stopped. Even with an evil watch after her, she pushed on and even made some friends along the way. Then she finally gets there, the Emerald City appears like a mirage, and you can see the elation in her expression when she realizes how close she is.

So, she runs, excited, through the poppies to get there faster, but what she doesn't know is that the evil witch made those poppies some sort of sleep time. It was always my opinion that this was one of the most brilliant parts of the movie. I was an older teen before I realized that opium, used for a variety of fucked-up drug uses, was derived from poppies. Now, no one said running through a field of them would get you knocked on your ass. However, the correlation was there.

And there was so much fucking more to it.

Dorothy didn't know about it. Most readers of the book or movie watchers didn't, either, but like real life, there were always obstacles. So goddamn close to the finish line or whatever you worked so hard for, and a field of powerful poppies knocks you on your ass.

It was metaphoric as shit, and I bought into every piece of it.

The poppies came in March, two months after the visit from Aaron.

They were the reminder I needed that things wouldn't always be easy. In fact, life could throw some seriously fucked-up shit at you, like falling in love with, and now living with, your best friend's ex-wife. How does that even happen?

Aaron finding out and the hysteria it brought was the field of poppies. Al and I were so close to having it all figured out, but there was one last obstacle, one more field of poppies to get through, before we reached our Emerald City.

But we made it through, and looking back, the journey was like walking through fire. Looking back a little closer? It was really fucking beautiful at times. A field of poppies was always going to be beautiful in the end.

I flipped open my laptop atop Al's, or rather our, kitchen counter to wait for the Skype call that was to be coming through soon. A rare Sunday when there was no crap work for us to do regarding business, and we could be us.

Clark Kent, the golden retriever puppy I got for Al, and well, me too, came bolting into the kitchen. He stopped abruptly and slid across the hardwood floors, bumping himself into the leg of one of the stools.

No doubt Al was on her way downstairs. Clark would always race her down and wait for her in the kitchen to make sure he got a treat. He was spoiled fucking rotten by her, and well, by me, too, I guess. I turned and reached up to the cabinet above the sink, pulling down his box of treats. After retrieving one, I knelt down on the floor.

"Hey there, buddy. How's my little nugget?"

He trotted over on his still uneasy, new legs. I held out my hand with the treat on it, and he wagged his fluffy tail with delight. In the end, I'd gotten my way with the dog issue. It was a tough sell, but when I brought him home, there was no way she could say no.

Alexis entered the kitchen, her hair done, wearing a bright pink T-shirt that read, "I'm a Baker—What's Your Superpower?" on it in black lettering. She stepped over to the coffeemaker and poured herself a cup as I continued to stare at her.

It eased me to see her without nerves anymore regarding the impending Skype call. She had found her peace. There was no greater fucking joy then seeing the girl you loved happy.

"What are you staring at?" she snapped.

Or seeing all sides of her, including the high-spirited attitude that kept me on my toes.

"You, baby," I said. "I was looking at you. Do you have a problem with that?"

She smiled, lifting her coffee cup to her mouth. "I love you," she said.

She had said it before so many times, and it only started after she met Delilah. I knew that wasn't an accident. It was what she needed. It was what her heart needed to let go of that pain.

Telling me about Sadie was the first step. It was what cracked her open, leaving her room finally to make peace with

Aaron and Delilah. The entire situation could've gone, and almost did, an entirely different direction. I often thought, in most cases, it would have—it probably should have.

But most cases weren't *us*.

They weren't Aaron and I.

They weren't Al and I.

They weren't Callie and Delilah and fucking all of us together.

And I'd never try to fucking explain it to outsiders, our beautifully dysfunctional "family," because it wasn't up to others' interpretation. It was only about us, and I could give a flying fuck if anyone *got* that. There was no room in my heart for it because it was too full of gratitude, that the allegiance and devotion of our circle had surpassed any kind of rational explanation.

None it and *all of it* fucking mattered.

Every time she spoke those three words, "I love you," it was like I'd never heard them before. There was such a sincerity, such truth, behind the term, and it was a massive comfort to know I never needed to question it, question her, because of it.

A ring from the laptop alerted us that the Skype call was coming through. I rushed over and pressed the button to connect.

Delilah's face popped up, all smiles and wild hair. "Hi!" she said, waving.

"Hey there, Nutter Butter! What's shakin'?" I asked.

"Is Miss Alexis ready for me? I have the apron on she sent me." She stepped back, modeling the red-and-white polka-dot apron Al had sent her.

"It looks perfect on you," I said.

I turned to Al, who was waiting until I finished up before stepping in.

"You heard the girl," I said. "She wants to know if Miss Alexis is ready?"

I moved out of the way, and Al took my place, grinning at the screen…at Delilah. "Hey there! Are you ready to get to work?" she asked.

"I am! I got all the ingredients ready that you told me to," Delilah said. "And Callie is here, too, in case I need help with something, even though I told her I wouldn't."

"Hi Callie," Al called.

"Hi!" she responded, a wave of a hand in the background notifying us she was, in fact, close by.

Al looked at me and gave me nod, letting me know to scram. She took these real-time baking lessons with Delilah seriously, and we both agreed that aside from Callie being nearby to help in case, it was something the two of them should do together alone.

The best part? It was Aaron's idea.

So I left them to get to business as I took care of some work stuff in the office and then took Clark Kent for a walk.

A few clouds in the sky when I left the house quickly turned to several, and it wasn't until I was far enough away from home that I realized it was going to rain.

Shit. Rain.

Oh. Rain!

I took to a jog to try and get back before it started, but Clark was still not up to my speed. The rain began to fall, and

I had no choice but to eventually pick him up, so we could run home. Of course, as we neared the final stretch, the rain ceased, and the sun was already trying to make an appearance.

The girls were just finishing up when I returned home and entered the kitchen. I'd neglected to ask what they were making, but judging by the mess on Al and at a glance at Delilah, it was a tad messy.

And so was I, soaked to the skin with rain and muddy paw prints from Clark Kent all over my clothes.

The crazy thing was I didn't even give a shit.

I was too mesmerized by the vision in front of me.

"My Nutter Butter and my baby. Both covered in sugar," I said.

They both giggled, and I left them to wrap things up and say their good-byes. After a change of clothes, I returned downstairs to find Al standing in front of the kitchen sink, looking out the window.

"Oh my God," Al said, staring out the window. "Did you see this?"

"What?"

Her head turned slowly, a smile brighter than the sun that had just emerged. "It's a rainbow."

About the Author

Melissa Marino is a full-time writer and part-time Storm-trooper collector. When she's not writing, you can find her watching *Friends* reruns, mastering her cupcake frosting swirl, and hunting for the perfect red lipstick. Melissa lives in Chicago with her husband, son, and very opinionated dachs-hund.

Learn more at:
  Melissa-Marino.com
  Twitter, @MelissaWrites2
  Facebook.com/MelissaMarinoBooks

Please turn the page for an excerpt from the first book in the
Bad Behavior series

So Twisted.

Available now!

Chapter One

CALLIE—

Is anyone else getting a wedgie from these damn things?" I shouted to the other females I was working with. I hurried to the other end of the bar as I adjusted my hot-pink bloomers that were under my extra short patent leather skirt. Our new uniforms were about as functional as wet toilet paper.

"Hey beautiful, how long does a guy have to wait to get a drink around here?" I turned and saw a barely legal guy at the other end of the bar, clearly not needing another cocktail.

Luckily, the DJ had decided that was the perfect time to crank the music, and like that, the cries of the drunken were silenced.

It was eleven o'clock and the night was young. The bar was packed, which was good for my bank account, but bad for my dignity. Every hour that went by at Venom, the downtown Chicago club I bartended at that catered to the newly twenty-one crowd, lowered the IQ of my customers.

"What can I get you?" I asked the dude heckling me.

He leaned in. "You can get me a double vodka, sexy."

"Is that it?" I said, making his drink.

"No," he slurred. He leaned in further, practically drooling over himself. "You can get me your phone number."

I rolled my eyes. "Sorry, sweetie. I don't date customers."

"Who said anything about dating? I just want to see that skirt on my bedroom floor in the morning."

"Ain't gonna happen. Anything else?" I said, handing him his drink.

"Yeah, I want those shiny, knee-high boots wrapped around…"

I cut him off before I could hear the rest. "Twelve dollars."

He reached in his pocket and pulled out a handful of crushed bills. He picked out a few and handed them to me. Something was crunchy in that wad of cash. Something damp, too. I wanted to vomit.

"There's more where this came from," he said with a wink.

Fuck my life.

"Wait just a second," Frat Boy Slim babbled. "You look familiar."

"Probably because you're looking right at me. Crazy how the mind works, huh?"

I attempted to step away, knowing that continuing a conversation with this guy would be as enjoyable as a two-day-old pulled pork sandwich that had been soaking in curdled milk, but he wouldn't let up.

"Wait!" he said, jumping and spilling half his vodka on his pink Lacoste shirt. "Aren't you in that um…math class…the one for teachers with me?"

"Mathematics in elementary school?" I asked.

He snapped his fingers at me. "Yes! That's the one. I knew I recognized you from someplace."

There was seriously no hope for our future if this was the kind of moron teaching our children.

"That must be it," I said. "Okay, then. I have to get back to work."

"Hold up. Do you live off campus? No way you still live in the dorms."

"No. I don't live in the dorms because I'm too old for that shit, and I only go part-time. Anything else?"

"Pfft," he spit, waving his arm around. "You ain't old. You can't be older than twenty-four or so."

I touched my nose, letting him know he got it right. "Einstein."

He nodded and snorted simultaneously. "Yeah. I'm pretty smart. And I think you are, too, so why don't you just tell me what time you get off so I can get you off?"

I wasn't sure if it was my disgusted look or the distraction of having a drink thrown in his face by the girl standing behind him who was listening to our conversation, but like magic, he disappeared.

I rubbed my temples, feeling the pain of a headache coming on. "Fuck my life," I said aloud before placing a smile on my face as fake as the skirt I was wearing before I approached the next customer. "Hey there. What can I get you?"

By the end of the evening—actually three o'clock in the morning—I was totally spent. As I walked out the back door, I stopped and unzipped my knee-high boots with the four-inch heels. I crossed the parking lot barefoot, and even though it was March in Chicago, the feel of the icy ground numbed my aching feet. After getting into my car and waiting a few minutes for it to heat up, I drove home. The streets were empty except for a few drunken stragglers, their arms draped over a new friend who will soon be a lover or maybe even an old lover who was never a friend. It hardly mattered which one it was because I was jealous all the same. Logically I knew half of them would be alone by morning, but for the night, they had someone close. They had deep kisses and warm bodies. All I had was hot chocolate and Garrett's Popcorn waiting for me at home.

Exhaustion hit me the moment I began the climb up the stairs to my apartment. My head pounded with pain, and every muscle in my legs screamed for rest. I dropped everything, except my phone, at the front door and dragged myself to the couch, where I collapsed. My bed would've been much more comfortable, but my room might as well have been a mile away at that point. I had just enough sense to set the alarm on my phone for seven a.m. so I had time in the morning for a quick shower before class. Hot chocolate and popcorn was going to have to wait.

* * *

I heard voices but refused to open my eyes. It would be admitting morning had arrived, and that couldn't be possible when I had just closed my eyes. The faint sound of my alarm grew louder and louder as I continued to deny the time.

Strong steps against our hardwood floors approached me, but then stopped abruptly and reversed. With a sigh, I peeled my eyelids open—which were stuck together from the glue of my false eyelashes and leftover makeup I hadn't bothered to wash off. I slapped my alarm off and cursed the sun for being, well, the sun.

"What is your problem?" Evelyn said, her voice raising. "I thought you were leaving?"

"Someone is on your couch. A woman, and she's in her underwear," an unfamiliar man voice answered.

"Will you knock it off? I told you I had fun and that I'd text you later," Evelyn said.

"It was fun, wasn't it?"

"Yes." She sighed. "So, see you later."

"But what about the girl in her underwear?" he asked.

"I'm not in my underwear," I shouted, opening my eyes.

Evelyn's head popped out of her bedroom door. "Oh. Yeah. Definitely not underwear."

A tall blond guy wearing a wrinkled white button-down and blue pants turned. He gave a quick nod and side smile, clearly hiding his embarrassment over his mistake.

"Hey there," he said, swinging a suit jacket over his shoulder. "I was just—"

"Leaving," Evelyn said, nudging him.

Evelyn's one-hit wonder began his walk of shame, but stopped in front of me. His eyes drifted down my body, stopping at my skirt.

"Yes?" I asked, sitting up.

His head tilted and he smiled. "You work at Venom?"

"For shit's sake," I said, standing and stomping to my room.

The last thing I heard before getting into the shower was Evelyn telling him he was an inconsiderate jackass with a small dick.

I love that girl.

While I was normally not a morning person, I was even less so when I'd only had three hours of sleep. I practically cried through my five-minute shower, but when the smell of coffee hit me, my spirits lifted slightly. When I came out of the bathroom, in my ratty robe and hair up in a towel, there was a cup waiting for me on the counter in the kitchen. She even put the right amount of my favorite peppermint mocha creamer in it.

I sat at the kitchen table, going through my class notes, when Evelyn came out of her room and breezed into the kitchen like the breath of fresh air she always was. Her long blond hair was curled into perfect waves, while her cream-colored blouse was tucked neatly into her black pencil skirt. I was lucky if I managed to leave the house wearing matching shoes.

"Thanks for the coffee," I said, yawning.

"No problem," she said, slipping on her black heels. "Everything good?"

I nodded. "Mm-hmm."

"You sure?"

I set my notes down and looked at her. She was nervously biting down on her lower lip, messing up her red lipstick. Something was up. She never ruined her lipstick unless she was nervous (which she hardly ever was) or she was getting lucky with a dude (which happened on a fairly regular basis).

I stood and crossed the kitchen. "What's up?"

"Nothing," Evelyn said.

I rolled my eyes at her as I poured myself another cup of coffee. "You're a terrible liar."

She twirled a lock of her hair and pressed her lips together tightly. "I'm worried about you."

"Worried about what?"

"Cal, you can't keep working like this." She moved and stood in front of me. "You're so exhausted between working these late hours and with school."

I took a sip and shrugged. "I don't have a choice right now. At least I'm not working two jobs anymore."

We had this conversation so many times before, and while I knew it only came from a place of concern, my situation wasn't by choice. Sometimes I wondered if she realized that.

"Look, you're sweet to worry, but we've been through this already. My student loans are through the roof, and while I know I can defer, it'll be more of an issue in the end. If I thought I could still pay rent and everything else by any other means besides bartending, I would, but that isn't happening. I'm just taking a larger course load now so I can finish next year."

She took hold of my hands. "Look, I was thinking I could ask Bridget if you could do some help around the office. With the wedding season coming…"

I shook my head. "Me, working for wedding planners? Seriously? Plus, I'd still be making more a few nights a week at Venom. The money is too good."

"I'm not trying to piss you off," she said. "I think that…"

I pulled my wet hair back, looking up at the ceiling to blink away the tears. "Ev. Please," I pleaded.

"Oh," she said, putting her arms around me. "I'm sorry. Please don't be sad."

I sighed and put my coffee cup down so I could hug her back. "You worry too much."

She shrugged when we pulled away. "Sometimes, although worrying is usually your specialty. But I know how hard you work, both with school and the bar, and I love you so stupid."

"I know. I love you, too, Blondie."

"I have to run." She walked over to the table and picked up her purse. "See you later?"

"Probably not. Work tonight."

Work. Work. Work.

* * *

I sat at a café by campus, the late afternoon sun glaring off the table's surface, reviewing material from my earlier class. I was on my third coffee of the day, but while the caffeine from my triple-shot latte was giving me just enough energy to keep my head up, it wouldn't last. My eyelids burned, and there was a serious nap in my future if I got everything done before work.

I returned to my notes but was interrupted when my phone rang. I dug it out of my purse, checking the caller ID. EVELYN.

"What's up?" I said.

"Hey, are you busy? I've got some news I think you might be interested in."

"Studying. Something going on?"

"Okay. Before I tell you anything, you have to promise me you won't get mad first."

"Why would I be mad?"

"I can't tell you that. You might get mad."

I put my pen down and took a sip of my mocha. "Fine. Go ahead."

"So, you're promising not to be mad?" she asked.

I didn't like where this was headed. Evelyn only asked me not to be mad at her when she did something I told her specifically not to do. The last time she pulled the "promise you won't be mad at me" bit, she came home with a ridiculously expensive handbag I'd admired when we were shopping together.

I knew I had to give in if I was ever going to find out what she was up to. "Okay, I promise I won't get mad. Tell me."

"I think I found you a job."

"Huh?"

"Hear me out. Okay, a few days ago I was at the office, and a client, Leslie Matthews, came in. She's hosting an event for the Junior League of Chicago. While we really don't do party planning, just weddings, Bridget does this yearly event for promotional purposes. I got to talking to Mrs. Matthews, and she was telling she was having knee replacement surgery in a few months."

I yawned. "Uh-huh."

"She told me she was worried because her son, Aaron, who's a single dad, really depends on her for when he's working. I met him at last year's event and recognized him as an owner of some of the clubs and boutique hotels we do weddings at. Anyway, he's looking for full-time help since Mrs. Matthews is going to be out of commission."

She paused, waiting for a response, but I had none.

I sighed and looked at the clock on the wall. *Come on, Evelyn, spit it out, I have a nap waiting for me.*

"Okayyyyy," I said. "Are you getting to the point?"

"Yes! Aaron needs a nanny, a live-in nanny," she said.

I thought for a second before responding. "This is really fascinating, Evelyn. I hope you alerted the *Tribune* to this development."

"Am I talking too fast for you?" She paused and sighed. "You could be his nanny."

"What? Why would I want to do that?"

"Because you can live in his house, which is amazing, rent-free and make more than what you're making at Venom."

I tapped my fingers on the table as I processed what she said. It wasn't totally crazy, considering I'd worked for several families over the years as a nanny and was studying to be a teacher. Plus, when my father died, my mom had to work multiple jobs, leaving me to care for my two younger sisters.

"Okay, okay, I know what you're thinking." She interrupted my thoughts. "I know you too well not to know that you're considering all the what-ifs, but seriously I think this could really go your way. Today, on the way to work, it just popped in my head. So, I called Mrs. Matthews, and long story short, I told her all about you, that you were an education major, still in school, and had been a nanny in the past. She got in touch with Aaron and he was thrilled. Remember when you had asked me to help you with your résumé a while back? I still had it on my computer so I sent it to him."

"You did what?" My voice soared an octave.

"He emailed me and asked if you were available for an interview tonight at seven. I said yes."

"Evelyn!"

"Nope. No getting mad remember?"

I could almost hear her smiling on the other end, proud of herself for putting this plan all together. If I was being honest, it did sound appealing. I loved working with kids; it was the whole reason I wanted to be a teacher. Plus, the idea of making more money so I could quit the hellish hours of working nights lightened the weight on my back.

"I don't know, Ev. What about my hours during the day for school and the rent for our place? There's a lot of things to consider."

"He knows you're still in school. I was clear with him about your need for flexibility. And as far as our rent, we'll cross that bridge when we get to it."

Was this something I could do? Was it something I *wanted* to do? I ran through a bunch of variables, considering worst-case scenarios and all the reasons why this probably wouldn't be a good idea. Evelyn was quiet, knowing I was processing it all. The possibilities were too enticing. An interview with this guy wouldn't hurt.

"First," I said. "Thank you. Second, I'm definitely interested, but I have to be at work at six, so I don't think I can meet him tonight."

"Callie, this is a huge opportunity for you. I think Venom will survive if you're a couple hours late."

She was right. If this played out as desirable as it sounded, I could throw my patent leather skirt in the Dumpster of that dreaded bar. "What should I do now? Should I call him to confirm?"

"Nope. I assured him you would be there."

"What if I'd said no?"

"You've forgotten who knows you best."

Again. She was right.

By the time I left the café shortly after, something inside me felt lighter. The feeling wasn't fleeting or riddled with uncertainty. It was just…promise. As I climbed the steps to the "L," I sent out all the positive vibes I had that this went well.

At seven o'clock on the dot, I stood outside the exquisite brownstone where Aaron Matthews and his daughter lived. A black wrought iron fence surrounded the brick house, while circle-topped windows decorated the front. I looked at the roof, adorned with hanging vines bare from the winter, but no doubt gorgeous in the summer. The vines intertwined through tall, thin pillars that ran the length of the roof.

I rang the doorbell and waited while I continued to admire the outside of his home. To the right of the door, I noticed a small Disney princess figure. I bent down to pick it up as I heard the door open.

"Hello there. Calliope?" a deep voice said.

"Hi." I lifted my face to look at him.

Then I almost fell over.

Oh. Hell. No.

Nope. Can't work for this guy.

My eyes scanning over him created a multi-visual experience, every bit of his presence capturing me all at once.

He was tall, very tall, with an athletic build and dark hair that curled slightly at the edges. He smiled, a smile that accentuated his perfectly straight teeth and full lips. When my eyes reached his, the real trouble started. They were blue, the color of the light, aqua edges of forget-me-not flowers, and piercing against his dark hair and features.

Forget-me-not. It was unlikely to happen.

"Are you all right? You look a little pale," he said, concerned. He moved from the doorway, stepping closer to me. "Do you feel faint?"

I took a deep breath and stood up. "Mr. Matthews, yes, I'm Calliope. Or Callie. Whatever. I'm so sorry. I'm just getting over a little cold and not quite myself yet."

Nice save.

He extended his hand to shake mine, gripping it tightly. "Nice to meet you, Calliope. And please, call me Aaron. Thank you for coming on such short notice, especially now that I know you haven't been well. Are you sure you're up for the interview?" he asked.

"Oh yes, of course. Ah. Here," I said, shoving the Disney princess at him.

He smiled and nodded, taking it from me. "Everywhere. They're absolutely everywhere. Thank you. Well, why don't we go in so we can talk?"

I followed him inside, desperately trying not to stare at his ass along the way and failing miserably. I reminded myself there was nothing wrong with a basic human reaction. We were animals by nature, and admiring another animal you found attractive was normal. Although…from where I stood, there wasn't much normal about the way he looked.

I unbuttoned my coat and looked around the exquisite home. Marble flooring lined the hallway and extended throughout as far as I could see. I trailed behind him down the large foyer, which connected to a narrow hall leading to the rest of the home. To my right was a formal dining room with a long glass-topped table and several high-back chairs.

If offered the job, it would've been far and away the most beautiful home I'd ever lived in. My meager background didn't lend itself to such expensive surroundings. It almost made me uncomfortable.

"Please sit down," he said, motioning to the table and chairs. "Can I get you something to drink?"

"No, thank you," I said, hanging my coat on the back of the chair. I looked across the table and saw a copy of my résumé and references that Evelyn had emailed earlier. I noticed a few notes in the margin.

"So, Calliope, why don't you tell me a little about yourself?"

"Well," I said, taking in a deep breath. "I'm a third-year elementary education major. I've been going part-time so I could balance work along with it, but I hope to graduate next spring, so I've taken on more classes this semester. I work nights at a downtown club, but that's been temporary. My goal has always been to work with children."

"Which one?"

"Which children?" I asked, confused.

"No," he said, laughing, his bright smile lifting the corner of his mouth into a handsome grin. "Which club?"

"Oh. Right. Duh. Um, Venom? It's near Rush—"

"And Division. Yes, I know it well."

"You do?"

"Don't act so surprised. I'm not that much of an old man at thirty-one."

"No," I said quickly. "Of course not. I didn't mean to insinuate."

He held up his hand, continuing to smile. "You were right to assume it isn't my type of crowd, but I used to be part owner of it. I sold off my piece some time ago, but it's good to know it still has some wonderful employees there."

He paused, his eyes running across my face, as his smile faded. There wasn't a sound surrounding us, but the energy in the room more than made up for the silence. The quiet sound of something brewing. Shivers rushed across my body.

"Have you always lived in Chicago?" he asked.

"No, but I never want to live anywhere else. I love it here."

"Agreed. Best city in the world."

He paused, glancing down at my résumé. "Your résumé is very thorough," he said, running his finger down the margin where his notes were. "I really asked for the interview to see if we'd be a good fit, or if rather, you'd be a good fit for us."

I nodded, waiting for him to continue.

Or maybe I was fixated on the fact that the way he said *fit*, a normal, everyday word, sounded so sexy.

Or maybe I realized my ogling was going to get me fired before I was hired.

"Why don't I tell you a little bit about us now?" He ran his hand through his hair and smiled. "I'm sure Evelyn has explained my situation. My mom's having surgery this summer, and I'll need someone full-time to help with my daughter."

As the word *daughter* left his mouth, his entire face lit up.

"What's her name?"

"Delilah and she's four. She's very smart and very high-energy. I love the idea of having someone with an education background. I'd love for her to go to the museums, take classes, and things like that."

"Absolutely."

"And I'm sure as is the case with many four-year-olds, she's very stubborn and isn't afraid to let her opinion be known."

"It's very common. Testing boundaries and all that."

"Well, she can definitely win top prize in the most dramatic tantrum competition. But she's sweet, and while I'm sure I'm biased, I think she's the most beautiful little girl, inside and out."

"Is she here? Can I meet her?"

"I thought it best that I meet with any candidate when she was not here. She's actually spending the night at my parents' tonight."

"Well, she sounds like a remarkable little girl."

"I think so," he said with a nod. "I understand you'll need some flexibility with your hours?"

"Yes. Three mornings a week I have class, but that's only for the next six weeks until summer. Obviously I'll be completely available then during the summer."

"It wouldn't be a problem. Even though my mom has been watching her while I worked from home, Delilah has been used to having me here. I wanted to ease her into someone new for the first few weeks. She's really only been looked after by family, so as you can imagine, she has one overprotective Daddy."

The way he said "Daddy" was so endearing I melted a little. "Totally understandable," I said.

"So, in the fall, you'll be in your final year?"

"Yes."

"That's wonderful." My eyes glanced over the white collared shirt he was wearing and to the small patch of chest hair that peeked through.

He slipped a piece of paper out from under my résumé and pushed it across to me. "Would this be acceptable to you?"

I looked at the paper and the number on it referring to the weekly salary he was offering. It was more than I'd made in a week at any job ever. My eyes looked it over again and again, as he tapped his pen on the table. This was in addition to the free room and board. My mind was blown.

"Very," I responded as calmly as possible. "Thank you."

"Of course that includes room and board, meals and such. I'd like to check out your references and verify the background check before we go any further. However, I do promise to call you by Monday with my decision regardless of what I decide."

"Great. Thank you."

We stood and I grabbed my coat from the back of the chair. He walked me to the front door, and as he opened it for me with one hand, his other hand brushed against my back. His touch, as light as it was, sent a shiver through my body. "Thank you again for coming on such a short notice."

"My pleasure."

I stepped outside and walked down the stairs as I buttoned my coat. I stopped at the bottom and turned. He still stood in the doorway, watching me. I smiled and waved.

He returned the smile, and even in the chilly temperature, my body grew warm all over. If offered this job, it might be the best employment opportunity ever or a mistake of epic proportions.

I went to work that night and the following, thinking of not much else besides Aaron. I worried that if I did move in, my infatuation would only increase and cause me to screw up one of the best jobs I might ever have. I mean, a child was involved with this. Plus, one bad reference from a prominent Chicago figure could jeopardize my future teaching career.

I spent Sunday mulling things over and decided to relax until I heard from him. He may not even offer me the position, and in that case, all of this was for nothing. From working and worrying all weekend, I was exhausted. After a long shower, I put on my most comfortable pajamas and climbed into bed.

Sleep came fast and hard, and I didn't wake until my phone buzzed on my nightstand the following morning with an incoming call. Groggy, I tried to identify the number on the caller ID, but it was no use.

"Hello," I said, my throat full of morning phlegm.

"Hi, Calliope? It's Aaron Matthews."

I shot up, clearing my throat. "Oh, hi. How are you?"

"Good. I'm sorry if I woke you, but I wanted to catch you before you went to class."

"Oh no," I lied. "I've been awake for ages."

"Well, the reason I am calling is that I would like to offer you the nanny position. Pending the rest of your references coming through as glowing as the others, of course. Plus, I'd like you to meet Delilah beforehand as well."

"Really?" I said excited. "That's—"

Fantastic?

Yes. I wanted to say it was fantastic. It was, but it was something else, too. The emotions I had when we met, the way my body responded, was not only out of character, but frightening. With my focus being solely on school and work for so long, I didn't have time to date, let alone even be completely attracted to someone. What would happen when we were living together day in and day out? That was a recipe for a very volatile situation.

"What do you think, Calliope? Will you be our nanny?" he asked eagerly.

I had a choice. Either I could turn down the job, fearing my initial emotions would filter into my daily life. Or I could stop worrying about what might happen, take hold of this amazing opportunity, and know I could handle anything that came my way.

I mean, was there really a choice?

"Yes, of course, Aaron. I'm thrilled to be your nanny."

www.ingramcontent.com/pod-product-compliance
Ingram Content Group UK Ltd.
Pitfield, Milton Keynes, MK11 3LW, UK
UKHW022259280225
455674UK00001B/95